The Pledge

ANN EL-NEMR

THE PLEDGE
ANN EL-NEMR

Published February 2015
Little Creek Books
Imprint of Jan-Carol Publishing, Inc.
All rights reserved

Copyright © Ann El-Nemr
Book Cover and Design by Tara Sizemore

This is a work of fiction. Any resemblance to actual persons, either living or dead, is entirely coincidental. All names, characters and events are the product of the author's imagination.

This book may not be reproduced in whole or part, in any matter whatsoever without written permission, with the exception of brief quotations within book reviews or articles.

ISBN: 978-1-939289-58-2
Library of Congress Control Number: 2015934816

You may contact the publisher:
Jan-Carol Publishing, Inc.
PO Box 701 Johnson City, TN 37605
E-mail: publisher@jancarolpublishing.com
Website: jancarolpublishing.com

"every story needs a book"

*To my longtime friends: who have embraced
and championed my new quest in life.*

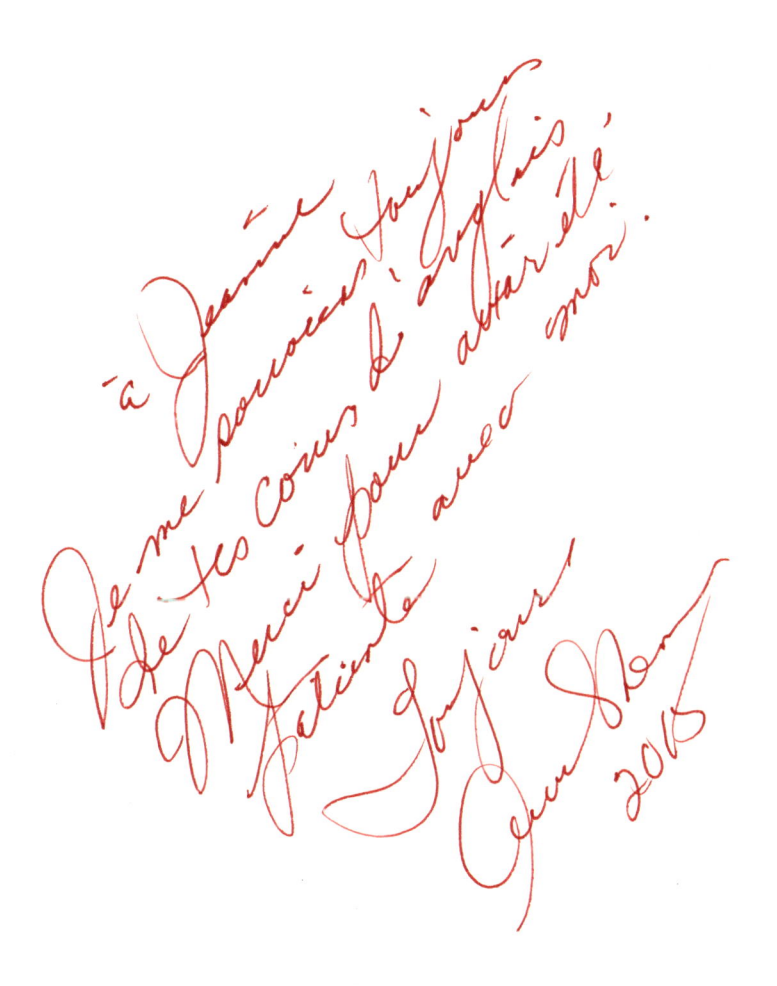

LETTER TO THE READER

As my journey continues in the writing world, I find myself loving every minute of my voyage. It gives me great pleasure to be able to put my ideas on paper for your entertainment. I love to hear from my readers as I go forward with every book I write. This book is a triangle of love and deceit with a surprise turn of events. Dalton receives a letter from his old friend a year after his death that asks him to honor the pledge they had taken while in college. He conceals the note from his fiancée as he goes into a direction he had never planned in his life. This adventure has many twists and turns as it progresses forward. The ending of *The Pledge* was unexpected to me until the last few chapters when I found the perfect conclusion. Sometimes life throws you a curve ball but in the end it all works out and that is how I decided to finish this book. Enjoy!

Yours truly,

Ann El-Nemr

ACKNOWLEDGMENTS

I want to thank my close friends for all the support you have given me, throughout the past year, while writing this book; especially my sister, Jacqueline Cormier, whom I love and has always encouraged me to see the bright side of things. To my children, Fouad, Badih and Amiranour; you are my life. You are always ready to assist and revitalize me with your humor when there is a bump in the road. "I love you the most."

INTRODUCTION

The Pledge started out as a romantic story but I couldn't keep myself from introducing a component of suspense and a third party to spice it up. The story begins in London, with Dalton, an attorney at a prominent law firm who is presented with a correspondence from his past. When he unexpectedly has to travel to Boston on business, an unforeseen encounter sparks his interest. He has not given any thought of meeting the mysterious woman in the letter until it happens. The drama materializes when Dalton's fiancée, Sidney, surprises him in Boston and interrupts his destiny. What will Sidney do to keep her man and how will she react to the betrayal? Who will Dalton choose and at what length will he go to conceal his secret? These questions are answered in this story, but with an unforeseen outcome.

Chapter 1

Outside, the bitter cold air of March whipped her long blond hair from left to right, hitting her in the face. Her cheeks were red and her eyes watered. She pulled the front of her coat together while she tried to shield herself from the freezing wind and she took her last step up on the small porch of her house. She reached into her pocket for her key and unlocked the door. Pulling the door open, she rushed inside into her warm home, closed the door, and leaned against the door.

"Thank God! I'm home," she said aloud to herself, grateful she was out of the shivering temperatures. She tapped her boots against the mat at the entrance to get rid of the snow.

Her husband had bought this place for them the previous year. It was only a two-bedroom home but they had loved the idea of being close to their work. The house was located on the North End of the city, and they had easy access to Hanover Street, where the restaurants and shops of the little Italy area were situated in Boston. It was an older brick building and they renovated it to its original beauty by redoing the woodwork on the floors and the high ceilings. She liked the warmth of the old house.

They enjoyed painting it together and remolding the rooms with help of friends. It had taken most of last year, but it had finally come together. They bought all new appliances and furniture before they moved in. It had been fun adding their personal touches here and there to make it cozy. They planned to live here forever and raise their children in the inner city.

She took her boots off and walked the short distance to the coat closet. After putting her coat away, she headed toward the kitchen to make herself a cup of tea to warm her tired bones. She dropped her pocketbook on one of the stools near the small granite island that graced the room. She took the kettle from the pantry, added water to it, and placed it on the burner.

She walked down the hallway to her bedroom, glancing at pictures of her husband that decorated the walls. As she entered the room, she pulled her black dress over her head and threw it on the nearby chair. She stepped over to her dresser and lifted the lid of a glass box that her husband had given her on her last birthday. She took off her wedding rings, earrings and dropped them into it. Out of a chest of drawers, she found a pair of sweatpants and shirt and slipped them on. As she changed, she heard the high-pitched sound of the kettle. She slowly walked back to the stove with her head bowed.

Suddenly her eyes pooled with tears, as they did on most nights. Her heart was heavy and she succumbed to an overwhelming feeling. She wiped the tears away from her eyes and poured the boiling water into her cup with a jasmine tea bag. She took her mug and went to the living room, not bothering to turn on a light, allowing the lights from the hallway to provide a dim illumination. She sat in her usual spot at the far end of the couch and placed her untouched tea on the side table.

She gazed at the large empty black chair across from her, which had been her husband's favorite spot. She still could hear his laughter in her head echoing between these walls as memories brought her back to the good times they'd had together in the past few years. What she missed the most was the soft words he would whisper to her at night when she was lying near his hard body. Another tear escaped down her cheek. She took a few steps forward to grab the pillow from his chair. She brought it to her nose and inhaled the musk scent of her late husband.

Her spirit broke every night when she remembered their special time. She sat alone again as recollections of him bombarded her. She pulled her knees against her chest as his face flashed through her mind with the memories of the three years she had spent with her only love. Today was the first anniversary of the death of her husband Mark. Tears started to flow freely as she thought of this. She was lonely and felt abandoned, her heart still breaking from the past events.

"Why? Why did you leave me when I still needed you?" She started to sob uncontrollably as she sank her head into his pillow. She remembered the tragedy of his death as if it just happened today.

A year ago in March, her husband Mark had been working late on a final legal contract in his law office at the other end of Boston. He called her around ten o'clock that evening. She could still hear the last words he had said to her. There had been a snowstorm raging outside and she had been worried for him. She should have told him to sleep at a nearby friend's house, but she hadn't because she wanted him next to her. She figured that since he didn't have far to drive, he should be okay.

"Hi, sweetheart," Mark had said, and she quickly noted how tired he sounded.

"Hey! How are you doing?" Annette had replied, upbeat as she sat watching the television.

"Great, but I will be better as soon as I'm beside you. I just wanted to let you know that I'm on my way home from the office," Mark had told her.

"I'll wait up for you. Be careful and don't drive too fast. The snow is coming down heavy here and the roads are very slippery," she had said, concerned as she looked outside her front window.

"Don't worry. I'll take my time. Don't wait up. Go to bed. It might take awhile for me to get home with all the traffic on Friday night. It seems everyone came out tonight," he had said to her, unworried.

"All right. I'll keep the bed warm. Love you," she had said to him. She brought her hand to her chest and tapped it twice, once for her and once for him. It reminded her that they were together, and she did it whenever he wasn't near her.

"Love you, too," he had told her, as she heard the click of the phone.

It was around two o'clock in the morning when the doorbell had rung. Annette turned around to touch Mark, but all she found was a cold, empty bed. She recalled her hand had swept the empty space. She opened her eyes and listened, but realized she did not hear or see him. The doorbell rang again. She pushed the blankets off the bed, grabbed her bathrobe, and slipped it on. She sat on the edge of the bed for a moment, listening for her husband's footsteps. When she heard nothing, she stood up and ran down the stairs toward the front door, thinking Mark had forgotten his key.

"I'm coming, darling," she yelled as she approached the front door. She pushed the curtain of the small door window open to make sure it was her husband.

What she saw froze her on the spot. Her heart started pounding hard against her chest and a cold sweat started to run down her back. With a shaky hand she unlocked the deadbolt and opened the door. The wind had blown snow inside the house, and forced her to take a step back as the freezing air hit her. They had come forward and closed the door behind them.

"Can I help you?" she asked almost in a whisper. Her eyes had been locked on them in fright as she wondered where her husband could be. She immediately thought something had happened to him.

"I'm Officer Jacob and this is Officer Cook. Are you Mrs. Annette Russell?" he asked in calm voice. Annette only nodded, her eyes fixed on them. She remembered a cold shiver passed over her body and her legs had become weak. She could hear her heartbeat in her ears and she could barely breathe. She hoped that their presence didn't have anything to do with Mark being late, but she knew better.

"Is your husband's name Mark Russell, Ma'am?" he continued without any expression on his face. Annette nodded again as she extended her hand toward the bench next to her for support.

"Oh! Dear God! What happened?" she finally asked in a trembling voice, her lips quivering.

"I'm sorry to tell you this, but your husband was in an accident on Storrow Drive this evening. He was brought to Mass. General Hospital with severe wounds. The doctors tried their best but he didn't make it. We are sorry for your loss." Officer Jacob tried to reach out to help her stand before she fell down on the floor.

Annette just stared at them in disbelief. Her mouth opened to speak, but nothing had come out. She wasn't been able to breathe and she felt as though someone was sitting on her chest, suffocating her. She had taken another step backwards, then her legs gave away and she had fallen to her knees. She pounded her fists against the floor.

"No, Nooooo. You're ... wrong," she screamed at them, shaking her head in denial. Her tears started to flow like a river. She choked on her words. She recalled how difficult it was to breathe. "It ... can't ... you have ... the wrong person. Oh! God! ... No, no, no." She continued shaking her head, unable to believe them at first, but as they helped her up, they had continued talking and affirming it was the truth. Her husband, her Mark, had died.

* * *

A half hour later, she was still crying as she tried to gain control of her emotions. Annette, still holding on to the pillow against her chest, walked to her bedroom. Her shoulders slumped forward as she took the difficult steps toward her bed. She lay under the sheets, still hugging his pillow. It was one of the only things that still held his scent. She pulled the blanket up to her chin, and then tucked herself into a fetal position. She closed her eyes, still feeling the tears run down her wet cheeks, as pain hammered through her head. She closed her eyes, wishing to escape to her dreams. She finally fell asleep after another twenty minutes of aching thoughts.

* * *

Women would be quick to label Dalton Rivers handsome. He was a man in his early thirties whose dark hair, tall stature, and toned body were the definition of attractive. He sat behind his mahogany desk in his law office, located on the third floor of a building in the city of London, England, which overlooked Piccadilly Circle. His eyes focused on documents he was reading—overdue corporate contracts that needed to be sent out immediately. The sun had already set in the sky behind him, but the rain still lingered into the early evening hours. Within the last year he had become the youngest partner at Jones and McCarthy Law Firm. He labored for long hours to prove to his other colleagues that he was worthy of this position. His office was uncomplicated and it consisted only of his huge desk and a few leather chairs for the clients. A small bar area to his right included a few bottles of whiskey and scotch, but the real attraction of this room was the huge windows behind his desk. They overlooked the bustling commotion of tourists down in the streets of one of the most famous square in London.

He loved his office, even though he could use a couple of paintings on the walls to make it homey. He hadn't had time to go shopping yet, though. The only picture on his desk was the one of his fiancée Sidney. She had given it to him for his birthday about a month ago. Dalton loved his position and had chosen to work in spite of his wealth. Not too many people knew about the fortune he had inherited about two years ago. He'd rather not tell his fellow partners about it, keeping his background humble. He'd rather go up the ladder on his own merits, not his money.

He was still absorbed in reading a document when he heard a knock at his door. He lifted his head, his eyes narrowing toward the intruder who was interrupting him. He frowned at being disturbed again. His secretary, Ginger, poked her head inside the room. She quickly came toward his desk and stopped in front of his desk.

"Sorry, Mr. Rivers, but there's a messenger here with a letter that won't take anyone's signature but yours," Ginger told him quietly while trying to give him a small smile.

"Fine, tell him to come in," Dalton said as he rolled his chair backwards a bit. He rubbed his face with his right hand. The secretary appeared again at the door of his office with a young man wearing a blue sweatshirt, holding a sandal bag and a helmet. He approached quickly with long strides and stood in front of Dalton's desk.

"Are you Mr. Dalton Rivers?" he asked Dalton politely while taking out a yellow envelope and a clipboard from his bag.

"Yes, I am," Dalton answered, annoyed at the intrusion. He reached over as the messenger gave him the clipboard.

"Sign here, please." He told him. Dalton signed, then was handed an envelope.

"Thank you," Dalton said, still irritated. He took the envelope in his hand and looked at it. As he inspected the outside of the envelope, he noticed it was from the law firm of Mackenzie and Brown in Boston, Massachusetts. Dalton leaned back in his chair and stared at the address on the envelope. He wondered if it was from Mark Russell. He was the only person Dalton had known from the Boston area who had kept in touch after graduating from law school. He had not spoken to him in over two years. They had been roommates in college. They first met in law school at Harvard University while he was studying abroad in the United States. Dalton had kept in touch with him, but in the last years he had been so preoccupied with his career that they had drifted apart.

Dalton reached over for the brass letter opener and held it tightly in his hand as he ripped the top of the envelope. He leaned his elbows on the edge of the desk and slipped the letter out. He started to read. His hand came up to his mouth and his eyes bulged out, then they watered a bit. His hand started to shake as he blinked the tears away. He didn't move from his spot as he studied the contents intently. His eyebrows came together as he continued to read the document.

Dalton carefully laid the letter on his desk. He closed his eyes to think. He didn't move a muscle as he tried to absorb the message. First, he had just found out he had lost a great friend, and then, there was the subject matter. He opened his eyes and analyzed the content of the letter again. He reread it one more time.

His time in college with his classmate flooded back to him, especially the day they had made in his opinion, a foolish agreement. He had never thought his buddy would go through with it or hold him to it.

"Well, what do you think?" He recalled Mark asking him as he extended his hand to bind the accord.

"You are crazy! You want me to love and take care of your not yet future wife if you die. You are really out of your bloody mind. What if I don't like her? What if she's ugly? What if I get married before you?" Dalton had answered, laughing at him. He had tried to walk away, but Mark had stood his ground, his arm outstretched at him. Mark continued nodding his way. His eyes had been locked on Dalton.

"She will be beautiful and intelligent. Come on! I'll feel better if I know there is someone for her if I die and I will do the same for you—unless one of us is already married to someone—okay?" Mark had replied seriously. Dalton had shaken his hand that day, but had never imagined Mark would go through with it or expected him to hold his end of the bargain. Dalton thought it was a joke. A year later after they had graduated with prestigious law degrees from Harvard Law School they had gone their separate ways. Dalton returned to England, where he had completely forgotten about this foolish agreement, until now. The letter read:

Dear Dalton,

If you are reading this letter, I am no longer with you on this earth. My death has been a year now to the day. I am writing to you because I am asking you to honor our agreement. As you well may not know, I was married a few years back and I want you to go meet my darling widow. I would like you to help her move on with her life. The time is now and I believe you are the right man for her to bring her happiness again. I understand we have not been close the last few years, but I know you can make her laugh again. Here in the package is an open plane ticket to Boston and some cash to purchase whatever you might need. Make her happy! I understand you have not met her, but I am convinced once you do, you will love her as much as I have loved her. By the way, she is not ugly! This is my last wish. I trust you will respect it and go meet her.

Love you, man.

Mark Russell

P.S. All the information you need is here.

Dalton put his hand inside the envelope and pulled out a picture of a woman, an airline ticket, an address in the Boston area, and a check in his name for ten thousand dollars. Dalton thought as he shook his head and ran his fingers through his black hair, unable to believe what had happened. He inhaled heavily then exhaled. He placed each article in front of him on his desk.

"What the bloody hell am I going to do with this?" he heard himself ask. He picked up everything and returned it all to the envelope. He opened the desk drawer and neatly placed the envelope inside before shutting the drawer.

He glanced at all the files that were stacked in front of him and needed attention. He needed to focus on the document he had been studying, not this letter. He leaned back in his chair, crossed his legs, and continued to review his sales contracts. He had too much work to do to even contemplate this foolish wish. He would deal with Mark's ridiculous ideas later, plus he was scheduled to marry a woman, Sidney, in a few months. He would send his widow the money. He had no time to go off to America and entertain a grieving widow, even though she was a pretty one with her long blonde hair and piercing blue eyes.

Chapter 2

Sidney Moore sat at the dining table in her one bedroom flat in south London. Her hands were on her lap. She looked at the dinner she had prepared for her fiancé. The meal was now cold and unappetizing. He was late, as usual even though he promised her he would be on time tonight. She studied the clock on the wall as the minutes ticked away. It was now almost ten o'clock. Two hours ago she had placed a pot roast with all the trimmings on the table. She had lit candles that had burned down to the wick, anticipating Dalton's arrival. She sat there peering at the gold tablecloth, fresh flowers, and her table arrangement until she couldn't stand it anymore.

A tear fell from her eye as she stood. She quickly wiped it away. She cupped her hand to blow out the reminder of the flames of the candlesticks. She reached over and grabbed the plate of the pot roast to bring back to the kitchen. She placed it on the counter and ripped a piece of foil paper from the box and covered it. She took hold of the dish, ready to put it in the refrigerator, but suddenly turned around and tossed the whole dinner into the garbage bin. She was furious. She could feel her ears heating up realizing that he had stood her up once again.

She walked to the living room, her shoulders drooping forward. She sat down on the sofa as she bit her lower lip. *"I will not cry. I'm stronger than that.*" She grabbed a bag that contained yesterday's English exams from her 5th grade class. She started to correct a paper, but the red pen she was holding ran out of ink. She threw it against the wall. "Damn you, Dalton," she screamed. She turned her head and looked at the telephone beside her on the table. Should she call him or just go to bed? He would only apologize.

It seemed that lately she was no longer Dalton's priority. He couldn't even call her to tell her he was being detained. When she called him he would become irritated at being disturbed from his workload. Sidney began wiping the tears that were now falling down her wet cheeks. She stood up, extended her hand, momentarily touching the receiver of the phone. She debated if she should or should not call him again. She decided not to ring him. She walked toward her bedroom, determined to look at the bright side.

He said he worked long hours for them, but would they ever be able to enjoy time together? She went to her dresser and stared at herself in the mirror. She was a strong person, but when it came to Dalton she wondered if the marriage would ever work. He was rarely home to spent time with her. She loved him enormously and he loved her but ... She had been the one pushing him to get married. *Maybe he wasn't ready for a commitment.* She placed her hand on her heart and made a fist. Another tear fell as she turned away from the dresser mirror.

She decided it was no use in waiting up for him and to go to bed. She quickly took her dress off, folded it and laid it on the chair. She pulled the bedspread back and slipped under the covers. The moonlight radiated upon the small room. Sidney laid still, her arms by her side as she looked up at the ceiling. She knew he had forgotten about tonight. *Tomorrow was another day and maybe it would be better,* she thought. She had to have a serious talk with him if this union was to ever succeed. She closed her eyes and tried to clear her mind so she could fall asleep.

An hour later Sidney still wasn't sleeping. She sat up in bed, pushed the covers back, and walked toward the living room. She eyed the phone, lifted the receiver, and dialed the familiar numbers to Dalton's cell phone. She held the phone tightly, her knuckles almost white as her heart beat fast against her chest. She was determined to appease this feeling of dread in her stomach that was stopping her from dozing off. She listened as it rang, then on the second ring she heard his voice. "Hello, this is Dalton Rivers," he answered. She wondered, as she bit her fingernail, *was he still at the office?*

"Hi, it's me," Sidney said in a low voice and waited.

"Oh! Lord! I am so sorry, Sidney. I completely forgot. I started reading legal briefs and lost track of time. I'll make it up to you, love," Dalton said to her. It didn't change the situation or the lump growing in her throat.

"It's all right. It was only dinner. I was just worried, that's all," she replied. She had to stop talking, afraid that the tears might start to flow again. She clenched her jaw tight and looked at the phone in her hand.

"No, no. I'll make it up to you. I am so sorry. I'll give you a call tomorrow and we will go out to the pub for dinner. How does that sound?" Dalton said in a hurry.

"Tomorrow then?" she said, but didn't wait for his reply and hung up the phone. She stood without moving. *I definitely have to have a heart-to-heart talk with him, even though it may hurt or pull us apart. But I cannot live this way. Tomorrow will be the day.*

She held her head high and walked back to the bedroom, numb, not feeling any better, but at least she was not weeping anymore. She felt conflicting feelings. She was angry and at the same time sad. Her mind was firmly made up. She sat on the side of her bed, and then slipped under the covers one more time to try to get some sleep. She no longer was going to be the nice girl. She was going to tell him how she felt.

* * *

Dalton held the phone in his hand and looked at it. "Damn it." Sidney had hung up on him or maybe they had been cut off, though he doubted it. She was a good woman, but a little demanding on some days. She should understand that his work was vital for his success at this firm. He looked at his wrist, casting his eyes upon his Breitling watch, a gift he had given himself after becoming a partner. It was late, almost eleven o'clock. He had completely lost track of time. How could he have forgotten the dinner? Did he really feel bad for missing the meal, though? Not really. His career was his primary concern now more than ever. He needed to prove himself to the firm. He was a new partner. He would make it up to her when he had time.

He massaged his neck then stretched his arms over his head. He had so much work that was backed up and really wanted to finish as soon as possible. He would give her a call tomorrow. It would be fine. He reached for his brown Italian-made pinstripe suit jacket that was hanging on the back of his chair. He slipped one sleeve on, then the other. He bent down and picked up his briefcase, opened it, and threw in the last couple of briefs he was working on. He snapped it closed and headed for the door. He would finish his work at home and come in early in the morning so he could leave earlier the next evening.

He rode the platform down to the street and stepped on to the busy street. Even at night the streets of London were bustling with all kinds of people—from tourists to Englishmen. He lifted his arm to hail a black cab. One stopped in front of him within minutes. He opened the cab door, sitting in the back as he usually did every night for the short drive home.

"Soho Central, Oxford Street, please," Dalton said to the driver. He placed his case beside him, closed his eyes and rested his head back to relax until he got to his flat.

* * *

The next morning Annette woke up to the music of her alarm clock. The sun was streaming through the shades as the light hit her in the face. She covered her eyes with her hand. She had forgotten to close the shades the night before. She turned on her side and reached over to shut off her alarm clock. It was seven o'clock. She had not had a good night. She had tossed and turned most of the night. She had woken up several times crying in her sleep. She raised her hand again to lightly brush her fingers across her swollen eyes.

She found the energy to push herself out of bed, take a hot shower and get moving to her daily job as an executive legal assistant. As the water washed her sleepiness away, she reminisced about the day she had first met Mark. He'd had an appointment with her boss at MacDonald and Paige law firm concerning the closing of a company named A and P. She sat across from him while she took notes for her boss in the conference room. She had a hard time keeping her eyes off him or her mind on her work. He looked so dashing in his dark brown designer suit with a bright blue tie that fit him without a fault. His hair was cut short to perfection, but it was his eyes that had kept her glancing back at him. She had never seen such golden brown eyes with long black eyelashes to top it all.

On his way out he had stopped at her desk. He grinned at her. She watched as he had taken a business card out of his pocket and discreetly said, "Here's my card. Give me a call tonight after work if you would like to have a drink." She had taken the card from him with a trembling hand. She could still feel her cheeks heating up. She knew she was blushing from ear to ear. She gave him a weak smile, but had not been able to utter a word. She only nodded at him. He leaned forwarded and whispered, "I don't bite. Call me, really!" He winked at her then he walked away.

A rush of sexual desire passed through her body at that instant, and she couldn't resist telephoning him after her workday was finished. She watched him as he walked to the elevator, his back straight, his head held high with his hands by his side, and disappeared. That had been the day she knew that he was the one. She now often wondered if she could or would ever love someone else as she had her dear, departed husband.

* * *

Dalton arrived at his office building earlier than usual the next morning, coffee in one hand and his briefcase in the other. In a hurried pace he marched toward his bureau, summoning his secretary, Ginger, to follow him as he passed her desk on his way to his office.

"Good morning, Ginger. Could you please order a dozen, no, two-dozen red roses and have them sent to my fiancée, Sidney. Just write: Meet me at Nobu Restaurant tonight, Metropolitan Hotel at eight o'clock. Oh! And Ginger, could you please make a reservation? You have the address, right?" he asked her. He didn't even wait for an answer. He continued walking, never stopping for a second until he sat in his chair behind his desk. He placed his attaché case on the top of his desk and his coffee to one side. He finally looked up at Ginger.

"Yes, sir. I will send the flowers and I will make a reservation. I also have your schedule for the day," she answered as she extended her hand to place his agenda before him next to his phone.

"You have a half hour before the partners' meeting in the conference room," she told him.

"Very well. Thank you. That will be all, Ginger," he replied as he lifted his head and glanced up at her again. He watched as she turned around to head back to her work. She was a very efficient lady; he had to give her that. Dalton tapped his fingers on the desk while he thought about how he was going to get out of work early to meet Sidney. He still had tons of work. He grabbed the cup of coffee and took a sip of it. It warmed his insides on the way down. He decided he would worry about it later, when the time came. He sent her flowers, so if he were a little late, so be it. She should understand. It's not like he had much choice with his line of work.

Seven o'clock came and went and Dalton was still in a meeting at a client's luxurious home in the town Barnes, located in the South-West side of London. They were discussing the sale of his client's company to a U.S. company. His client, Mr. Paul Reynolds was an older, gray hair gentleman in his seventies, with many health problems, and was set in his ways. He was opinionated and held a tight ship on all his legal matters. He made most of his money with his beverage company, which featured his famous family tea beverage, Morning Tea in England. He now wanted to sell the rights and the entire company to an American corporation called First Drink. He basically wanted to close this deal so he could retire completely and try to enjoy the rest of his life. But lately the two parties had been having differences in opinion. There had been an inconsistency with the financial statements and it had led to a disagreement on the final sale price.

"I need you to go to Boston and personally take charge of these negotiations for me. I have had enough of their bloody bull crap with the CEO, CFO, and whoever else is at First Drink. If they don't want to buy at my price then that's just fine by me, but I have had enough. I am going to give it one more try and if the company doesn't want to give me my price, well to hell with them," he said harshly. Paul was not happy with the new terms of the agreement that had just been faxed to Dalton today.

Dalton sat in the study of the man's house, wondering how in the world he was going to find the time to go to the United States on such short notice with his overload of work. Mr. Reynolds was one of the firm's biggest clients. Dalton followed Paul slow movements without moving his head as he got up from his chair. Paul grabbed his cane, which was next to his thigh, and hobbled to the bar area. Dalton noticed a limp in his stride. With his free hand, Paul poured himself a Scotch in a tumbler, raised it to his mouth and gulped it down.

"Would you care for a drink, Dalton? I hate to drink alone, but right now I have to calm my nerves before I dissolve this contract all together." Paul lifted the Scotch crystal decanter toward Dalton. He didn't wait for an answer before he poured himself another drink.

"No, thank you. Paul, we need to be realistic. I ... really don't think that it is necessary for me to go to Boston. I will talk to my partners tomorrow and try to amend the agreement to your satisfaction without losing any capital," Dalton said while shuffling his briefs back and forth. He was trying to concentrate on the legal points supporting his client's side. He noticed Paul didn't take kindly to his answer by the way he pursed his lips and scowled. Dalton shifted his weight in his seat from one side to another. He cast his eyes upon the contract again, trying to find a resolution for his client. He could not afford to displease him. *Paul Reynolds is one of the bigger accounts of his law firm*, he reminded himself. Paul walked back and sat across from him with his half-full tumbler in one hand. He placed it on the coffee table in front of him and laid his cane by his side.

"Dalton, I truly do not believe we can come to an accord with these acquisitions unless you go to Boston and talk to them face to face. You need to pound some sense into these Americans and make them give me what I require to close this deal. I am in no physical condition to travel that far with my leg," he answered, then rubbed his knee with the palm of his hand. He glanced up at Dalton, a bit embarrassed that he had showed one of his weaknesses. He cast his eyes downwards for just an instant, then suddenly looked up and said in a confident voice, "That's what I want. This is why I pay you and your firm the fucking money I do. Do my bidding. Now get your bloody ass over there and do your job," Paul said as he stared at Dalton. He was direct and didn't want to hear no for his answer. He was showing the true colors of a rich entrepreneur.

"Well, let me talk to the other partners then I shall get back to you tomorrow. I definitely will do my best." Dalton gathered his files, opened his briefcase and carefully rested the papers in it, closed it, and snapped it shut. He picked up his case, anxious to go meet Sidney. He extended his right hand to Paul, which Paul shook firmly.

"I will call you tomorrow. Please, don't bother getting up. I will see myself out. Good day," Dalton said as he maneuvered around the chairs. He marched down the long corridor, and sighed as soon as he saw the front door. He kept his pace steady, counting every step until he grasped the handle of the front door. He pushed the handle down, the door open and he felt the cool air against his face. He noticed his driver approaching and was thankful he was attentive. He lifted his wrist to eye level and glanced at his watch. It was half past eight. He was late once again and in big trouble with Sidney.

It would still take a half hour to get to Nobu restaurant, and that was discounting traffic and the rain. He sat down in the vehicle as fast as he could then said, "Please, take me to Nobu restaurant as quickly as you can manage." He decided he would call ahead to let her know he was coming. This way she might not be as angry for having to wait on him alone. He put his hand in his jacket pocket, searching for his phone, but he did not find it. "Damn." He had forgotten his cell at the office. *"Now what?"* he thought. He had no choice but to prepare himself for whatever Sidney was going to do. She would at least be upset with him for not calling, and he envisioned another shouting match about why he hadn't at least called her beforehand to let her know he was going to be late.

Dalton rested his head on the back of the seat. He looked at the ceiling of the car and thought, *"I'm in deep shit now, and in more ways than one."*

Chapter 3

Nobu was a famous Japanese restaurant located in the Metropolitan Hotel on Old Park Lane in London. The restaurant occupied a large part of the first floor of the hotel. It had a flair for the contemporary with its décor including leather booths and wood tables. Large windows overlooked Hyde Park, which was across the street. It was one of the largest Royal parks situated in London. Nobu was always a favorite spot of many famous patrons, who demanded delicious sushi and impeccable service. The restaurant was owned and operated by a well-known chef called Nobu Matsuhisa, whose excellent reputation stemmed from the exquisite dishes he produced.

It was where Sidney and Dalton had first met two years ago while having sushi at the stylish bar area. Since that day, it had been Sidney's favorite place to eat.

* * *

Sidney received the flowers during the early morning hours. They were beautiful and she was delighted, but she didn't feel the same way about them now. A black cab had dropped her off fifteen minutes before their reservation. She was dressed in a sexy little black dress that hugged her hips and was a bit shorter than what she usually wore. She also knew Dalton liked the dress because she had long, lean legs that he admired.

John, the maître d' recognized her and greeted her as soon as she stepped in.

"Good evening, Miss Moore. How are you this evening? May I take your coat?" John said to her as she approached his counter at the front of the restaurant.

"Good evening to you, John. Yes, thank you." Sidney took off her jacket to give it to John, who preceded to hand it off to the lady at the coat check.

"Is Mr. Rivers joining you for dinner this evening? By the way, you look beautiful," he told her politely as he smiled at her. Sidney was not used to compliments from men, so her cheeks instantly turned pink. She glanced to her side for a second, smiled, and then just nodded at the man.

"Please, follow me. Your table is ready," he said as he grabbed two large menus from the pile. They walked through the filled restaurant, all eyes on them until she was seated in a corner booth by the window. John pulled the small table out a few inches so she could slide in, then laid the two menus down on their table and said, "Have a nice evening, Miss. Moore. I'll keep an eye out for Mr. Rivers for you. Your waiter will be with you momentarily." Sidney thanked him and watched him retrace his steps toward the front entrance of the restaurant.

An hour passed and Dalton still hadn't shown up yet. He was extremely late and she was fuming. She was now casting her eyes anywhere except at the people who surrounded her in the room. She had already ordered an appetizer to nibble on and she had finished her Cosmopolitan. She was feeling uncomfortable about having sat alone for so long. She kept fidgeting in her seat.

She looked at her watch discreetly one more time. It was now nine o'clock and she had not heard from Dalton. She had tried to telephone

THE PLEDGE

him, but his phone had gone directly to voicemail. He could have called if he was going to be this late. *This was the last straw,* she thought. She could not take it anymore. He would probably use his work as an excuse. What good was it to send her roses to apologize when his feelings weren't in it?

She flagged the waiter with her hand. She casually gave him her apologies while playing with her cloth napkin under the table. She avoided eye contact with the server as she shyly asked him for the check. She picked up her napkin, folded it, and placed it on the corner of the table. She got up from the table, held her breath, kept her head high, and walked out of the dining area as quickly as she could. She imagined all the patrons in the restaurant looking in her direction as she was leaving. She didn't even acknowledge John's nod on the way out. She picked up her jacket from the coat check lady without a word. She was too humiliated to speak to anyone. Her fiancé had stood her up again. *How dare he?*

The outside cool air combined with the rain brought her back to reality. She held her coat closed at the throat area as the raindrops hit her face. She ran down the block to flag a cab as tears mixed in with the rain on her face. She gave the driver her address in a feeble voice, not wanting him to notice she was crying. She sat quietly in the taxi. Not another word was spoken between them as he drove her to her flat. She turned her head and watched the rain hit and roll down the side window of the cab.

She didn't register the scenery flying by her. She felt nothing but sorrow. *How had their relationship deteriorated so quickly?* The darkness engulfed the night as she clasped her clutch bag tighter. She headed home, disappointed that their romance was going in a downward spiral. She would not take second place to his job. She was his wife-to-be and she should be his first priority.

* * *

The town car dropped Dalton at the front entrance of Nobu. He quickly paid the driver and jumped out of the vehicle. In three long strides he was standing in front of the maître d'.

"Sorry I'm late, John. Is my fiancée, Sidney, at our usual table?" he asked as he took a step to his right pass John's shoulder to scan the dining area for Sidney.

"I'm sorry, sir, but she left about fifteen minutes ago," John answered him politely.

"Bloody hell," Dalton said under his breath as he was undoing the buttons of his shirt and loosening his tie.

"Sorry, sir," John said again and excused himself to help other customers. Dalton turned on his heels and walked outside. He stood immobile at the entrance of the restaurant, getting wet from the falling rain. He kept thinking she must be livid at him. He needed to go talk to her immediately so she could understand why he was late. Hopefully she would comprehend, but he doubted it. She must have gone home. He knew she was furious with him. He had stood her up two days in a row, but this time was worst. He had left her waiting for him in a public place. How was he going to make it up to her?

Fifteen minutes later Dalton stood in front of her apartment door. He took a deep breath then exhaled. He paused and closed his eyes, trying to compose his thoughts before he rang her doorbell. He pushed the button then he heard the sound of the bell echo inside. He waited patiently as he shifted his weight from one foot to the other. He felt a wave of nausea come over him. Why? He was not sure. He hadn't planned this, so he hoped she wouldn't be too upset and that she would understand that sometimes he had no choice. It wasn't his fault. He had to devote a lot of time to his work since he was a new law partner. And that meant long hours.

If she really loved him, she would be able to grasp the importance of his work. He was doing this for their future. Well, that was what he had told her. He didn't need the money, but he wanted the prestige and recognition that would come with the job. This was going to be another fight; he could feel it in his gut. He heard the door chain rattle as the door opened slightly. Sidney stood on the other side. Her eyes were red and her face was wet. He cast his eyes downward and pouted his lower lip, sulking.

"I am so, so sorry, Sidney. It wasn't my fault. I was with a client and I did try to leave, but couldn't. Then I was going to call you, but I had forgotten my phone at the office, so I couldn't call. Please, let me in so we can talk," Dalton said as fast as he could. He placed his hand on the side of the door.

"I am really mad at you right now. It might not be a good time to talk," Sidney answered him. He could tell she was very irritated with him. She would not even look at him. She stood her ground and he noticed she hadn't opened the door yet.

"Please, open the door. Let me explain. I'll make it up to you, I promise. Let me in, please," he pleaded. She didn't move for at least a minute, but then she stepped aside to let him enter. He rushed in and closed the door behind him. He didn't move or breathe; he just waited for her to unleash her wrath upon him.

"I can't believe you embarrassed me that way. I was so humiliated. I think we should rethink our relationship. I don't seem to be your prime concern; otherwise you would have been there. I sat there while everyone looked at me. You ... you ..." Tears were filling her eyes as she turned her head away from him. He reached over to touch her arm, but she shrugged him away. Sidney walked to the sofa and sank into it. Dalton slowly moved toward her one step at a time, and then sat next to her. His knee pressed lightly against hers. She didn't pull away, so he felt he was gaining ground.

"I am truly sorry. The client kept me longer than I had anticipated. Forgive me?" he said as he gently touched her knee with his fingers. She lifted her head and narrowed her eyes at him.

"It's always the same bloody excuse: your clients. I'm frazzled by your excuses. What about me? I really don't think we should get married because you ... you keep leaving me behind without any regrets," she said, then slapped his hand away from her knee and stood to face him.

"I'm tired of you walking all over me, and then, all you do is just give me excuses. Well, I've had enough of apologies. If you want this future marriage to work, you are going to have to change your bloody ways," she said loudly. She was staring straight at him and kept rolling her engagement ring on her finger.

"Just give me another chance so I can show you I really am sorry and I love you. My work is demanding, I know, and I will try to do better. I promise," he implored. He bent his head down, pressed his hands together, and looked at his shoes. He braced himself for her reprisal, but she didn't say anything for a few minutes. There was dead silence. He lifted his head and looked up at her. He gave her a small smile.

"This is your last chance, otherwise I'm through. I cannot live like that." She crossed her arms on her chest. Dalton stood in front of her. He wrapped his arms around her waist. She didn't really resist his embrace. He kissed her softly on the lips. She tried pulling away by turning her head, but he held her tightly against his chest as he rushed his lips on hers once more. She gave him a weak smile.

"I'm really sorry," he told her as he held her against him.

"Did you eat yet?" she asked him quietly.

"Not yet." He held her closer and kissed her deeper. He knew then she was no longer mad. She wiggled out of his grip to walk to her tiny kitchen to make him a sandwich. He watched her as she prepared his food, all the while debating how he was going to tell her he might have to leave her to go to America for a least a few weeks. He would handle that tomorrow after he spoke to his partners. Why get her all hot under the collar again when he wasn't one hundred percent sure if he had to go or not.

THE PLEDGE

* * *

The next morning Dalton arrived at his office early as usual with his cup of coffee. He needed to speak to his partners as soon as possible about the closing of Paul Reynolds' Company. He went directly to Bob Jones' office, one of the senior partners, to discuss the deal. Dalton sat down across from Bob as he explained the circumstances. He tried to reason with him that it wasn't necessary for him to go to Boston, but in the end the final decision came down to the senior partners. The decision was made. He would have to go to MacDonald and Paige law firm to negotiate this deal in person. He probably would be able to close this deal faster in person and just be done with it. Dalton wasn't pleased as he walked out of the senior partner's office, but since he was the youngest partner, he had no choice about the decision. They had made it clear. He would have to go. It would be to his benefit, and the firm's, if he could secure this indenture quickly.

As he headed back toward his office, he decided that it was the right thing to do as far as his career was concerned. He had to fly out this evening on the red eye flight to Boston. He entered his office without a word to his secretary. His thoughts embroiled in his dilemma. He sat down behind his desk to think, turning his chair around to glance out the window at the people rushing down on the street. He peeked at Sidney's picture beside him. *What am I going to tell her?* He raked his hand through his locks as a few strands fell forward on his forehead. He had too much work to do as it was and he wasn't going to fret over what she would say. She had to accept it.

He opened his desk drawer to look for his Mont Blanc pen when he eyed the envelope from Mark. He reached in and touched it lightly. Mark had taken this agreement seriously and now what was he to do? He opened the envelope and tilted it to let the picture of Annette slide out. She was a ravishing woman, he had to give her that, but he already had a woman, Sidney. He placed the picture back into the envelope, but for some unknown reason he threw it in his briefcase. He snapped the case shut and headed back to his flat to pack for this trip. A thought was in the back of his mind. *Maybe, just maybe, he would have time to go meet Annette. He would never have to mention it to anyone,* he mused as he hurriedly walked out of the office.

He was not in the mood for another confrontation with Sidney. He needed to return home to retrieve his passport, pack for at least a few weeks, and get going to the airport. His secretary was in the process of making all the preparations for his flight and hotel. She would call him later. He had a feeling it was not going to go smooth with the First Drink attorneys, so he wanted to be prepared for this major deal. He was not going to go back to Boston a second time. He would have plenty of time, seven hours to be exact, to work while on this transatlantic flight. He decided he would ask Sidney to come join him after his work was done. That way she wouldn't chop his head off when he told her where he was going and for how long he was planning to be gone. They might be able to enjoy some time together after the deal was closed.

All had gone well with Sidney, especially when he had asked her to join him later on in Boston. She was excited at the prospect of spending time with him without any work. He told her he would book her a flight and informed her where he would be staying in Boston. He would call her when he was about ready to close his arrangement to come meet him that way she would not waste her time sitting in a hotel room by herself while he worked.

* * *

Dalton was sitting in seat 3A in the first class cabin of a British Airways airplane and his flight was bound to America. Dalton had been working since he first sat down. His eyelids were heavy and he was blinking to keep the fatigue away for the last hour. He brought his hand up to his face and pinched the bridge of his nose. He couldn't concentrate anymore, so he finally gave into his tiredness. He tucked his contracts away in his carry-on. He reached up and turned off the overhead light, then he pushed the button to recline his seat to lie down. He kicked off his shoes, adjusted his pillow under his head with his right hand, he pulled the blanket over his shoulders. If he were to be in form to deal with the closing the next day, he really needed to catch a few hours of sleep. It didn't take long. Dalton was fast asleep within seconds. The next thing he knew he had missed breakfast completely. The steward was tapping his shoulder telling him to straighten his seat. They were approaching Boston and were preparing for landing.

Chapter 4

Annette was at her desk, diligently drafting documents and researching titles for her boss, Mr. Paige, when her phone rang. She reached over and brought the phone to her ear.

"Good morning, Mr. Paige's office. How may I help you?" she said, suspending her work as she put the brief down on her desk and answered the call.

"Good morning. My name is Dalton Rivers. I'm Mr. Paul Reynolds's attorney from London. I just wanted to confirm my appointment with Mr. Paige at three o'clock this afternoon," Dalton said to her.

"Good morning, sir. My name is Annette. I am Mr. Paige's assistant. You are all set for three o'clock. Can I help you with anything else, sir?" she asked while tapping her pen on her desk, intrigued by his thick British accent. She always thought that the way that they pronounced their words was alluring.

"No, thank you. That will be all. Good day," he answered. The line went dead. She sat there with the phone in her hand, looking at it while fantasizing about what this man with the accent might look like. Since he was representing such a prominent law firm, she figured he was probably an older, distinguished British gentleman who smoked a pipe and dressed in three-piece plaid suits. He had to look like that to be able to speak for a company like Morning Tea, but his voice was so sexy ... *Oh well*, she thought, putting down the receiver and returning to her duties. She would find out soon enough when he arrived at their office.

* * *

Dalton finally arrived in Boston. He was a bit tired, but he would deal with the jetlag and the time difference. He arranged to have a town car to pick him up from the airport. The ride gave Dalton time to admire the cityscape, but his mind quickly went back to his purpose of the trip. The first thing he had done when he had landed was to confirm his appointment with Mr. Paige. He couldn't help but notice the softness in the voice of the girl who had answered the phone at Mr. Paige's office. *It must be the American accent*, he thought, and dismissed it. He was on his way to the Ritz Carlton on Avery Street in Boston. He was glad that he still had a few hours before his meeting. He wanted to shower after that long transatlantic flight, and he still needed to go over a few more documents.

He entered the lobby, registered at the front desk of the hotel, and was soon on his way. He took the elevator up to the tenth floor, where his room was located. He slid his hotel card into the slot of his room door and opened it. His suite consisted of a living room area, two baths, and a separate bedroom area. It was elegant, spacious, decorated in blue with yellow accents, and featured modern, mahogany furniture.

He dropped his briefcase next to the sofa as he waited for the bellboy to bring up his luggage. He walked over to the large windows, pushed the colorful drapes back and admired a view of the Boston Commons. He brought his hand up and unfastened his tie then took off his Valentino suit jacket. He dropped it on the back of the leather chair near his bed. He looked around in the bathrooms, and walked back to the living room couch where he sat down and opened his briefcase. He laid out some of his legal briefs on the coffee table in front of him. He started examining the terms of the agreements once again so that he would be prepared for the battle of this afternoon's meeting. He hoped he could manage to close this deal by the end of next week so he would have free time to explore the city. He cast his eyes toward his opened briefcase.

Suddenly, he was distracted.

He saw Mark's yellow envelope sticking out of the folder in his briefcase, as if to taunt him. He pondered for a minute, rapping his fingers on the table while he wondered what she really was like and if she knew about Mark's letter. She certainly was stunning with those captivating blue eyes—he had to give her that. *Maybe, just maybe, if he had time next week, he could ... Stop ...* This had been the second time this thought had crossed his mind. It was not a good idea to play with fire. He shook his head from side to side. This was ridiculous. He was here to work, not to chase a skirt around town. He returned his attention back to his contracts, dismissing the notion from his mind. He had been sent here to do work for a powerful company, not to go meet his dead friend's wife. And he was engaged to Sidney anyway. Just the same, why was he so preoccupied with her?

Fifteen minutes later the bellhop brought Dalton's luggage. Dalton tipped him ten dollars and proceeded to hang up his clothes. He showered and shaved quickly. He stood in front of the mirror in the bathroom with his grey Yves St. Laurent suit, his black and white pin stripe shirt, and his wine-colored tie. He picked up a comb from his toiletry bag and slicked his hair back one more time, then grabbed the bottle of Burberry cologne from the marble countertop and sprayed it twice toward his suit.

He took one last look in the mirror and he was ready for the deal of his life. He had to close this as soon as possible. He reached for the hotel phone, dialed the reception, and asked them to call him a town car. He picked up his briefcase, and with long strides he headed out the door of his hotel room, on his way to MacDonald and Paige's offices on

State Street. The attorneys' offices were located in the heart of Boston. It was two fifteen in the afternoon, allowing him plenty of time to get to his destination.

The driver dropped him off right in front of the attorneys' building. He walked into the lobby of the building and took the elevator up to the seventh floor. The doors opened into a large reception area with a signboard that read "MacDonald and Paige" on a brassy insignia. Several brown leather chairs stood to his left in the waiting area for the clients and esquires that had business with them. There was a young girl sitting at a reception desk that was facing him. As he approached her, she looked up and smiled at him.

"Good afternoon. How may I help you?" she asked politely as he noticed how she discreetly scrutinize him with her eyes.

"My name is Dalton Rivers. I have an appointment with Robert Paige at three o'clock," he answered, and smiled back at her.

"One moment, please." she replied and shyly looked away. He watched her as she checked her appointment book. She picked up the receiver of the phone and punched in a number. He heard her say, "Mr. Rivers is here for Mr. Paige." She listened to the person on the other end of the line, and then hung up the phone. She looked up at him again, smiled, and said, "You may have a seat. Someone will be right with you. Can I get you a beverage? Coffee? Water?" she questioned, and extended her hand to show him the direction of the waiting area.

"No, thank you. I'm all set," Dalton replied as she returned to her work. He walked to one of the chairs and sat down, placing his briefcase next to him. He crossed his leg and placed his hands on the arms of the chair. There was a coffee table in front of him that had several magazines and a Boston Globe newspaper. Dalton reached over and picked up the daily newspaper. He might as well read to pass the time while waiting, since he was early. He had been reading the local news for about ten minutes when he heard a quiet voice say. "Mr. Rivers, my name is Annette Russell. I'm Mr. Paige's assistant. Nice to meet you."

As Dalton lifted his eyes from the newspaper, his heart started to race immediately. He was staring into a familiar pair of baby blue eyes. His mouth instantly became dry. He couldn't believe it. The picture that Mark had sent! It was the woman in the photograph! He was meeting the woman in the picture he had received from Mark. He couldn't move; he just sat there holding the newspaper while looking up at her. Finally he heard his name again. "Mr. Rivers?" Annette said with a puzzled look on her face. She extended her hand toward him. He finally noticed her hand. He placed the paper down on the table and smiled at her while trying to compose himself. He reached out and shook her hand.

"Sorry. Nice to meet you, Annette," he managed to say. As he stood up, his legs felt weak from the shock of the encounter.

For some unknown reason, when he touched her he felt a strong desire pass through his loins. He couldn't let go of her hand. Her touch was so soft. He could smell her floral perfume. He had been caught off guard. She was gazing right into his eyes, and the rich blue of her irises was absolutely mesmerizing. Her beauty hypnotized him. He realized he was still holding her hand and immediately let go. He rubbed his hand against his pant leg. A little embarrassed he said, "So sorry. After you." He just grinned at her.

"If you'll follow me, I'll take you to the conference room," she told him. He picked up his briefcase with a slight tremble in his hand. He accompanied her close behind, watching her skirt flow as her hips moved from one side to the other. Her luscious blonde hair bounced on her shoulders as she walked in front of him. He wanted to stretch out his hand and run his fingers through her hair. This was not happening. He had to regain control of himself. He stood upright, chest out, and he looked straight ahead as he continued to follow behind her.

"Did you have a pleasant flight?" she asked as he trailed her. She turned to glance at him, and the aroma of her floral perfume drove him wild with lust.

"Yes ... yes, it was good. Thank you," he replied, still distracted by her. He tightened his grip on his attaché case. He was stunned that a woman could cause him to forget everything around him. He couldn't fathom what was wrong with him. She had some sort of magnetic pull on him and he couldn't get away. He directed his sight to look straight ahead. He thanked God when they arrived at a conference room. He was trying not to look unprofessional or foolish.

"If you'll have a seat, Mr. Paige will be right in. Make yourself at home," she said and turned to leave.

"Thank you," he mumbled as he eyed her walking away. He hurried in, placed his hand flat on the table, and exhaled so he could concentrate. He took the nearest seat at the table. He was relieved he was alone. He slowly took his documents out of his briefcase. This was going to be an interesting meeting, especially if she came back into the room. He really hoped she didn't otherwise ...

How was he going to focus knowing who she really was and not being able to say anything to her? He had to concentrate and keep his mind on this deal, not that woman. Maybe after he was done with this business he would talk to her. He kept looking out the door at the chance she might walk by while he waited for Paige to arrive into the conference room. His leg was bobbing under the table as he glanced around the room, trying to exclude her from his mind. He placed his hand on his knee to stop it from bouncing. His desire was so unexpected and he was aghast at his reaction. He knew he would be in trouble if his nerves got the best of him.

"Pay attention to your work," he mumbled to himself.

"Mr. Rivers, my name is Robert Paige. So nice to meet you," a small balding man in his late fifties walked in with a bunch of files under his arm. He was well groomed, wearing a two-piece brown suit. He extended his hand over to Dalton and shook it. He dropped his files on the table as he sat across from him.

"The same here, Mr. Paige. And please, call me Dalton," Dalton told him with a sigh of relief; grateful Annette hadn't followed him into the meeting room. Now he could focus his energy on his work.

"Would you care for something to drink before we begin? Coffee? Soda? Or water? I can have my assistant get it for you," he asked him as he began to sort his briefs. Dalton really wanted to see her again, but he didn't need any distractions. He was having enough problems keeping his mind on work without having her in the room.

"No, no, I'm fine at the moment. Thank you," Dalton said as he started reading his acquisitions and getting ready to start the negotiations.

"Very well then. Shall we begin? I know we have a lot to cover," Robert said, then opened his files and took his briefs out.

* * *

Annette was now safely sitting at her desk, amazed that she had made it this far without fumbling her words, or worse, making a fool of herself in front of Dalton Rivers. She was trying to calm her nerves, but her whole body was still shaking. She glanced once more toward the room where her boss and Dalton were in a meeting. She had not expected to have such strong reaction when she first met this man. He was so good-looking; so drop-dead gorgeous in his newly pressed suit. She loved his black hair and how he slicked it back. She figured he couldn't be more than thirty-five. He had such a sexy voice, and the British accent fit his demeanor. He was intriguing.

He was the first man since Mark's death that had caught her complete attention. She was remembering the dimples in his cheeks when he had smiled at her. She touched her hand and could still feel his strong grip. The way that he looked into her eyes had surprised her the most. It was as if he knew her. She usually didn't react this way when attorneys came to this office, but this man had left a serious impression.

She tried to return to her work, but it was slow. She couldn't get him out of her mind. She hoped she would be able to see him again before he left at the end of the day. *How was it possible he had captured her interests so quickly?* This feeling was what she felt when she first met Mark. He was the only one to ever make her feel this way. She never dreamed that she would feel it again after he had died. Yet in spite of the fact that she only met this man, Dalton, moments ago, she was thinking about him sexually. *How could this be happening?*

"This is not me. It's totally ridiculous," she said to herself.

The minutes turned into hours, but she still couldn't keep from thinking about him. It was now almost six o'clock at night. Mr. Paige and Mr. Rivers were still discussing the contracts. Annette was about to leave for the evening, so she walked to the conference room and gently knocked on the door. She turned the knob and peeked her head inside. She instantly noticed how his head whipped around to look at her.

"Did you need anything else before I leave, Mr. Paige?" she asked not wanting to look at Dalton and keeping her eyes on her boss.

"Yes, Annette. One more thing, please. We are just about done for the evening. Could you check and see if you could get us a reservation for dinner at Island Creek Oyster Bar down the street?" Robert asked her politely.

She nodded, smiled, and asked. "Sure, no problem. For how many people?" She kept her eyes on Robert. She feared if she glanced at the Englishman, she might embarrass herself by stumbling over her words.

"Three. Why don't you join us?" she heard Dalton say. She spun her head toward him and looked at him, then at her boss. She was speechless.

"That's a great idea. Why don't you join us? It's up to her," replied Robert, unfazed. "We are all done for the day," he continued. She turned to face Dalton, surprised at the invitation as she blushed. She could feel her cheeks burning. Her mouth opened, but then she closed it. She did go out to dinner once in a while with clients and her boss, but usually it was business. Mr. Paige had been kind and loving like a father to her since she had lost her husband. They were very close friends. Dalton just sat there. He tilted his head and grinned at her.

"I'm sorry, but I can't tonight. Maybe another time," she answered quickly.

"Another time, then," she heard Dalton say. Then he smiled at her, showing her those dimples once again. She swallowed hard. She felt a bit flattered by the invitation, but did not address his issue.

"I will be right back." She closed the door as fast as she could. She braced her back against the door for support. Oh! My God! That was forward. Why hadn't she accepted it? She had been thinking of him all day. She had not been able to keep her mind on her work. She had made excuses to peak at him through the door when it was open. Now she had just denied his offer to dinner. What was the matter with her?

It wouldn't have been appropriate to accept his offer since she was attracted to him and her boss still had to work to finish with him. The attorneys that came to the office had never lured her out to dinner. *Robert was going to be there anyway. It might be awkward*, she told herself. What was she thinking? She slowly sat down at her desk. She found the number of the restaurant and called to make a reservation for two for dinner. Her mind was not on her work.

She could not believe what had just happened. This man had asked her to dinner. How bold of him! They had just met. But that was what she had really wanted, so why not accept? She wondered if she was overthinking this. He was just being polite, that was all. It was not like she had never been asked to dinner before she had gotten married. She glanced at her husband's picture near her on her desk, feeling a bit guilty to have thought of accepting his invitation. Now she had to return to the conference room to tell them about the reservation. This time she decided to make her entrance quick and precise then leave the room. She knocked on the door and only took one step into the room.

"You are all set, Mr. Paige. You have a reservation at the Island Creek Oyster Bar for seven o'clock," she said, bracing her hand against the doorknob of the door for support. She was ready for anything else he might throw at her.

"Thank you, Annette. Have a good night and see you tomorrow." She nodded, trying to concentrate and not look at Dalton, but she dared to take one last swift glimpse toward his way. He was just sitting there smiling her way. It took all her strength to quickly pull the door shut. What was she doing? Flirting? What was she going to do tomorrow when she saw him again? *This was absurd. This man must flirt with all the women he met. It didn't mean anything.* She walked back to her desk, put on her coat, and left the office. For some unknown reason she was kind of excited thinking about the next day. It was something that had not happened in a long time. She couldn't wait to see him again. She wondered if he would try to ask her out again.

Chapter 5

Annette had not been able to think of anything else but Dalton all evening. This had never happened to her in her life. Her mind was consumed with thoughts of him. She felt guilty about the desires and curiosity she felt toward a man she had only just met. She knew he wasn't married. She hadn't noticed a wedding band on his left hand, but she knew that didn't mean anything these days. It was eleven o'clock at night and still she was unable to sleep, so she grabbed her laptop from the night table next to her bed.

She wanted to know more about him. She felt ashamed that she was thinking of snooping on this man, but it would be harmless if she just looked him up on the Internet. She made the decision to see what she could find. She googled his name on her computer and up popped his picture with all kind of facts. He certainly was a handsome and appealing man. He was also the youngest partner at Jones and McCarthy, one of oldest firms in London. Impressive! He was single! He had gone to Harvard Law School and he graduated the same year as Mark. It was an odd coincidence and she couldn't help but wonder if he had known Mark. If she had a chance, she was definitely going to ask him about it.

She was overdoing it. She was looking up a man she had just met this afternoon—at her office of all places. "This is crazy. You sound like a stalker," she said and shut down her laptop. After closing it, she reached over to place it back on her night table. She slid down into her bed, pulled the blankets up, and closed her eyes, longing to dream about Dalton. Tomorrow was a new day and she hoped Mr. Dalton Rivers would be as mysterious as he had been today.

* * *

The next morning Dalton awoke feeling well rested. He had a good night's sleep. He was ready to go back to work. He left the hotel and was greeted by his driver of his town car. He couldn't wait to get to the law firm to see Annette again. His thoughts had been on Annette most of last night. He was disappointed that she hadn't accepted his dinner invitation, but it had been at the spur of the moment and not very tactful. The words had just sprung out of his mouth without thinking.

He wanted to spend time with her, but he would have to be more gallant next time. He would ask her again today, but in a more delicate, private way. He was curious about her. He needed to know more about this woman. He wanted to know about her than anyone he had ever encountered in years. This was really strange. *How had he accidently run across his roommate's widow?* She was in most of his thoughts when not working on this sale, and still ...

He had discreetly inquired about her at dinner the previous evening through Robert.

"So Robert, if I may. Tell me about your assistant Annette," Dalton asked in passing conversation as he sipped his red wine.

"She is a great girl, exceptional worker. She lost her husband in a car accident last year. I wish she would start going out again. It would do her good. Why interested?" Robert said with his eyebrows raised, looking at Dalton as he lifted his single malt to his mouth to gulp it down.

"Well, I do fancy her and she is a stunning woman, I must say!" Dalton replied without thinking to whom he was talking or what he had just revealed. He reached over and stuffed an oyster with bread in his mouth.

"I kind of took her under my wing when her husband died, and she's like a daughter to me. She has been with me for quite a few years. If I was only a few years younger and not happily married ... I wish you luck." Robert laughed. He returned to eating his swordfish. The rest of the evening had gone by without another mention of Annette.

* * *

Dalton was sitting in the backseat of his town car, looking out the window on his way back to the attorneys' office when he asked the driver, "Could you stop here, please?"

The driver eyed him in his rearview mirror.

"Yes, sir." He began to pull over to the curb and stopped as soon as he could.

Dalton rapidly opened his door and said, "Could you wait here? I'll be right back. I just want to run into this store for a moment." The driver nodded as he watched Dalton run inside. A few minutes later Dalton exited the store with a brown paper bag in his hand. He was back in the car and on his way to the law office.

He had gotten up this morning with Annette on his mind, so he arrived early at the law firm. She wasn't there when he arrived. He was disappointed when another girl instead of Annette escorted him into the meeting room. He had hoped he would have time to talk to her before he started work with Robert. He felt more confident today as he approached the conference room. He took his papers out quickly and prepared for his appointment. He reached into his case and removed the small paper bag. He stood up before Robert came to the room and with long strides, his heart pounding fast; he sneaked to Annette's station. He placed the bag on her desk. He hurried back to his previous seat in the conference room. Dalton smiled to himself, hoping she would like what he had bought her. He waited patiently for Robert to arrive and start going over the numbers of the closing again.

* * *

Annette was late arriving at work today. She had a lame excuse and she felt guilty about it. Well, just a little bit. It was silly, but she hadn't been able to make a decision this morning on what to wear—the blue dress or the purple one. She knew Dalton would be there again today, and for the first time in a long time she wanted to look exceptionally nice ... for him. She wanted to be noticed. She finally made up her mind and picked the blue one. *My eyes stand out more with the blue. Well, that was what Mark used to say,* she thought.

She hurried to her desk with great haste the minute she entered the office floor, but with the heels she wore, it was virtually impossible to quicken her pace much. She hoped Robert wouldn't note her tardiness, but she knew better. He was very perceptive when it came to her, just like a protective father. He was already in the conference room working when she sat down at her station. She threw her purse under her desk, sat down, and tried to catch her breath for a minute from running down the hallway. She stood up again and she walked to the coffee machine in the firm's small kitchen, which was located in the back of the offices, as she did every morning. She grabbed her mug and poured herself a cup of coffee. She brought it to her mouth and sipped it on her way back to her desk, trying to calm down. This was absurd. She had to relax.

She noticed a brown paper bag on the top of her desk by her phone. She hadn't seen it when she had first sat down. She placed her cup of coffee beside her computer, extended her hand, and grasped it. She opened it to peek inside. Her eyebrows shot up as she looked around, wondering who had left her such an unexpected delight. It was a large cinnamon roll with lots of frosting. Her hand could feel it was still warm.

"Mmm!" she expressed as she took it out and placed it on one of the napkins. She carefully picked it up, brought it to her mouth and bit into it. "Nice!" She licked her fingers one at a time, hoping no one was watching her as she devoured the cinnamon roll. She was famished since she didn't have time to have breakfast this morning. She assumed it was her friend Abby's doing. She was one of the other paralegals in the office and she sometimes brought Annette food. She must have dropped it off when she was out. Annette would have to thank her when she saw her.

She kept an eye on the conference room, hoping to get a glimpse of Dalton again, but she didn't hear from Robert until midmorning when he asked her to bring in additional documents. She immediately found them. She headed to the conference room, her heart beating faster as she brought them to him. She knocked on the door lightly when she heard Dalton's voice.

"Come in," he said. She entered the room. She stopped abruptly, still holding on to the doorknob. Her mouth opened. Robert wasn't in the room. She took a step forward toward the table and said, "Mr. Paige asked for these documents." She placed them on Robert's side of the table without looking directly at Dalton.

"He went to the men's room," she heard him say as she turned her head to sneak a look at him.

"Oh! He did. Could you please tell him I brought the files he asked for?" she replied, a little embarrassed about repeating herself. She smiled. There was complete silence. She didn't know what to say to him. She was tongue-tied, so she started to return back to her desk when he spoke again.

"Did you enjoy your cinnamon bun?" he asked, grinning at her. She caught a glimpse of his dimples as she turned to face him.

"It was from you!" she exclaimed, surprised. She placed her hand in front of her mouth and sucked her breath in.

"Yes. Did you enjoy it? It was sort of an apology gift for bombarding you last night for dinner," he said. He was sitting motionless, his hands clasped in front of him. His eyes were glued to her.

He frowned after she still hadn't responded, so she finally said, "Oh! Yes. It was ... delectable, thank you. It was very considerate of you, but you didn't offend me by asking me out to dinner."

She could feel her cheeks ablaze again and she knew she was blushing. It always happened when she was tense. She started to turn around again to return to her desk when he said, "So, does that mean you will go to dinner with me this evening? I'm sure you could recommend a nice place." She froze on the spot. She stood straight as a board, closed her eyes, trying to calm herself. Her heart began beating fast against her chest. She slowly lifted her gaze to face him. She put her hands into her pockets instantly so he wouldn't see them trembling.

"Well, I ... suppose I could ... that is, if you ... I would like that." She couldn't believe it. She couldn't speak and her tongue was like sandpaper. She was so nervous. She needed a glass of water to quench her thirst! She felt like she was making a fool of herself, but she gave him a shy smile.

"Perfect! We can leave after I finish work with Robert today. Why don't you make a reservation? Anywhere you prefer," he said. He smiled broadly showing his pearly white teeth. All she could do was nod slightly and reply, "Okay." She hurried out of the room and went back to her desk. She sat motionless for at least five minutes, not able to concentrate on anything. She had a date. Her stomach was quivering. She tried to relax. It was only dinner, she kept telling herself, but it was her first ... her first real date since Mark had died.

"It will be all right," she kept telling herself. "Stop fidgeting, for God's sake, and get back to work."

For the rest of the day she was trapped in a whirlwind of work. Thank God! She hadn't seen him again all day. Yet she had trouble with all of her work. All she could think of was: him. It all had happened so fast. She hadn't had time to process anything. She had said yes.

* * *

Dalton loved her shyness and how she tried to hide her shock from him when she learned that he had purchased the cinnamon roll for her. He couldn't wait for the end of the day. He debated whether he should tell her about the letter. It might freak her out and he didn't know her yet. Plus, she seemed nervous enough. By six o'clock he couldn't stand another minute of looking at numbers and discussing the sale. He put his spreadsheets down and said, "Robert would you mind terribly if we continued tomorrow?"

"No, no. It's been a long day. You must be exhausted with the time change and all," Robert answered and gathered his files to put them away. "We can resume tomorrow. Not a problem," he told him.

"Yes, thank you. But I do have another reason for cutting the day early. I asked Annette out for dinner again and she accepted. I hope you don't mind," he said, sorry afterwards he had mentioned it unsure what Robert might think.

"That's fabulous. She needs to start going out again. Go and have a great time. We can continue later. It's going to take us many more days anyway," Robert answered him. He got up, shook Dalton hand, and walked out of the room, leaving Dalton alone.

Dalton slipped on his suit jacket on. He picked up his briefcase. He was holding it tight as he strolled down to Annette's desk. When he approached her area he surveyed it but he didn't see her. He decided to wait. Maybe she had gone to another room. He leaned his shoulder against the wall and checked his watch. It was only five after six. Minutes ticked away, and fifteen minutes later Dalton noticed the receptionist go by. "Excuse me, Miss. Would you know where I could find Annette?" he asked her. He was getting curious as to why she hadn't come back to her desk.

"I'm sorry, but she left about an hour ago," she replied, then started to walk away, but Dalton needed more details.

"I'm sorry, would you know if she is coming back? Was she sick or something?"

"I saw her leave. I don't think she will be returning today. She had all her stuff with her. I think she was going home for the evening." She gave him a quick smile and then she went on her way down the hallway. Dalton watched her walk away, stunned.

He just stood there mystified. What had happened? What had made her change her mind and not want to go to dinner with him? Maybe he had pressured her too much. He was disappointed, but maybe she really didn't want to have dinner with him. She had just been trying to be nice to him by accepting. Maybe she hadn't wanted to offend him. Why hadn't she just said no? The more he thought about it, he remembered she had seemed extremely agitated when he had asked her out. He recalled what Robert had said: she didn't date. He headed back to his hotel for a room service dinner and an early night in.

* * *

Annette sat by herself on the sofa in her living room, staring at her husband's picture that was on the end table. She had felt guilty all day after she had accepted the dinner invitation from Dalton. How could she move on with her life when all she wanted was her husband back? She knew it wasn't possible, but her heart broke to pieces every time she thought about him. She still loved him—even though he was dead.

She knew in her heart that she had to start going out again and meeting new people. She still was young. She couldn't grieve over Mark's death forever, but she was still filled with sorrow. It didn't feel right yet. She thought about Dalton, how sweet and considerate he had been today by buying her sweets. She was afraid of losing the feelings she still had for her husband. She felt like she was being unfaithful to Mark. "He is no longer here," she told herself over and over. "You have to move on. Mark would have wanted you to do so." Why hadn't she stayed at the office? She felt ashamed and mortified that she had not been mature enough to talk to the man face to face. She should have explained her position rather than leaving him waiting for her without a reason. A tear fell from the corner of her eye, but she let it fall. "What am I going to say to him tomorrow?" she mumbled to herself. She rubbed her hands together, thinking.

She did like the man a lot. He made her feel excited to be alive again. It was a feeling she had not felt in a long time, so why deny it? Her heart skipped a beat just thinking about him. She didn't know much about him, but for the love of God, she had googled the man. She definitely was attracted to him. It brought a giggle out of her as she bowed her head. She placed her hands in front of her face, embarrassed at what she had done. She had stood him up without an explanation. He didn't deserve that.

Today had been overwhelming. She hadn't expected the invitation. She wondered what he thought of her now that she had fled to hide in her house instead of telling him the truth. She decided tomorrow she would apologize for standing him up. She hoped she could get a rain check on that dinner. What was she going to tell him when she saw him? She decided she would tell him the truth: that she had been afraid and was really sorry she had stood him up—or something like that. She laughed. She got up walked to her bedroom, brushed her teeth, and went to bed. She was tired. She had not slept that great since Dalton had walked into her life.

Chapter 6

Dalton couldn't believe she had gone home yesterday. Annette had stood him up. That had never happened to him. Maybe she had been sick or maybe she really didn't feel the same way as he did. He couldn't wait to see her again to find out her reason. Dalton decided to pick up another cinnamon roll for her. He placed it on her desk on his way to meet Robert in the conference room. This time he left a note inside the bag that read: "My apologies if I was too direct yesterday. I hope we can be friends. Please accept this token as a peace offering, signed: Dalton."

The hours flew by. By midafternoon he still had not seen her or heard from Annette. He wondered if she wasn't feeling well again or was just avoiding him. All through the day it always had been another girl who would deliver the briefs they needed for the closing. He didn't even leave for lunch. They had ordered in. He had gone by her desk, but she was nowhere to be found. He had debated asking Robert if she were sick, but didn't dare. Dalton felt a bit uncomfortable. He had been stood up and he wondered if Robert knew about it, because he had not mentioned the date.

Two days had gone by without seeing her or a word from her. Today was going to be one of his last days at this law firm. Everything was in order. The two parties had finally agreed on a price of the closing and he had faxed the contracts to Paul to sign. The deal was done. If he didn't see her today, he might never see her again. He wanted to find her so he could talk to her and tell her he was sorry for the misunderstanding or for offending her.

He desperately longed to see her blue eyes one more time, just so he could say goodbye, and tell her that it had been a pleasure meeting her. Maybe the next time he was in Boston they might be able to have coffee or something. She had not waited for him. He was hoping she would at least explain why, but he would not pressure her unless she volunteered the information. He was disappointed that they couldn't fix the misunderstanding before he departed, and it was eating him up.

It was four o'clock in the afternoon when another paralegal appeared in the conference room while he was packing up his documents to leave and return to the hotel.

"Mr. Rivers, this is for you," she said, then she handed him a small white envelope. He looked up at her as she handed him an envelope. She turned around right away and left the room without another word. Dalton ripped it open and read the small card. A smile appeared on his face. He couldn't believe his luck. He automatically felt a sense of relief come over him. He would see her again. It was an invitation to dinner this evening at six o'clock at Hennessey's Pub on Union Street, Boston. He examined the card. It was not signed, but in his heart he knew it was Annette. Who besides her knew that he was in Boston? Who else would invite him out? It had to be Annette. Didn't she know that the British usually didn't go to Irish pubs? He laughed, and was delighted he still had a chance to see her. He tossed his files in his briefcase and walked out of the law office.

The timing of letter only gave him enough time to go back to his hotel, shower, and change into more casual attire. He was thrilled at the prospect of seeing her again. He placed the card in his coat pocket and he walked briskly to the elevator, all the while thinking if he should tell her about the letter or keep it a secret. He would play it by ear first to see how the date unrolled, and then, make his decision. He had never been so excited to go meet a woman as he was this evening. *Funny how things turned out.* He wondered if Mark had felt the same as he did on his first date with Annette.

A yellow cab dropped him off at the front door of the Hennessey Pub. He grabbed the front door handle and pulled hard. He strolled inside slowly. He abruptly stopped to admire the décor. *How delightful!* He thought. This place looked like an authentic Irish Pub with its old rustic wooded chairs and tables. A few pieces of stained glass Irish emblems and Irish flags were hung on the walls, along with several carved wooden signs. *How Irish!* He chuckled. A couple of timber booths stood in the back of the pub, but the fully-stocked bar in front of him was what was impressive. It seemed to have a wide range of beers on tap and single malt whiskeys.

A wood fireplace in the back area warmed the customers from the cold weather brewing outside. It wasn't a large place, but it was quaint. Patrons were sampling ale with friends and laughter filled the air. It was packed with people of all walks of life, from college kids to business people in suits, all gathered together eating, drinking, and having a good time. A band of young artists were strumming on guitars and violins in the background on a small stage, singing old Irish songs. It set the mood for a jolly time. This was her type of place. She wouldn't feel threatened with him. It was cozy and there were lot of people around her. He had to find her.

He first cast his eyes toward the bar area. He moved forward at a slow pace, scanning the scene for her. There wasn't much room to maneuver around the table, but he made his way forward. He noticed a blonde woman with her hair tied back in a ponytail at the bar. She was wearing a blue sweater and blue jeans, her coat hanging on the back of her chair. She was sitting by herself, drinking a mug of tap beer. He knew it was Annette.

He unhurriedly approached her from behind. He extended his hand as he gently stroked the top of her arm. He let his hand slide down to her elbow. She turned her head toward him. She glanced at his hand that was resting on her arm. She looked up at Dalton. Her eyes sparkled in the dim light. The smile she gave him made his whole body lust for her.

"Hi, I'm glad you decided to come. I was afraid you might not show," she said to him, keeping her focus on his face. He moved his body closer to hers, moving between the chairs that were filled with other customers. He could smell her lavender perfume and it engulfed his sexual senses. It made him want her even more, but he knew he would have to take it slow. He didn't want to her to retreat away from him again. He placed one arm protectively around the back of her chair and his other hand on the side of the bar. He was inches from her and if he leaned just a few inches, he could kiss her, but he didn't want to scare her away. As he examined her face more closely, he noticed freckles around her nose peeking through her makeup. He hadn't noticed them before. Strands of her hair had fallen out of her ponytail. He wanted to rearrange them, but didn't dare. She looked lovely.

"I'm pleased you invited me. After the last time I saw you, I wasn't sure you wanted anything to do with me." He couldn't keep himself from staring at her blue eyes. When she opened her mouth, all he wanted to do was crash his mouth down on her luscious lips.

"I'm so sorry about that. I wasn't prepared for you. You caught me off guard and I didn't know how to deal with it. This is all new to me. Dating again, I mean. I hate to admit it, but you are the first date I have had since my husband died last year," she answered as she turned her head away, avoiding his gaze. He noticed she shifted her leg away from him. He knew she was a little sad and probably uncomfortable. He would have to gain her trust.

She took a sip of her beer and asked, "What can I get you to drink? Tonight, it's my treat for standing you up the other night." She touched his hand slightly, but she pulled it away swiftly. Dalton noticed she was tapping her finger on her knee. She was nervous, which was understandable since she hadn't dated since Mark's death. He knew this was a big step for her and he was not going to blow the only chance he had to get to know her. He would take it unhurriedly and try not to scare her away again. With his index finger, he pointed at her glass.

"I'll have whatever you're drinking. Ale is fine," he said. He grinned at her. She smiled back. He watched as she flagged the bartender and signaled for two more beers. The bartender nodded. They observed as he filled two more mugs of beer and placed them in front of them. Dalton lifted his mug toward Annette. "Cheers! To our new friendship," he said as he took a gulp of his drink then licked his lips. "Not bad, I must say."

A brunette lady was standing next to him holding menus as she interrupted them by touching Annette on her shoulder with her hand. "Your booth is ready, Annette, if you'll accompany me," she said to them. The woman started walking towards the back of the room. Annette gathered her coat under her arm and she started to follow her, as did Dalton.

He sat across from her as she slid into the last booth in the back of the pub. Thank God! It was less noisy in this spot, at least, and they could talk more quietly without too many distractions.

"You must come here often since they know you by your first name," he said. He could tell she was still anxious, her eyes darting everywhere but at him.

"Yes, I do. So, how are you enjoying your stay in Boston? Have you had time to visit the city yet?" she asked him as she opened her menu and kept her eyes downcast into it.

"Now that you are sitting with me, I'm liking it much more. And thank you for offering to show me the city tomorrow," Dalton said to her, taking advantage of the opportunity to spend more time with her. She started to giggle as she brought her menu in front of her face.

"You are too funny. How do you know I want to ..." she stopped speaking she seemed to be thinking about what he had said, then she faced him and said, "Very well, you're on. I'll show you the city, but first I will have to ask Robert for time off," she answered with a mimic of his British accent.

"Ohhh!" he replied, laughing at the poor accent she had just tried to pull off. "What if I asked him? I'm sure I can convince him. I really need a tour guide if I'm going to enjoy my last days here," he answered her with smirk on his face. He returned to his menu.

"Thanks, but I can do it," she said. She closed her menu and intertwined her fingers on top of it, ready to order.

The waitress returned a few minutes later to take care of their order. They both ordered the specialty of the house—Irish American burgers—and more ale. He watched Annette as the server grabbed the menus, thanked them, and left them to their conversation. She moved her hands around her ale mug. She peered at the wood table that had carved names into it. He detected a slight tremor in her hands, but didn't say anything.

"So tell me about yourself?" she asked as they waited for their food.

"What would you like to know? I live in London. I am an attorney. I'm a very adorable, trustworthy person and I love movies," he answered, picking on her. He looked up. She was shaking her head.

"An attorney? Really? Wow! What an interesting career." He could tell she was warming up and she seemed more comfortable with him. At least she was joking. She didn't seem as shy, at least. She was participating in the conversation and she was having fun. Her laugh brought joy to his heart for some reason. "Where did you go to school?" she inquired. She pulled over the bowl of popcorn the server had dropped off while they waited for their burgers. She started popping a few pieces in her mouth and munched on them.

"I studied here in Cambridge, I graduated from Harvard Law School ten years ago, then I returned home to London to find a job," he replied, hoping she would not question him about the law school ... but it was not meant to be.

"Really? My late husband went to Harvard Law, too. The same school ... Maybe you knew him. His name was Mark Russell. He graduated in 1995," she said. She became quiet and distant right after she uttered the words. Dalton could see tears swimming in her eyes. He reached over and gently touched her hand with his. It seemed to bring her back to life.

"Yes, I knew him. He was in some of my classes. He was a great man. I am so sorry for your loss. I will never forget him," he said while he kept rubbing her hand with his thumb. She looked up, but didn't pull her hand away. She surprised him by wrapping her fingers around his and squeezing his hand lightly.

"I'm sorry. I don't mean to ... "she whispered to him regretfully, but she didn't look at him.

"It's all right. So where are we going tomorrow? We could take a duck tour and have lunch at Faneuil Hall or ..." He tried to change the subject. He couldn't bear to see her sad.

"You have it all set, don't you? All right, then, I will show you the city even though you seem to know it quite well," she said with a smile. The waitress arrived with their food. She placed the burgers and fries in front of them. "Let me know if you need anything else," the server told them.

"How about one more beer each," Dalton ordered. He glanced at Annette, who was nodding. They ate and talked for hours about their dreams and their lives. The only thing he had not mentioned was Sidney.

It was close to midnight and many beers later when she announced with a chuckle, "It's late. I think it's time to go home. I've had more than my share of alcohol. It's time to go home." He could tell she felt tipsy with all the beer she had consumed. She kept giggling and she was more open about herself now than she had been all night.

"I had a great time. I can't wait for tomorrow. I'll accompany you home," he said, but he knew the instant he had said it, something was wrong. She became silent and not one word spoken. She swiftly put on her coat. She averted his eyes and fumbled for her keys in her pocketbook.

"I didn't mean ... I meant we can share a cab," he replied quickly as he winked at her. He nodded at her, a bit embarrassed. They slid out of their booth and they walked outside where a taxi was waiting. The cabbie first took Annette home. The drive to her home wasn't far. She placed her hand on his knee, but he didn't move it. She was becoming friendlier and he was pleased. Just her touch on his skin made him hot all over. When the driver parked in front of her house, Dalton pushed his door open then jumped into the street. He walked around the car to open her door as she stepped out. He poked his head into the car to talk to the driver. "Could you wait for me, please? I'll be right back," Dalton said, and the cabbie nodded.

"I'll walk you to your door," he told Annette as he followed her close behind.

"It's not necessary. I'll be fine," she answered, but he didn't listen to her. He took her hand in his as he approached the door of her house. They stood at the entrance of her house.

"Thank you for a fabulous time," she said, but then he saw her lips part to say another word, Dalton couldn't resist. He surrounded her waist with his hands and he pulled her against his body. She didn't protest or back away. He gently cupped her face with his palms, and brought his mouth down on hers. Their tongues danced together as he pressed his hips closer to hers. He could feel her arms caressing his back. An erection mounting, his whole body was aching for her. His desire was intensifying. He pulled away, looked down at her as he kissed her again on the cheek lightly.

"Thanks for a great evening. I can't wait until tomorrow," he said. He let go of her even though he would have preferred not to. He watched her as she turned the key into the lock of the front door. He was wishing she would invite him in, but it was not meant to be. She said, "Bye," and the door closed. She disappeared behind the door.

* * *

Annette leaned against the closed front door, trying to catch her breath and stop the weakness she had in her legs. She had never been kissed like that. Her husband had not kissed as good as Dalton. She took a step forward, trying to regain her balance by holding on to the wall on her way to her bedroom. The sexual attraction that man transmitted was unlike anything she had ever experienced. She still could hear his British accent ringing in her mind and she absolutely loved the tone in her ears. She still could feel a tingle on her lips from his kiss as she brushed a finger on her upper lip.

She loved how his warm body fitted so well against hers. She was happy she had decided to invite him out. She felt a little guilty she stood him up before, but it was now resolved. She couldn't wait to see him again the following day. She wanted to know more about this man. She needed to feel him against her at least one more time. *How could she like everything about him? He was perfect. She had just met him, but maybe he was her second chance at happiness after all.* She really wanted to believe it.

She undressed and threw her jeans and sweater on the chair in her bedroom. She crept under the blankets of her bed, wearing only her underwear. She closed her eyes. Her head sank into the feathered pillow while it spun, either from all the beer or maybe from his kiss. She didn't care, because tonight was one of the few nights she was going to fall asleep content without crying herself to sleep, not even a tear.

* * *

Dalton arrived at his hotel room when he heard his cell phone ring. He stuck his hand in his coat pocket and looked the phone. When he saw the caller's number displayed, "Crap," he heard himself say. He didn't want to talk to her. What was he to do? He had been so preoccupied with work and Annette he had completely forgotten about her ... his fiancée, Sidney.

Chapter 7

Dalton sat on the edge of his bed in his hotel room. He stared at the phone in his hand, trying to decide what he was going to tell Sidney. He had been gone almost a week and still hadn't talked to her. No wonder she was calling. He knew he had to call her back, but all he could think of at the moment was Annette. He stood up and paced the length of the room back and forth. He really didn't want to talk to her presently, but how could he delay this conversation? He dialed her number and listened as the phone rang. With the time difference between them, it was morning in London, so he had no choice, otherwise she would be calling him all night. He wouldn't be able to sleep.

"Hello, Dalton. I'm so glad you called. I was getting worried. I hadn't heard from you. How is work?" Sidney asked him, all bright and cheery.

"I'm so sorry; I've been extremely busy with work. How are you?" he answered as he closed his eyes, trying to sound happy to hear her voice, but he wasn't. His mind was elsewhere. It was on Annette.

"Everything is great. I can't wait to see you. I have been shopping for this trip all week. I'm so excited. I bought new clothes and a few things for you. How's your work advancing? You should be almost done, right?" she asked him again enthusiastically.

"Oh! It's a bloody mess! I don't even have time to think. I am so swamped and ..." he lied. He saw his way out to gain more time. Time to spend with Annette was all he really wanted. He wasn't going to lie to her again, but what the hell. It would be worth it and she would never find out anyway.

"I have been working day and night. It's a lot of debating back and forth. I don't know if I'll be able to conclude before you arrive. You should delay your arrival until I know how it's going to go for the next few days. Just a couple more days to a week at the most," he told her.

"I'm really sorry to hear that. I could still come and be a tourist around town. I wouldn't bother you. I miss you. I want to be with you," Sidney pleaded to Dalton's deaf ears.

"The problem is I wouldn't have any time for you. I wouldn't be able to concentrate on work. I would worry about you. What kind of trip would that be? I truly think you should postpone until I tell you," he told her hoping she wouldn't catch the lie or put up a fuss. He heard her sigh on the other end of the phone, and then there was complete silence.

"Sidney, darling, it's not I don't want you to come, but I want to be able to spend time with you. You can understand that, now can't you?" he asked her softly while glancing out the window at the snow starting to fall. He recalled Annette mentioned that a snowstorm was in the forecast. He hoped the weather wouldn't stop their meeting tomorrow.

"I suppose ... I don't have too much time off work. I guess I can wait. I'll reschedule my flight, but I was so looking forward to this trip." He could hear her disappointment in her voice, but it did not deter him.

"I won't be able to focus on my work if I know you are here alone. I would rather you wait until next week. I should be done with this assignment." He tried to sound positive, but deep down all he wanted or needed was time to see what would develop with Annette.

"I wouldn't be alone and I don't mind if you—" she tried once again, but Dalton interrupted her immediately.

"Sidney, please, I need to finish ... so just wait. I will see you next week," he firmly added. He could tell she was not happy. There was complete silence again at the other end of the phone. He raked his fingers through his hair and bit the inside of his bottom lip. He waited, hoping she would agree.

"Fine, I'll wait. Complete what you have to at work and call me in a few days to let me know where you are at, okay? I love you," she answered him.

"Thank you. I will call you later," he told her and hung up the phone. He didn't tell her he loved her. He felt a small lump in his throat for lying to her. She was his fiancée, but she was not his new priority at the moment. Annette was. He sat down on the couch with his phone in his hand. He directed his sight to his briefcase and leaned down to picked up. He clicked the brackets and opened it. He pulled the yellow envelope out and held it in his hands. He slipped the contents out on the coffee table. He stared at Annette's picture wondering how she would feel if she knew what he had in his possession and all that he knew about her. He licked his lips as he gently brushed his fingers over her image. "You truly are one of a kind, inside and out," he said, he laid the photograph down on the coffee table in front of him. He stood up, took one last glance at the picture, and walked to his bed when a smile crossed his face.

He didn't feel bad anymore for lying to Sidney. He just wanted to spend as much time with Annette before Sidney arrived. It was late. He wanted to wake up early so he would have the whole day with Annette. He undressed and decided he would surprise her with coffee and bagels in the morning. He sat on the edge of his bed once again, grabbed his alarm clock, and pushed the buttons to set it for seven o'clock. He laid down in the dark, lifted his arms over his head, placed his hands behind his head, interlaced his fingers, and closed his eyes. He smiled as he remembered Annette's laughter, her touch, and especially her kiss.

* * *

Sidney just sat at her kitchen table, stunned while holding the phone receiver in her hand as tears swam in her eyes. She thought they were going to spend quality time together and have a good time. She raised her hand and wiped away the tears. She was not going to let him bring her down. Not after all the preparations she had done for this trip—buying new clothes, having her hair cut, and having to take extra time off from her job. She would call her boss to extend her vacation time. She was going to try to prolong it by at least two weeks. Dalton was going to have to pay for her expenses while she was in America because her budget was gone. *But he hadn't called her since he had arrived to America. Why?* Now he needed more time for his work, cutting their vacation short. Boy, did she have a surprise for him.

Why didn't he want her there by his side? Did he really need that much time for work? He told her it wouldn't take him but a few more days to close the deal. Now it had been over a week. What was he doing with all his free time? Was he really working? She had doubts. She wouldn't bother him if she went. He could still work as late as he wanted. She could occupy her time with other things like sightseeing or shopping. There was a lot for her to do. She was not afraid to be alone in a large city. But no, he wouldn't agree.

Something was not right. She could feel it in her belly. She had known this man for years. He wasn't talking to her as he usually did. He was hiding something behind his work. What was she to do? Maybe he was getting cold feet with the upcoming wedding. She resolved to find out what was going on. She would give him his extra days, but after that she was going to fly to Boston, with or without his blessing, to confront him.

THE PLEDGE

This was supposed to be their escape vacation—just the two of them spending a week away from everyone before their nuptials. She wasn't going to let him ruin it for her with his work. *She loved this man, but hoped he was being honest with her otherwise....* She stood up from her spot, gathered her books and her pocketbook. She walked to her front door and left to go to work.

* * *

Annette waited anxiously for Dalton. She had been up since the break of dawn. He was late. She kept pacing the floor of her living room, trying to pass the time. She pushed the curtain back from her front window once again. She stood immobile for a minute while she watched the snowflakes fall rapidly. The wind was blowing the snow sideways into a drift of deep snow. It brought back horrible memories of her late husband. She wondered if she should call him to cancel their rendezvous since the snowfall was increasing rapidly. Maybe he had changed his mind and he wasn't coming. *No, no, not by the way he had kissed her last night. He was just delayed.* She returned to sit down on the sofa. She picked up a magazine lying next to her. She flipped through the pages without paying much attention to the articles or the pictures. Dalton was on her mind. *Where could he be? He had said eight, hadn't he? Yes, she was sure. But the snow might have held him up,* she reassured herself.

The city was on a storm alert. The area expected over a foot of snow within a short period of time. She had tossed and turned all night thinking of silly things like what to wear, and whether she should invite him in or just leave when he arrived at the door. She geared up and was ready to go visit the city since seven o'clock that morning, but while she watched the morning the news, she found out there was a fast approaching snowstorm coming to the region. She peeked at the clock on the wall. It was ten past eight. "*He's coming. Stop fidgeting and relax,*" she thought and kept telling herself over and over. She jumped up from her spot when she heard the telephone ring. She grabbed the receiver and answered immediately.

"Hello," she said hoping it was Dalton.

"Good morning, Annette. I'm sorry I'm late. I'm on my way. I was delayed because of the snow and the traffic. I should be there shortly," Dalton said to her cheerfully. She smiled to herself, and some of her uneasiness disappeared when she heard his voice.

"Thank you for calling. I was getting worried. I thought you might have decided not to come because of the snow," she replied not wanting him to know how restless she had been.

"No, I'm on my way. I shall be there shortly, okay," he said joyfully.

"Great. Please be careful and I'll see you soon. Bye," she replied as she hung up the phone. Relieved, Annette returned the phone to its proper place. She walked to the wall mirror in the hallway to look at herself one last time before Dalton arrived. "I still have circles under my eyes from lack of sleep," she whispered to herself. She wiggled her nose and made a grimace. "Nothing I can do now." She had to learn to unwind.

She looked at her hands, which had started to sweat. She had butterflies in her stomach anticipating his arrival. She felt just as excited as a teenager going to prom with a new boy. He was coming and was on his way. She made two fists, opened them, and then wiped her palms on her blue jeans. She could feel a knot in her stomach from the suspense of seeing him again.

Thirty minutes later Dalton hadn't arrived. This was insane. *Where was he?* He wasn't that far from her. Fright and worry engulfed her. A cold sweat came over her as she thought back to the last time a man had been late to her house. "This is not the same as Mark. Don't even go there," she told herself. She unintentionally resumed marching up and down the corridor of her home. Realizing that she was pacing, she sat down on the couch in the living room and watched the snow come down from the front window.

At last the doorbell rang. She sprang out of her seat and ran to the door. She stopped in front of it and sighed with relief. She opened the door wide as the snow flew into the entrance. He walked in rapidly, wiped his feet on the mat and rubbed his hands together.

"Come in. It's nasty outside," Annette said as casually as possible while closing the door behind him. Before she could say anything else, he leaned forward to kiss her lightly on the mouth. The contact sent a shiver down her spine. She was so grateful he was there.

"How are you this fine morning?" he asked, his eyes locked on hers.

"Much better now that you are here," she answered as she laughed out of nervousness. She was trying to avoid his stare by moving away from him. She noticed he was carrying a pastry bag. He had dropped it on the bench next to the entrance when he had entered. So to change the subject, she pointed at the paper bag.

"What's this?" She aimed her finger at the bag. He bent down and picked it up. He held it in his hand.

"Oh! Yes! This is for you. I planned on coming to surprise you with breakfast, but I have to confess, I overslept. I think I'm still jetlagged from the time change. So I brought you this instead." His dimples showed as he smiled. She extended her hand out and took the bag from him.

"What is it?" she asked but she already knew what it was. The aroma flooded her nostrils. She closed her eyes just for a brief instant, inhaling it. She walked toward the kitchen, signaling him forward so he followed her close behind. She stopped at the kitchen island, opened the top of the bag, and peeked inside.

"Cinnamon rolls! How did you know they were my favorite? Thanks. Have a seat. Would you like coffee? It's not very nice outside. How are the roads?" She bombarded him with questions as she watched him take off his coat and place it on the back of the stool. He pulled out the chair, sat down and placed one foot on the base of the other chair.

"Well, I figured since you ate the first one, you must like them." She could feel the heat going to her ears. She was sure she was blushing. She turned toward the cupboard, took out two mugs, and placed them in front of him. She could sense he was watching her every move. He had this sexy grin on his face. She poured the coffee into the cups without looking at him.

"Cream? Sugar?" she asked as she stretched out her arm to grab the handle of the refrigerator for the cream.

"Black, just as is. Thank you," he answered as he brought the mug to his lips to take a sip.

"So, do you still want to venture outside in this storm? It's supposed to be pretty bad. I should have checked the weather to see how much snow before making plans. We could have organized it for another day. It won't be much fun trying to maneuver around the city sites today, and some of the places might be close. We will have to call in advance to make sure they're opened." She was babbling as she reached into the bag and took out the pastries. She placed the cinnamon rolls on plates. She moved one in front of him and the other beside him. She traced the counter with her hand as she went to sit down next to him. Her right leg accidently brushed against his. She pulled it away even though she liked the feel of his leg next to hers.

"We don't have to go anywhere if you don't want to. I'm satisfied just sitting here talking with you or just watching a movie as long as you are near me. I'll be just fine," he answered. He took a bite of his cinnamon roll and started to chew. His eyes opened wide.

"Wow! I really didn't know this was that good! I should have bought more," he said in between bites. They both started to laugh. It eased the tension Annette felt inside. She watched him as he licked his fingers, just like she had done with the first cinnamon roll that he had given to her. She wished she could pass her tongue over his fingers. *Stop it!* She regained her composure and carefully took a small bite of her roll.

"Very well. If that's what you want to do, it's fine with me. We will make it a day and we can order Chinese food or pizza later on. We can watch TV and ... talk," she said. She was trying not to be obvious that she was hoping that he would kiss her again like he had the previous night.

"Mmm! That sounds perfect," he answered and placed his hand on her knee and caressed it lightly. It sent chills down her whole body. She desired this man. She really yearned for what might happen later on, but for now she had to refrain.

This was definitely going to be an interesting day with him by her side. Annette just kept on smiling. She kept eating her pastry quietly, not wanting to disrupt the moment. She hadn't felt this at ease or attracted to a man since her husband had passed away over a year ago.

The hours passed as the snowstorm intensified outside. They could hear the wind howling outside the house. There was almost no visibility. It definitely was a Northeaster passing through the New England area. Barely any cars travelled down her street and not even tire tracks were visible since Dalton had arrived at her home. On television, the meteorologist had broadcasted at least a foot of snow would accumulate during the day.

Annette was sitting on the floor in front of her sofa in the living room next to Dalton watching the weather channel on the evening news. She was munching on a bowl of Lays chips, feeding Dalton from time to time. His thighs would touch hers every time he moved, and he had wrapped his arm around her shoulders. They occupied their afternoon watching the movie channel, discussing their lives, playing backgammon, and eating Chinese food that they had ordered earlier for a late lunch.

She had noticed the way his fingers played with her hair and how he caressed her cheek lightly with his hand when he spoke to her. It made her feel desired again, and she loosened up. She wasn't so edgy with him. He would stop talking in the middle of a sentence just to stare at her, and then grin, showing her his dimples, which she loved so much. He was so attentive to her needs all day. He would get up to fetch her beverage or cover her shoulders with the afghan resting on the chair when she was chilly. The man was so giving. He was handsome and his accent drove her wild with sexual passion. Every time he smirked at her, she would crave to touch more of him, but he had kept his distance. He had been a perfect gentleman all day, which was to her surprise. He hadn't even tried to kiss her. She had expected him to make a pass at her, but he had refrained from it. They were now discussing what they could do this weekend since they had lost the day being cooped up in her house. She loved her time with Dalton today because she had gotten to know him. She trusted him.

"So, what about tomorrow? Are you up to go sightseeing since we missed today?" she asked him as she reached across his side of the couch for the television remote.

"I don't care what we do as long as you're with me," Dalton answered her. She was flabbergasted by his response. She hadn't thought he liked her that much.

"That's so nice of you to say. There might not be much to do, but we could always build a snowman tomorrow," Annette joked as she cast her eyes away from him once again. She put the bowl of chips down beside her and pushed herself up from the floor. She took a few steps toward the window to look outside. She could feel his eyes watching her. She had caught him a few times observing her every move. She was flattered. It had been like this all day. She reached out with her hand to push the curtain to peek out the window at the storm.

"The snow is not stopping. We are snow bound." She laughed out of nervousness, feeling a little on edge as she wondered what was going to happen now that the sun had gone down and he probably needed to return to his hotel. She eyeballed the snowflakes that were furiously whipping around her street.

She heard him stand up, but she didn't budge from where she was standing. The next thing she knew he was beside her. He wrapped his arms around her waist from behind, his chin resting on her shoulder.

"Yes, we are snowbound and I like it, but ... " he whispered in her ear as he started to nibble on her earlobe with his mouth. It sent a sexual jolt of electricity right down to her toes. She could feel the warmth of his body pressing against her back. He pivoted her around, all the while gliding his hands around her waist so she was facing him.

She let the curtain fall from her fingers and she placed her hands on his chest. She lifted her chin up as his lips came crashing down on hers. His arms cocooned tightly around her. She moved her hips to meet his and their tongues danced for what seemed an eternity. She heard him moan as he kissed her. She had been patient, waiting for another one of these kisses. He pulled his head away, still holding her near to his body. She admired his features in the moonlight as she tried to control the lust shooting through her body. She sensed his excitement against her. She wanted to make love to this man right now. Never in her life had she done anything so impulsive like this, but she didn't care. She didn't want to let this chance pass her by. She was ready to give in to all her urges.

"I have to leave now or I might not be able to leave later," he whispered to her. He started to pull away from her, but she held on to him, gripping his shirt with her fists.

"Stay. I don't want you to leave," Annette replied in a low voice. She couldn't believe she had said it, but it was the truth. She glided her hands nervously up his chest to his neck and enveloped her mouth on his. She prepared herself for whatever he would offer her on this snowy night without any regrets. She took his hand in hers. He didn't resist as she led him toward her bedroom.

Chapter 8

The next morning the sunrays were streaming through the windows of Annette's bedroom. The snow had stopped falling when Dalton woke up. He was alone in her king size bed. The gold sheets mixed perfectly against the dark wood of the bedroom set. He spotted their clothes scattered on the floor. He chuckled, reminiscing of the passionate night they had shared together. He turned toward her side of the bed and saw a picture of Mark in a silver frame on her nightstand. He looked at the alarm clock. It read nine o'clock. *Wow! I slept late*, he thought.

Annette had slipped out of the bed without waking him. He picked up his phone from the night table. He had missed three calls with a voicemail from each. He scrolled down with his thumb and noticed they were all from Sidney. He didn't want her to spoil his mood so he placed it back on the side table without a care. He didn't want to hear her ranting about where he was.

He could still smell Annette's perfume on her pillow and he wished she hadn't gotten up. Not just yet. He still craved her. He looked around the room as he stretched his arms, and sat on the edge of the bed. He stood up and walked to the bathroom located on the other side of the room.

He jumped into the shower. He positioned his head under the hot water, washing their lovemaking away. *There would be other nights*, he thought. He stepped out, grabbed a towel off the rack, dried himself, and then wrapped it around his waist just below his muscular abs. He headed to the kitchen to find Annette. As he approached the kitchen, he came to a halt so he could observe her. He could hear her humming a song, wearing only a large pink t-shirt, her hair disheveled from all the lovemaking of the previous night. She looked irresistible. *How could I have become so intrigued by this woman in such a short amount of time?* When she was near him he couldn't think straight. He was obsessed with her.

He wanted to spend all his free time with her. He didn't understand how a woman could take hold of him in such little time, but he accepted it. His sight was focused on her. She was scrambling eggs over a skillet. He leaned his back on the edge of the wall as he crossed his arms across his chest and watched her every gesture for a minute. He was already getting aroused just watching her. She was so appealing. She must have heard him because she looked up and became aware of him. She puckered up her lips and blew him a kiss with her hand.

"Hey! Good morning. Are you hungry?" She tilted her head at him then she gave him a broad smile.

"Are you going to help or just stand there watching me?" she asked him as she beat the eggs then dropped them in the saucepan.

"Oh! I'm definitely hungry, but not for eggs," he answered her as he moved toward her with a seductive grin. Two long strides later he had her bundled in his arms as he nuzzled his face in her neck, kissing his way up to her lips. He broke away from her just long enough to take the skillet of eggs from her hand and remove it from the burner. He reached past her with the other hand to turn off the stove knob.

He lifted her up in his arms as she started to giggle. It was music to his ears. She glided her arms around his neck as she cuddled closer to him. She felt weightless as he carried her toward the bedroom, all the time indulging his passion on her. He felt his towel fall to the floor. He was ready for another round of lovemaking with her.

* * *

Days passed by and the weekend went by without a single word from Dalton. Sidney had been up most of the last night, her mind going where she shouldn't let it go, but Dalton was her life. She loved him more than her own existence. She would do anything to keep him. Anything! She had not moved from her chair in her living room for hours. She hadn't eaten or showered in two days. She had fallen asleep after waiting up for hours for a reply from her fiancé. It never came. The light of the morning woke her. She felt stiff from sleeping upright. She moved her head from side to side while rubbing the back of her neck with her hand. She glanced down, grabbed her phone once again from the side table, lifted it, and then scanned through it. Nothing! Not even a text message. She had left numerous messages at the Ritz Carlton hotel and on his personal phone, but the hotel had told her that while he was still registered at the hotel, he had not retrieved his messages yet.

Why was he not returning her calls? Where was he? She had left him voice messages and she had texted him. Where could he be? Maybe he was hurt, but she doubted that was the case. He was a tall, large, fit man. He was in perfect health, but still ... He had played football in college and he wasn't afraid of anything. What was he doing at all hours of the night without her and not answering her calls? But more importantly, who was he with? A jolt of jealousy came over her as she tried to not think of it.

Sidney knew he wasn't at work it was the middle of the night when she had last called him. She was worried about him. Dalton always had wandering eyes when there were beautiful ladies nearby. She caught him looking at other women many times, but up until now, she hadn't fretted because he had always come home to her.

She recalled the latest incident, which happened two weeks earlier. They were sitting at a bar having a cocktail. She was talking to him but his eyes weren't on her. He was looking at the lady who was having a drink two stools down. She turned her head to see what had distracted him, and then she had seen the woman—a tall, slim brunette wearing a short, tight red dress. The woman was leaning against the counter, her low-cut dress exposing her breasts. She was staring back at Dalton. Suddenly, she winked at him and smiled.

"Dalton, darling, did you hear what I just asked you?" Sidney said to him as she tapped him on the arm. His eyes refocused back to her.

"I'm sorry, love, what did you ask me?" he replied and his vision returned to Sidney. He acted as if he hadn't done anything wrong ... but she had seen him leer at the other woman.

"Let's go find a table," Sidney suggested as she stood up and picked up her cocktail.

"Sure, anything you want." He followed her without a word, but she had known what he had been doing. She had not mentioned the lady, but she had seen him looking at her from time to time during the evening. Sidney became so annoyed by his behavior that she ended going home earlier than planned. It had not been the only time she had caught him over the years. She thought he had done it just to frustrate her, so she had kept quiet.

Now, he was far from her and she didn't trust him. He had always been a ladies' man. Jealousy was arriving at her door again and she didn't like it one bit. She decided to try to get a hold of him one more time. If he didn't answer, she would modify her travel plans. She had hoped he would change his mind at the last minute and tell her to come join him, but it hadn't happened. She dialed his number and waited. She bit her lower lip as she listened to the phone ring. She heard the click to voicemail, but this time she was not going to leave a message. She was determined.

She closed her phone and briskly walked to her bedroom. She kneeled down in front of her bed, reached under it, and pulled her suitcase out. She raised the bag and dropped it on the top of her bed. She unzipped it and took a step sideways to her dresser, slid the drawer open, looked inside, and started throwing clothes and toiletries into her suitcase.

Finally she closed it shut. She hurried to shower and dress. She was ready to go within an hour. It was a bold move, but she would not sit here and wait. She was tired of wondering if her man was all right or if he was with another woman. Sidney had to know. She was willing to travel across the world to find him. She could barely breathe as she checked her list. She had her passport, the address of the hotel where Dalton was staying, cash, and her ticket, which she would change once she arrived at Heathrow Airport. She would be there tomorrow. She was going to America to find out what her fiancé was up to and why he was being so distant from her. She loved him and would not give him up without a fight. She was ready.

* * *

Annette spent the most enjoyable weekend with Dalton. She was starting to move on from the past. It felt great to have found another man to share her life with. First, they had been snow-bound in her home for two days. They had talked for hours about themselves and she felt like she had known him forever. They had been inseparable for the last few days. The only time they were apart was when he had gone back to his hotel to pick up a change of clothes. They had spent their time visiting the city and making love.

When she woke up this morning, a sense of fear crept upon her. He would be leaving in less of a week to return to London. *What would she do then?* She was lying motionless in bed, her eyes closed, listening to his shallow breathing against her neck. He snuggled close to her, and his arm wrapped around her waist as he slept.

She wondered what would happen after he left. The last few days had been the happiest in a long time. She was herself again, laughing, enjoying life, and feeling untroubled again. She didn't want him to leave, but what was she to say? "I want you to stay with me. Don't go back to London." Yes, that sounded about right, but she knew things didn't work that way. He probably was just having a good time with her until he returned back to his work and to his life in London. She hoped she was wrong and that the past two weeks would leave an impression on him. This was going to be one of their last days together before she returned to work tomorrow. But at least they would have one more night together. She turned to lie on her back. She heard him say, "Good morning, gorgeous." She felt his hand advance to fondle her belly. It brought a smile to her face.

"Good morning, handsome. What would you like to do today?" she asked him. She felt him cuddle closer and kiss her lightly on the mouth. She heard him moan as she felt a bulge growing against her thigh.

"We could stay in bed," he answered as the corner of his mouth lifted upward.

"We are not staying in bed all day. Why don't we go down to Newbury Street? We could do some window shopping, and then have lunch at one of the bistros," Annette suggested as he snuggled closer and pulled her on top of him.

"Ahh! Do we have too?" he asked, acting just like a child who didn't want to do something.

"Yes, we do have to. Now, let's get going," she giggled and gently pushed him away so she could slide off him. She sat up next to him. She crossed her arms on her chest, simpering at him.

"Okay, okay. We'll go. But first I need to shower. Why don't you join me? It will go faster." He smirked at her. She laughed out loud even harder.

"Now, you know if I do that we will never get going. So, get up before I have to punish you for not listening," she teased. She got out of bed, stood in front of him for a moment before grabbing her robe and turning around to go make coffee.

"Wait, I want to be punished. Come back," he yelled softly. She kept on walking, still laughing. But then she stopped abruptly, choosing to jump back in bed to punish him by slapping him on the butt.

"Now, you are in big trouble," she told him as she kissed him passionately.

* * *

An hour later Dalton was still in bed. He had never felt this comfortable with anyone in his life. He loved to make her giggle and her smile brought joy to his heart. He did not want to leave her side since that first night with her. Now he understood why Mark had married her. Anyone would fall for her once they really got to know her. He was glad it was him and he had been given this opportunity. Other than the trip back to the hotel, after the snow had died down to gather some clothes, he had not budged from her house for the last five days. He could stay here with her forever, but he knew there would be complications ... Sidney. He would deal with that later.

He pushed the sheets off his body and walked to the bathroom to wash up. He didn't want to interrupt his time with her. He would call Sidney later and tell her not to come to Boston. He would think of something to tell her. He was going to spend as much time he could with Annette. He didn't want to admit to himself, but it was true. He was developing feelings for her. They were feelings he had never thought possible: feelings of being whole. He didn't have those types of sentiments with Sidney. He never had and never would. He hurried to wash and dress. He met her in the kitchen after he was ready.

"Okay, I'm ready," he said to her as he marched toward her. She was sitting at the counter drinking a cup of coffee. She was wearing only an oversized t-shirt that fell down below her butt. It was a man's shirt—probably Mark's.

"You are always ready," she said, chuckling. He watched her as she got up from the stool to go poured him a cup of coffee. She handed the cup to him.

"Sit. Stay put. Do not move. I won't be long and then, we are going to leave this house," she ordered as she pointed her finger at his cup of coffee. "Drink."

"Yes, mum," he answered playfully as she disappeared down the hall. He took his phone out of his pocket to scan his emails and noticed that Sidney had left several more messages. He had to fix her habit of calling him all the time as soon as possible. He deleted the messages. He didn't have the patience for her at the moment. By the time he had finished his coffee and called a taxi, Annette was coming out of the bedroom. She was wearing a red cashmere sweater with a pair of tight True Religion jeans that accentuated her curves to the fullest. Her hair was pulled back in a ponytail and she wore red lipstick.

He whistled at her. The one thing he loved about her was how he already knew how to make her blush. She stuck out her tongue at him and said, "Ha! Ha! Let's go." She grabbed his coat and threw it at him as she put hers on. They were approaching the door when his phone buzzed once again. He retrieved it quickly to look. She stopped walking and stood beside him as he read the message. He moved the cellphone away from her sight so she couldn't see the content. He replaced it in his pocket. She was watching him. "Anything important?" she questioned casually.

"Nothing that can't wait. Let's go. The cab is here. I'm starving," he answered. He took her hand in his after she locked the door and he strolled away from everything. She was beside him and he was in a good mood. Nothing was going to change that.

Chapter 9

Twelve hours later, Sidney landed in America. She passed through immigration and customs. She walked towards the main entrance of terminal E at Boston Logan Airport. The bitter chill and the snow immediately assaulted her as she stepped outside. She was not used to the cold. London rarely had snow and the temperatures were usually in the 50s in March.

She buttoned up her coat to the top and pulled her hat down over her ears. She looked around and tried to orient herself with her surroundings. She glanced to her right and noticed people were waiting for taxis. She headed towards them as she tried to maneuver her suitcase between people. Finally it was her turn. The driver took her bags and placed them in the trunk. She sat inside the cab as fast as she could. She rubbed her bare hands together, trying to warm them up. She hated the cold weather and it was worse here, especially in the middle of their winter, but she soon would have Dalton to keep her warm. That thought alone was the only thing that could take away the chill she was feeling deep inside.

"The Ritz Carlton on Avery Street, please," she told the driver when he sat back behind the wheel. He nodded and took off driving toward the city. She looked out the window and admired the Boston skyline.

THE PLEDGE

They crossed the William Tunnel and within fifteen minutes the car stopped in front of the hotel. She paid the driver fifteen dollars, picked up her bags, and walked inside to the reception area with her suitcase in tow. The young lady at the front desk smiled at her and said, "Good morning. Welcome to the Ritz Carlton. How may I help you?"

"Good morning. My name is Sidney Moore. My fiancé, Dalton Rivers, has a reservation here and I'm here to meet up with him," she told her as she passed her the hotel reservation sheet Dalton left for her before he had departed London.

"Very well. Let me check." Sidney watched her as she searched for Dalton's booking on her computer. "Here we are, Dalton Rivers and Sidney Moore." She took out a key card and swiped it in a machine. She wrote the room number down on the sleeve of the envelope for her.

"Your room is on the tenth floor. Here is your key and room number. The elevators are on the right behind this wall." She handed her the key as she pointed the way.

"Thank you," Sidney replied, glad she had arrived at the hotel.

"Have a nice stay. Can I help you with anything else?" the receptionist asked her while smiling.

"No, that will be all. Thank you." Sidney grabbed the handle of her bag and wheeled it toward the elevator. She waited for the platform doors to open, entered, then pushed the button for floor number ten. She was excited to see Dalton. It had been almost ten days since she had last seen him. It was Sunday, so she knew he wouldn't be at work today. When the lift doors opened, she found her way down the hall to his room. She decided to surprise him, so she rang the doorbell and waited. Her heart was racing. She had missed him so much and couldn't wait for him to hold her. But to her surprise, no one answered.

Where could he be? She swiped the card and opened the door slowly.

"Dalton, are you here, darling?" she yelled out as she entered, but the rooms were empty. She went to look around, but he was nowhere to be found. He must have gone out for a while; maybe to get a bite to eat or something. He should return soon. He didn't know too many people in town. Sidney was disappointed he wasn't here, but she was tired from the flight and could use a nice hot bath. It would give her time to freshen up before he came back. She hung her coat in the closet and made herself at home until her love came back.

* * *

Dalton and Annette spent the last hour hand and hand walking down Newbury Street. Annette had gone into a few stores to browse around, but she hadn't purchase anything. It was Sunday afternoon, so the area was filled with patrons. The sidewalks were still covered with snow from the last storm, so it was difficult to navigate on the sidewalks. Dalton looked at Annette's pink cheeks and red nose. She looked as if she was freezing from the low temperatures. He certainly was cold as he lifted the collar of his coat to guard against the rawness of the wind. Dalton decided to stop to eat. He noticed a bistro, Sonsie, up ahead on Newbury Street.

"I'm famished. Are you hungry yet? This restaurant up ahead looks pretty good. What do you think?" Dalton said as he looked at her. Her lips were trembling slightly from the cold. She just nodded at him.

"That looks great. They have a Sunday brunch that is fabulous and I'm freezing," Annette replied.

"Perfect, let's go in." They headed for the entrance of the bistro. Dalton liked the ambiance of the restaurant. It had a long bar to the left and tables covered by white tablecloths with black leather chairs. There was a row of single tables for two against the opposite wall. It was a cozy place, but it was booming with people at the same time. The crowd was young and alive, even in the early afternoon. Many individuals were having drinks and laughing while they were having lunch.

The young man at the entrance greeted them, and found a table for them against the wall near a window. Dalton liked that they were seated right away. A waitress came by and asked them if they would like a beverage.

"Sure. I'll have a dry gin martini with two olives," Dalton said and looked at Annette for her order.

"I'll have a Blood Mary, I guess," she answered as she took her coat off her shoulders.

"Very well. Would you like to order an appetizer?" the waitress inquired as she looked at them and waited with her notepad and pen.

"Yes, I'm starving. Bring us an order of calamari and an order of mussels for now," Dalton answered as he glanced at the appetizers on the menu.

"Great, I'll be right back with your drinks," the server said and turned to get the cocktails. Dalton noticed Annette was giggling behind her menu.

"What's so funny?" he asked her as he smiled at her from across the table. He reached over to lower her menu so he could see her face.

"Well, you really are hungry, aren't you?" she said to him. "You didn't give her time to say hi before you were ordering food." She gently slapped his hand away from her menu. He laughed as he admired her blue eyes twinkle.

"Yes, I am," he said, all the while returning to look at the menu.

"So tell me, what are you going to do this week? You know I am returning to work tomorrow. You are going to be all by yourself," she told Dalton, keeping her eyes glued to her menu.

"I suppose I will have to see you every day after work. I will probably do some work at my hotel room and do a little sightseeing by myself. But just so you know, it won't be the same without you," he answered her. He really wanted to spend as much time with her as possible, but he understood she had to work. He extended his hand over and touched her elbow with his fingers. She glanced up and winked at him.

"Maybe you could stop by one day and we could go to lunch, or I could skip lunch and go home earlier," she suggested to him.

"Oh! That sounds much better. Skip lunch or we could meet ..." he proposed as he returned her wink. She giggled quietly, her blue eyes sparkling with joy. She glided her hand toward his hand. She brushed her soft skin against his. It made him want to feel her closer, but right now he relished the contact, however slight it might be.

"I don't think I'd be able to return to work if we met at lunch," she answered him.

"Mmmm! I like that," Dalton replied as he smiled at her and sent her a kiss with his lips.

Their server arrived with their drinks and placed them on the table. Dalton wanted to order lunch right away. Annette ordered a salad while Dalton took the grilled chicken and pasta. The afternoon passed in a blink of an eye, and before they knew it, the sun was already setting outside. They had been in the bistro for the last three hours, having more drinks and eating. The chemistry between them was undeniable. They held hands and their eyes were only on each other. They fed each other small bites of their food and laughed together. They expressed their plans to each other for the future and savored their time together.

"If you'll excuse me for a moment. With all these drinks, I have to use the ladies' room again," she revealed as she finished the last drops of her third Bloody Mary. She pushed away from the table and stood up to leave as Dalton's phone pinged again from a text message. He had ignored them all day. There was no one he wanted to talk to but Annette.

"Would you like another?" he asked her as he pointed to her empty glass. She smiled and leaned close to his ear. He could smell her fragrance again as she bent near him. He closed his eyes and inhaled her aroma.

She whispered softly, "If I have another drink, you might have to take home and then you might take advantage of me." She left him with that message as she walked away. He smiled, and watched her head to the back of the restaurant toward the ladies' room. He reached into his pocket to retrieve his phone. It had been buzzing all day. He swiped it opened and he was stunned. His mouth opened. For a moment he was unable to move an inch. He held the phone tightly in his hand. His thumb scrolled down the contents of his cell phone. He tried to stay calm, so he took deep breaths. He was so mad at this woman and he had to gain control of his emotions before Annette returned to her seat. The message was from Sidney. It read: I'm in Boston and waiting for you at your hotel.

"Bloody hell!" he said under his breath and put his phone away.

* * *

Annette was in the ladies' room, the palms of her hands resting on the counter as she looked at her image in the mirror. She felt tipsy and she was lightheaded. She had been drinking for hours and having a great time with Dalton. She couldn't understand how in the last ten days she could be falling for a man she barely knew. It was like the angels had heard her cries. They had answered her prayers by sending her Dalton. It was a new beginning. She thought it would never ever happen after her husband's passing. She had not wept in days, and that alone was a big event in her mind.

Now, as she examined herself in the mirror, tears started to burn her eyes. It was the alcohol taking over her feelings and she couldn't let it take her. It finally hit her all of a sudden. Dalton was from another country on the other end of the world. He would have to return to London eventually. His world was not in Boston. His life was elsewhere. He belonged to a prominent law firm and he had just made partner. He wouldn't throw all this away to stay with her. This was an impossible situation. Tears trickled down her cheek. She quickly grabbed a tissue and wiped them away. She blew her nose and threw the tissue away in the garbage bin. She didn't want him to know she had been crying. It would ruin their day together. She didn't want that to happen. They were so happy.

How stupid could she be to get involved with a man who would probably leave within the next week and break her heart? What was she going to do then? She turned on the cold water and splashed it on her face. She grabbed another towel to rub her face dry. She would worry about it later. Right now she was going to enjoy every moment she had with him. Tomorrow was another day. For the time being he was with her and that was all that counted. She opened the bathroom door and walked with her head held high. She walked as straight as she could, though it was difficult given how much alcohol she had consumed this afternoon. She was back at the table with a smile on her face.

* * *

Sidney had been sitting on the couch watching television at the hotel alone all day, waiting patiently for Dalton to return. She had taken a hot bath and a short nap. She stored all her clothes away in the closet and raided the mini bar, but all she found was junk food. It was now late afternoon and she was getting a little upset because she had left Dalton multiple messages on his phone. She had also texted him several times, but he hadn't responded.

Where was he? What could he be doing that would keep him away all day and prevent him from taking the time to answer her? She was now wondering if it had been a bad idea to come to Boston to surprise him. *He would have to return to his room eventually, though.*

Here she was in a strange city, by herself and unable to contact her fiancé. Something was not right. She could feel it. She shooed away the notion. He was fine. She was overreacting ... but he had been away all day. Maybe he was in a meeting and couldn't respond. *Hell, it only took a few seconds to text her a message, though,* she thought. Her mind was in a maze. Why hadn't he answered her? It weighed heavy on her.

THE PLEDGE

She rubbed her forehead with the tips of her fingers. Her forehead throbbed with pain. She was developing a headache so she lay down to rest her head until he came back. She was going to question him when he returned. Again, she now had doubts. Maybe she shouldn't have come. Well, she soon would find out what he had been up to. He had been distant the last two weeks when she had spoken to him, and now he was ignoring her.

She wondered if he was getting cold feet and didn't want to marry her anymore. No, he loved her. He was probably stressed with the mound of work he had been assigned since he had become a partner in his law firm. That was all. It was the pressure of his new position. But he had changed toward her in the past few months. She had to be more understanding. She didn't want to anger him, or worse, alienate him. He was her life, her only love. She would not be able to live without him. He was part of her and she never wanted be separated from him. She would do anything to keep him by her side. Anything!

Chapter 10

Dalton sat immobile. For a few minutes he didn't move a muscle. He started playing with the utensils on the table, rearranging them one by one in a straight line as he mused. He couldn't believe Sidney was here. What was he going to do? He didn't fancy her anymore now that he had met Annette. How was he going to tell her without breaking her heart? It was an impossible task. He took his beer in his hand and gulped the rest of it down. He closed his eyes to try to think, but nothing was coming through. He decided he wasn't going to do anything until he returned to the hotel. He would deal with this problem later.

Annette had to work in the morning. He would get back to the hotel when he was ready, not before. She was only going to lecture him for not answering her calls, so why rush back? He already knew the outcome. He knew Sidney was probably furious with him by now. He had seen all the messages, but he hadn't answered any. He saw Annette coming back from the ladies' room. His eyes were fixed on her as he followed her every move. He grinned her way until she sat down. He watched as her delicate hand took her napkin and replaced it on her lap.

"You're back. I missed you. I thought you might have gotten lost," he teased. "Did you want anything else before I ask the waitress for the check?" he asked her as she settled back in her seat.

She looked up at him and said, "Dear Lord, no. I've definitely had enough to drink. No thank you. Besides, I have to work tomorrow morning." He stretched out his hand over to touch hers that was resting on the top of the table and massaged it gently.

"Very good. Then let's get out of here." He raised his arm to flag the server to bring the check. He noticed while he was signing the tab that she had bowed her head as if she was preoccupied with something. Though he was curious, he didn't ask her what she was thinking about. He figured she would tell him in time. She looked up straight at him. He put his credit card down on the table and glanced up at her. She smiled his way.

"I have to work in the morning but would you like to come over for dinner tomorrow night? I make a mean steak," she said to him as she twirled her napkin a bit. She seemed nervous that he might refuse her.

"Sure, that sounds perfect. I'll take mine medium rare, please," he replied right away. He accepted without hesitation. He wanted to spend as much time with her as possible. She beamed from ear to ear when he told her. He would find a way to attend.

"How does six-thirty sound? It will give me time to start dinner without any interruptions from you," she said and clapped her hands lightly with joy.

"Ah really? I interrupt you?" he teased her, smirking at her. The waitress arrived at the table. Dalton reached over and grabbed his card. He passed it to the server. He watched as she slid his card on a portable pay machine, then she gave him his receipt to sign. He picked up the pen, added a tip, and they were done.

He extended his hand to Annette and she placed her tiny hand in his. He guided her toward the front door of the restaurant. They walked hand in hand back to Annette's house. The chill of the late afternoon gave him the chance to wrap his arm around her shoulder. He pulled her close against him. Their bodies rubbed against each other. They had spent a magnificent day doing nothing in particular, just browsing around town.

Half an hour later he stood in the entrance of her house. He started kissing the nape of her neck while she was trying to put the key into the lock to open the door. As soon as the door was open, they stepped inside. He slipped his hand around her waist and drew her near to his body. Her arms went up around his neck. He pressed his lips against hers. He gave her one of those kisses that would drive any woman wild. An electric sensation went down his entire body. It eventually became so intense that he had to pull away from her. He held her at arm's length. He gave her a predatory look and then growled at her. She giggled at him as she took her coat off and hung it up in the closet. He knew she had to work the next day and that he shouldn't stay late, but he had hoped that maybe ...

"I think you should go now, otherwise I may not make it into work tomorrow morning and Robert won't be happy," she said in between his kisses. She smelled so good and inviting, but he refrained.

"Would it be that bad?" he asked as she shook her head at him. "Very well. Good night. I shall see you tomorrow night for supper." He reluctantly let go of her waist and kissed her nose one last time. He turned around, took hold of the handle of the door, and turned the knob. He closed the door behind him. He decided he might as well walk back to the hotel. It would give him time to think about what he was going to say to Sidney. He slowly returned to the Ritz Carlton to face her.

An hour later Dalton stopped when he arrived at the front door of the hotel. He had lifted the collar of his coat and rammed his hands into his pockets. He stood outside on the sidewalk, trying to get his thoughts straight. He gazed at the passing cars. *What am I going to do with Sidney?* He turned and entered. The doorman greeted him as he opened the door for him. He walked into the reception area, and his eyes went straight to the bar area. He debated if he should stop and get one last drink before he went upstairs to the room. *No, better to have a level head.* He had enough to drink today.

He moved toward the elevators and pushed the lift button to go up. He closed his fists tight, his nails digging into his palms until they hurt. He needed to calm down. It wasn't her fault. Sidney was here, but she didn't know what was going on. He stepped into the elevator. He watched the number increase as the tenth floor neared. He sighed and bent his head down until the doors opened. He took a step forward, stopped, and strolled to his hotel room, reading every number on the doors in the hallway.

Finally he arrived at his room. He took out his room card from his pant pocket. He scanned his card in the slot of his room. He heard the click of the door. He pushed it open slowly with the tips of his fingers. As soon as the door opened, Sidney accosted him.

"Hi, darling. I thought I'd surprised you and come to meet you early," Sidney said as he saw her running toward him from the bedroom. She was like a cougar attacking her prey. Her arms went up and around his neck. She kissed him hard on the lips, but he did not respond to her. He never moved from his spot and did not embrace her. Not one word came out of his mouth. He was rooted, just staring at her. He gently took her arms off from around his neck and he softly pushed her back.

"I thought you were supposed to wait for me to tell you when to come. What are you doing here?" he questioned her harshly. She took a step back, just glaring at him with her mouth open.

"I figured you must be almost done with work. I wanted to surprise you. Aren't you delighted to see me? I missed you so much. I definitely wasn't expecting this reaction!" she said standing still in front of him. She crossed her arms upon her chest.

"It's not that I'm not happy to see you, but I wish I had known you were coming. I would have been prepared for you," he replied as he took a step beside her. He went toward the bathroom.

"Prepared for me? What are you talking about? Where were you? I have been waiting here since this morning. I called and texted you several times, but you never answered me." She turned around and followed him closely into the bathroom. She leaned on the archway, fiddling with her fingers, waiting for him to answer.

"I was busy," it was the only thing he responded as he proceeded to undress for bed.

"Busy? What do you mean busy? I just flew across the world for you, and all you can tell me when you see me is that you were occupied," she said as she crossed her arms again and stared at him.

"Listen, I'm tired and we can talk about it tomorrow. I'm going to bed," he said firmly. He could feel her eyes on him, but she didn't say anything. He grabbed his toothbrush, applied paste on the brush, and cleaned his teeth. He dropped the toothbrush in the tumbler, walked past her without another word, not even glancing her way. He set foot into the bedroom. Dalton pushed the bedspread off and he slid under the covers of the bed. He turned to face the wall, tucked his arms under his pillow, and closed his eyes. His thoughts were about the last two weeks he had spent with Annette. Sidney didn't say another word, but he heard her open the closet door and grab the extra blanket. She moved toward the bed and picked up the pillow from the other side of the bed. She slammed the bedroom door and walked away to go sleep on the couch in the living room.

* * *

Sidney was heartbroken and furious at the same time. He had ignored her and had given her no explanation. How dare he treat her that way? She was his fiancée. She could not believe he wasn't more enthusiastic to see her. And the greeting he had given her ... He hadn't even responded to her kiss and he hadn't embraced her. She kept trying to keep her tears from falling. She wanted to be strong. She pushed the tears away with her back of her palms. He had said he was busy! *What kind of answer was that?* He brushed her aside as if he didn't want her there. She threw her pillow and blanket on the sofa. She sat down on the edge of the couch, fuming. She bowed her chin low; her heart was in her throat. She would not cry.

She really wanted to sleep by his side, to be close to him and make love to him. He had even denied her that. *Why?* She was so mad she wanted to scream at him, but she thought *it is better to say nothing than to have a full-blown fight on their first day of vacation*. She sat back with a heavy heart and pulled the blanket around her waist. She placed both her hands over her mouth, not wanting to let him hear her cry. Tears fell down her cheeks. She was not strong enough. She patted the tears dry right away. She didn't want Dalton to know, so she tried to gain control of her emotions. She clenched the side of the arm of her resting place. She would not cry anymore. *Why was he like this? What had made him change since he had left London?*

Tomorrow she would question him. Maybe he would be more receptive and answer her. She laid still. Finally she grabbed the blanket to cover her entire body. She sank her head into the pillow. It took her a while to clear her mind. She closed her wet eyes. What had she done to make him push her away? She didn't have an answer. Her mind was in a whirlwind. Tomorrow was a new day. She was patient and the answers would come in time. After countless hours of speculating why he was so cold toward her, she dozed off into a deep sleep.

* * *

Annette sat at her desk, trying to concentrate on her work, but her mind kept drifting back to the last two weeks she had spent with

Dalton. She could not wait to see him this evening. She picked up a pen and began writing a list of things she had to buy for dinner. She raised her pen to her mouth and gently chewed on it. Then, she had a marvelous idea. Why not invite a few of her close friends to come to dinner? She wanted everyone to meet him, even though Dalton wouldn't be here for a long time. She decided that it would be a simple dinner party.

She picked up the phone and brought it to her ear. She dialed her friend Helen's number. Helen's husband John had gone to college and graduated with Mark. John and Helen had married right after her husband's graduation. She and Mark had remained friends with them. She listened as the phone rang, beating her pen on her desktop.

"Hello," she heard Helen's voice say. Annette was happy she caught her at home.

"Hi, Helen. It's Annette. How are you?" she said cheerfully as she rearranged the papers on her desk into a row.

"Great. How about you, sweetie? I haven't seen or heard from you in ages. What have you been up to?" Helen asked her joyfully. How Annette had missed hearing from her!

"I'm doing well. I just called to see if you were available for dinner this evening? I understand it's a short notice, but I wanted you to meet this guy I recently met." Annette giggled and crossed her finger, hoping they could attend.

"A man you say! Well, well," she laughed. "We would love to come. You will have to tell me all about him. I don't see any problems. I'll call John and let him know. What time would you like us to be there?" she asked. Annette smiled to herself, pleased they were going to meet Dalton at dinner.

"How about around seven o'clock? Would that work?" she replied to Helen as she added two more steaks to her list.

"That will be good. I'll bring the wine," Helen said. "I can't wait to see you. I'm glad you called. It's been such a long time. We will have a lot to catch up on."

"Perfect. I'll see you at seven. Bye." Annette was thrilled they were coming. She hung up the phone. She wrote down a few more items and put her checklist in her pocket. She talked to Helen often, but she had not felt like entertaining anyone until now. They called and invited over her many times since Mark had died, but she had only accepted their invitations twice in the last year. She didn't have the heart to go and she wasn't in the mood to celebrate much. She had not seen the couple in months. They used to spend so much time together before her husband's death. They were longtime friends.

She returned to the task of finishing her work so she could try to leave early. She still had to stop by the grocery store to pick up a few articles and then head home to prepare supper.

The hours passed by rapidly. The next thing she knew it was six-thirty. She had worked nonstop in the kitchen for the last hour. Everything was ready. She had done all her errands and she had gotten home by five-thirty. She chopped up a salad, prepared a crab dip for an appetizer with crackers, and marinated the steaks.

She had even had time to change into a red chiffon dress that hugged her body perfectly. She put her hair up with another bobby pin. She examined her work in the mirror, but made a face of distaste. She was having difficulty. She was not satisfied with her hairdo, so at the last second decided to leave it down. She fluffed her hair with the tips of her fingers. Dalton liked it down around her shoulders anyway. He had told her he loved how it bounced around when she moved. She raised her hands up one more time to rearrange her hair. She took a step back to admire herself in the mirror, and returned to the kitchen, satisfied with the outcome.

She searched for a corkscrew in the drawer. She picked up a bottle of white Pinot Grigio and opened it. She poured herself a glass before she placed it in an ice bucket to chill. She brought the glass up to her lips and took a sip. She then opened a bottle of red merlot and set it on the marble kitchen counter to let it breathe.

She grabbed her glass carried it to the living room where she sat down in a chair while she waited impatiently for her guests to arrive for dinner. She moved from one chair to another by the window. She wished they were already here. She was restless, thinking it might have been a bad idea to invite Helen and John so early in her and Dalton's relationship. She reached for a book on the end table. She tried to focus to read, but to no avail. She sat motionless, looking at the pages while lost in thought.

Dalton didn't know them. What if he didn't get along with them? Or what if they didn't like him? Then what? She was overanalyzing the situation. She put the book back in its original spot. She finished her wine and then went back to the kitchen to refill her glass. She could feel her body relaxing as she drank. She had not invited many people to her house in the last year, so she was a bundle of nerves. It would be fine. She rubbed her hands together as she glanced around the room to make sure everything was perfect for her guests. She was ready.

* * *

Dalton woke up around five o'clock in the morning. He laid in bed, motionless, his hands tucked behind his head. For an hour now he had been trying to figure out what he was going to say to and do about Sidney. He really didn't want her here, but at the same time he really didn't want to hurt her. He knew deep down he could not have it both ways. He knew it was a fact of life that when a relationship ended, at least one person would end up hurt. Sidney was a good woman with a big heart and she deserved the truth.

He would try to explain his situation to Sidney in good time. His immediate concern was what he was going to tell her about this evening. He really wanted to see Annette. He told her he would come to dinner. He scratched his chin while he deliberated his next move. Finally he found a temporary solution to his problem. He decided he would spend the day sightseeing with Sidney, he would tell her he had a business dinner this evening that he could not miss. That was it!

He rose out of bed and silently tiptoed into the bathroom. He turned the shower on and he stepped inside. He then snatched a towel off of the railing and dried off. He dressed as fast as he could into a pair of Hugo Boss black jeans with a black Brioni sweater. He combed his black hair back, placed his comb back on the washbasin, and turned around to go talk to Sidney. He went to the living room area where she had slept the previous night. He stopped about ten feet from her. He stood still as he looked down at Sidney, who was sleeping soundly. He didn't want to wake her, so he passed by her without a sound, opened the hotel door, and with long strides he sneaked out of the room.

He took the lift down to the main lobby to the small restaurant called Artisan Bistro. He ordered an assortment of muffins and croissants with two cups of tea to go. He watched as the server brought his purchase to him. He opened the bag and glanced inside to make sure his order was correct. He held the bag with both hands as he returned to his hotel suite. He hoped Sidney would be awake when he arrived back to the room. He wanted to try to smooth things over a little with her before he had to break her heart.

He swiped his hotel card to unlock the door. He pushed the door with his free hand and slowly walked in with his purchases. He noticed Sidney sitting on the couch with her arms folded in front of her. Her eyes were focused on the flat screen television as she watched the news. He gently dropped the food on the coffee table in front of her; he sat next to her on the sofa. Neither one spoke nor did she look his way.

"I thought you might be hungry this morning. I bought you muffins, croissants, and a tea," he softly said to her, but she just sat there. She turned her head; eyes slanted and stared at him. She didn't say a word or move from her spot; she just kept her eyes on him. He could tell she was angry with him and that it was not going to be easy to persuade her to be on his side.

"I'm sorry Sidney. I wasn't expecting you to just show up. I have been working long hours and I was tired," he told her, but not a peep came out from her. She seemed pretty mad.

"I picked up your favorite, a blueberry muffin. I also brought you a cup of tea as a peace offering," he said to her as he pushed the bag toward her. He knew they were her favorite morning pastries.

"Thank you," was all she said. He smiled at her, but she did not reciprocate. He felt a glimmer of hope when she reached for the bag. He watched as she took the cup of tea out from the bag and took a sip. He could tell she was starting to loosen up a little.

"I have the day off, so I thought we could spend it together and go visit the city. We could go to Faneuil Hall and maybe have lunch. You could do some shopping and we could walk around town, if you want," he offered to her. He noticed she had brought the bag over and taken the blueberry muffin out. She bit into it, and replaced it in the bag. She raised her head and nodded at him.

"Okay, I would like that. This muffin is really delicious." She picked up her tea and stood up. "I'll get ready," she said, bent down and kissed him on the cheek. She passed by him and headed for the bathroom with her cup of tea.

Dalton pushed back in his seat and sighed. He grabbed his hot tea and sipped it slowly. He leaned forward and picked up the remote control to the television. He occupied himself with the TV while she was getting dressed. A half hour later Sidney appeared in front of him. Dalton checked his wristwatch. It was only ten after nine in the morning. They had all day to visit the city. They strolled out of the hotel on their way to Faneuil Hall, hand in hand. He didn't want to ruin her whole day, so he decided he would talk to her about his dinner engagement this evening when they came back. He hated to do this to her, but he didn't have much choice at the moment.

* * *

Sidney was trying to hurry. She was multitasking as fast as she could manage. She brushed her teeth, combed her hair, and got dressed in record time. She couldn't believe she had her man back. He had been so sweet this morning when he had arrived with breakfast. How could she not forgive him? She had to agree that she should not have come without first notifying him. He must have been extremely fatigued last night with all the long hours he had been working. He was stressed. She had to be more understanding and try not to get on his nerves.

She dressed in a pair of blue jeans and a brown sweater. They were the first things she saw in her closet, so she grabbed them. She applied lipstick to her lips and took one last look in the mirror. She picked up her pocketbook and swung it around her shoulder. She couldn't get out of the bathroom fast enough to go meet with Dalton in the other room. He was taking her sightseeing. They were going to spend the whole day together and she was excited. She kept hopping around the room while singing a tune in her head. She was also pleased he had taken some time off to so that he could spend time with her. This was what she had been dreaming would happen with this vacation. She was going to be more attentive to his needs and tonight she would make love to him like it was the first time. Sidney ran up to Dalton as he stood. She lifted herself on her toes and kissed him on the lips. "I'm all yours," she said as she slipped her arm into his.

"Okay, let's go," he replied without too much emotion. He bent down and picked up his coat. He slipped it on and reached for the door handle.

"Where are we going first?" she asked him, excited to be in America. It was her first trip abroad and she wanted to experience the whole city, taste unfamiliar foods, and browse the stores for new fashions.

"Let's go to Faneuil Market Place first. We can take a tour of the city if you want, then we can have lunch in the market area. They have all kinds of ethnic food—unless you would prefer a sit down lunch?" he said as he kept on walking toward the elevator.

"That sounds like a plan. I would like to eat at the market, if you don't mind. That way we can try different foods. That would be fun. I'll follow your lead," Sidney answered. She didn't care where she went as long as Dalton was by her side.

"All right, we'll make the decisions as we go," he replied without looking at her. They asked the doorman to flag them a cab. They only waited a few minutes before they were on their way. Sidney sat close to him in the backseat. She could feel his thigh touching hers. She placed her hand on his knee, but she noticed he ignored it. Usually Dalton would have covered it with his hand, but unfortunately he just stared straight ahead. She was not sure why he was still distant with her. It had to be his work. He had a lot on his mind. Once they got going around town, she was certain he would be more receptive to her and his attitude would improve toward her.

"Have you visited the city since you have been here? I mean, where we are going today?" she asked, trying to make conversation. He never even glanced at her, his eyes fixated on the road in front of them.

"I have seen the city many times. I came to college here, remember?" He answered her without expression. She watched as he shifted his weight away from her.

"Can we go see Harvard?" she asked, hoping he would like to see it with her.

"We won't have time today," he answered her as he looked out the cab's window.

"That's okay. You can show it to me another day. We have enough to do today," she said, biting the inside of her cheek. She kept quiet for the rest of the fare until the driver dropped them off in front of Government Center. She stepped out upon the sidewalk while waiting for him to pay the cabby. She was examining the skyscrapers around her. She was ready for whatever the day brought. She was on vacation with her fiancé and that was all she cared about at this instant. She was going to make the most of every day she had with him. She had a whole week with Dalton to soften his mood and show him how much she loved him.

Chapter 11

Dalton and Sidney spent the whole day together visiting the city. They took a Duck Tour around town to see the popular sights. They walked down into the Market Place to taste a variety of foods the merchants sold from fudge to homemade dumplings along the alley. Sidney loved it a lot. Finally, they dropped by the Faneuil Market Place Human Vital exposition. Dalton had been patient with Sidney. He had kept his cool the whole day, ignoring all the sexual passes that she had thrown at him. He hadn't gotten mad, but he had disregarded them.

It was the end of the day and they were sitting at one of the window tables at a Starbucks coffee shop. They were watching people going by as they were drinking hot chocolate before heading back to the hotel. Sidney was agreeable all day. She seemed to be having a good time. She laughed and joked with Dalton, even though he was uninterested in what she said. Dalton looked at his watch and winced. It was almost five o'clock. It was time to get going. He still needed to get back to the hotel to shower before he met Annette for dinner at her place. He couldn't wait to see her.

"Are you almost done? I have to get back to the hotel," Dalton said as he tapped his fingers against his cup while waiting for her to finish her drink. She glanced up at him over her mug.

"Why? What's the rush? Why don't we go out to dinner tonight at one of those famous restaurants? We could—" she started to say, but Dalton lifted his hand up to cut her short.

"I can't go to dinner with you. I already have plans," he told her in a monotone tone. He watched her eyes widen and her mouth open as she stared at him. He stood up, gathered his coffee cup in his hand and threw it out into the garbage bin next to them.

"What do you mean you have plans? With whom? You said you had the day off," she questioned him vexed, but she didn't raise her voice. He knew she was not pleased about being left alone once again for the evening, but he didn't care how she felt. He needed to leave now.

"It's a business dinner," Dalton said. He turned and picked up her empty cup in his hand to dump it out.

"Why didn't you mention it earlier? I thought you were done with work today and that we were going to spend time together. It's our vacation, remember?" she said as she stared at him, waiting for a response. He didn't feel like answering any more questions. He wanted to leave to go find Annette. He knew Sidney was furious, but it didn't faze him. He observed as her lips pinched together. She picked up her phone from the table and shoved it in her pocket. She rose from the table.

"The least you could have done was tell me about it. And by the way, who are you having dinner with?" she said as she placed her hands on her hips.

"No one you know. It's business," he replied. He started walking away from her and toward the front door, leaving her standing by herself in the store. He pushed the glass door and stepped upon the street, not even waiting to see if she was following him. He lifted the collar of his jacket, tucked his hands in his pocket, and stepped away from her. He was returning to the hotel with or without her.

* * *

Sidney could not believe what she had just heard as she left the coffee shop. What the bloody hell was going on? Why was he suddenly being so cold and mysterious to her about dinner? What had she ever done to him to be treated this way? Something was definitely not right. Many questions were going through her mind as she slowly trailed behind him as they walked back to the hotel. He never turned around to see if she was following him. She knew he was avoiding her. *What was the matter with him?* He entered the lobby and went directly to the elevators. Not a word was spoken to her all the way back. She arrived at the room a minute later, still shadowing him.

She entered, took off her coat, and went to sit on the couch in the suite. Silence envelope the suite. He didn't say a word. She waited for him to wash, and watched him as he changed his clothes and prepared himself to go out to dinner. Her heart was pounding in her chest. She had to try one more time to find out where he was headed before he disappeared into the evening night. So when he was almost ready to leave, she went to talk to him. Maybe he would be in a better mood and answer her questions. She got her courage up and went to find him. She was trying to hold her angry feelings back and not cause an argument. She clamped her teeth tight keeping her arms by her side, and went to him.

"Dalton, darling, why are you being so secretive about this dinner? Who are you having dinner with?" she asked again in a soft voice as she approached him in the bathroom. She leaned against the door archway. He didn't answer her. He just continued combing his hair and then sprayed cologne on. He cast his eyes up briefly and looked at her in the mirror; he turned around to face her.

"It's just a business dinner. I didn't want to ruin your day—that's why I didn't tell you until now." He came forward and didn't even kiss her on the cheek.

"I have to go. I'm late," he said as he bypassed her; his pace was hurried as he headed for the exit. She heard the click of the door close behind her. She couldn't move. Her mind was wild with all kinds of ideas about where he was going and with whom.

Suddenly she turned, snatched her pocketbook, and put on her coat. She ran for the door. She didn't wait for the elevator to come up to the floor. She pushed the exit door to the stairs and took them two at a time down to the lobby of the hotel. She was breathing hard by the time she reached the main floor. She stopped, bent in half, hands on her knees as she took long breaths. She straightened up and walked as fast as she could toward the entrance.

She saw Dalton standing outside as the doorman was holding the door of a cab. She hid behind a pile of suitcase on a trolley by the front entrance and observed Dalton get into the taxi then leave. As soon as the car took off she came out of her hiding place and ran directly to the doorman. "I need a taxi. Please hurry. I'm late for an appointment," she said to him. He immediately signaled the next one in line to come forward. He opened the door and she hopped into it.

"Could you follow that cab in front? Over there, please," she pointed to the yellow car in front that had stopped at the traffic light.

"No problem," the driver said. He clicked the meter and shifted the car into gear.

"Don't follow too close, okay?" Sidney told him. He looked at her in his rearview mirror and just nodded. She searched in her bag and found her black wool hat. She placed it on her head and tucked her hair under it. She pulled it down low over her face. She lifted the hood of her coat up then sat back as she watched Dalton's cab roll down the street.

She truly wanted to know if his dinner was really a business dinner or if he was meeting ... a woman. She wouldn't think of that until she had proof. He had always been faithful to her but ... *Dalton better not be cheating on her.* She couldn't bear to lose him to another woman. Dalton was her life and she would fight for him. She would do what had to be done to keep him, but first she had to make sure he wasn't an adulterer. She didn't believe he would do such a thing to hurt her. He loved her.

* * *

Annette raced around the house all day preparing dinner and making sure everything was perfect. She wanted to introduce Dalton to her best friends. She had just laid out the hot appetizer on the stove top, chilled the wine, and was lighting candles one by one when she heard the doorbell ring. She took off her apron and crammed it in one of the island drawers. She straightened the front of her dress with her hands and checked her lipstick in the mirror before she quickly strolled to the front door. She checked the peephole then swung the door open.

"Hi, guys. It's so nice to see you. Come on in!" Annette said to her friends as they stepped inside. She leaned forward to embrace and kissed them.

"It's been a long time. I was so glad to hear from you. We have so much to catch up on," Helen said as she took off her coat and gave it to Annette. Annette smiled at her guests while she hung up their coats in the entrance closet.

"First let's go in and have a glass of wine." She led the way to the small kitchen bar as they followed close behind. "White or red?" she asked them as she took out two wine glasses from the cupboard and placed them in front of her guests. She grabbed the bottles and held both up for them to choose. Both of her friends said white would be fine, so she poured them each a glass.

"So, tell me about the mystery man," Helen said as she took her wine from Annette's hand and sat next to her at the kitchen island.

"Well, his name is Dalton Rivers. He's an attorney. I met him at work a few weeks ago and he is an absolute doll," Annette told her as she sat next to her and sipped her glass of wine.

THE PLEDGE

"Dalton Rivers. That name sounds familiar. Do you know where he went to school?" John asked Annette as he sat down on one of her kitchen stools and dipped a cracker into her crab dip.

"As a matter of fact, he went to Harvard. He graduated the same year as you and Mark did. Do you know him?" She eyed John, seeking more information about Dalton.

"I can't place the name, but it will come to me in time. Maybe when I meet him it will ring a bell," John answered her as he kept munching on the crab dip and crackers. Annette could see he was preoccupied. She watched him as he frowned, trying to remember. They continued to catch up on their news while they waited for Dalton to arrive to the house. A half hour later she heard the doorbell ring.

"That must be Dalton. Excuse me," she told them.

Annette rushed to the door to open it. As soon as Dalton set foot inside the house, he came forward and kissed her on the lips and said, "Hi, gorgeous. If you want to skip dinner, I really don't mind." She could feel the heat rise to her face. She hoped her friends hadn't heard him.

She took his hands in hers, looked him straight in the eyes, and whispered, "I wish I could, but I invited a few friends to dinner." She tilted her head toward the kitchen.

Dalton squeezed her hands, grinned at her, and said in a low voice, "Too bad." He turned his head and looked toward her guests, who were watching them from afar.

"Come on. I'll introduce you," Annette told him as she led him by the hand to the island.

"Everyone, I would like you to meet Dalton Rivers. These are good friends of mine, John and Helen Glass," Annette said with a broad smile on her face. Helen was the first to come forward to shake his hand, and then John approached.

"Nice to meet you. You must be special to her, because she hasn't entertained for some time, and here we are," John told him as he shook his hand. He took a gulp of his wine.

"That's nice to know," Dalton replied as he turned to Annette to wink at her. She offered him a glass of red wine. He took a glass of merlot and sipped it.

"Why don't you boys go sit in the living room while us girls talk and I start dinner?" Annette suggested to the men.

"Good, I'm starving!" exclaimed John. She smiled at them, as she angled her head in the direction of the living room.

"Sure, no problem. I suppose you have a lot to talk about," John replied as he looked at his wife and started laughing. He walked toward the other room. He signaled for Dalton to follow him into the living room. Dalton obliged without a word.

"John, I know how you love hockey. Just to let you know, the remote for the TV is on the coffee table if you want to watch the game," Annette yelled John's way, giggling as she raised her glass of wine to Dalton.

John just said, "Thanks," as he sat down in Mark's chair.

* * *

Dalton sat on the edge of the couch with his glass of wine. He had a knot stuck in his stomach and he felt like he was walking on glass. He would have to be careful how he approached this man. He recognized John the instant he saw him sitting in Annette's kitchen. Dalton never gave any indication that he recognized John. He hoped John didn't remember him. Dalton felt sweat crawling down his back as he played with the rim of his glass, following its contour. He was speechless, but he had to try to distract him.

"So, you like hockey? What is your favorite team? " Dalton asked John as he picked up the remote from the coffee table and passed it to him. John took it in his hand and clicked the television on. He scanned the sports channels until he found the Boston Bruins game against the Montreal Canadians.

"The Boston Bruins are my favorite, of course. I hope you don't mind. I have a passion for hockey. I used to play in college but after that ... " John shrugged as he continued to watch the tube. He leaned back into his chair and placed his foot on his knee.

"I don't know much about hockey. I personally prefer football," Dalton replied. He was glad they weren't in the kitchen. He was nervous that John would recall who he was. Dalton rested his back against the sofa.

"Annette said you were an attorney and that you graduated from Harvard. We already have something in common. I also attended Harvard. Go Crimsons!" John said casually as he kept an eye on the game. Dalton felt a chill pass through him. He was feeling uncomfortable about the statement. He squirmed in his seat, but he was not going to pursue the subject. He was afraid it might be revealed that he had been Mark's roommate. He bit his lower lip, trying to figure out what to say to John without giving anything away.

"You should say 'Go Bruins!' Do you know the score?" Dalton asked him, pretending he was interested in the game even though he didn't give a damn. But he continued to question John about the game and the players as means of conversation. Dalton got up from his chair during a commercial break to refill his glass of wine. He smiled Annette's way and winked at her again. He filled his glass, and discreetly guzzled it to try to ease the tension he felt as he examined John sitting on the chair.

The evening passed without another mention of Harvard. Dalton averted a conflict. It would have put him in the position to either lie to Annette or tell her the truth. But he might lose Annette if he told her the truth. He was not prepared to do that at this time. One day he would explain the letter to her, but not now. He needed more time with her before he plunged forward with it.

Dinner went without a hitch. They had finished eating and they were having coffee at the kitchen counter when Helen said, "We should do this again before you return to London. I'll give Annette a call soon."

"That sounds great, thanks," Dalton answered, hoping they never got together again. Annette went to retrieve their coats from the closet and hand them to her company. Dalton watched as they put them on, smiled, and waved goodbye. They were gone in minutes. Dalton felt relieved when Annette closed the front door and locked it. Now he would be able to really relax. It felt like a hefty load just had lifted off his shoulders. He sighed heavily.

"Come over here," Dalton said to Annette as he pulled her closer to him. He placed his fingers under her chin and lifted it up towards his face. He gently touched her lips with his mouth once, and enveloped his whole mouth on hers. He pulled back, traced his tongue up to her earlobe. He could feel her hands gripping his backside. He paused to inhale her skin. "I couldn't wait for them to leave. I've been waiting all evening to do that. That was torture," Dalton joked as he pulled her against him as he felt an erection growing. He could feel her breasts rubbing against him. He heard a faint moan come from her. It drove him wild. He scooped her up in his arms. He carried her light body to her bedroom, all the while kissing her while preparing for a delightful evening of lovemaking.

* * *

Sidney followed Dalton's taxi until she saw it stop. "Keep going! Pull the car up the next block, please," she almost yelled at the driver of her taxi. She scooted down low in the back seat when they passed the other yellow cab so Dalton would not see her. She rose up from her hiding spot after they had passed by. She took a peek over the backseat to determine which house Dalton was entering.

She noticed the driver was observing her from his rearview mirror. He was probably wondering what the bloody hell she was doing. She forced a smile at him and said, "That's my fiancé. I just wanted to know where—" she halted as the man lifted his hand at her. He didn't want to hear her.

"Listen, lady, I really don't care what you do. If you want to stay here, the meter will keep running, just so you know." Sidney looked back at the house and watched as Dalton walked inside. This was not a business dinner. *What was he doing in this part of town?* She also noticed he didn't even have his briefcase with him. If it was business, he would have his case. She glanced back at the house one more time while she considered if she should check it out or go back to the hotel. What if Dalton saw her snooping around? He would be furious. She raised her hand and bit her fingernails. She was trying to make up her mind what to do.

"Hey! Miss, are we staying or are we going?" she heard the driver say. He sounded annoyed. She whipped her head around and peered at him.

"Could you wait for me if I paid you?" She asked him, irritated that he was pressuring her to make a decision.

"Pay me what you owe me now, and I'll keep the meter running from there. How long will you be?" he inquired as he clicked the meter. The driver grabbed his time sheet and wrote something down.

"I shouldn't be more than maybe ten or fifteen minutes. Would that be suitable? Here's a twenty. We can settle the rest when I come back," Sidney told the driver. She reached over the seat and gave him two twenty-dollar bills.

"Sure, that will do," he answered. "Fifteen minutes. After that I'm gone, understood?" he blurted out. She nodded. She grabbed the door handle and opened the door. She started walking toward the house with her head bowed low. She couldn't just go up to the front door and say, "Hi, I'm looking for Dalton." She must be crazy. She kept a steady pace until she was almost in front of the house when she saw a small alleyway that separated the houses.

She instantly turned into it. She sneaked into the narrow alley without thinking. She ran in and froze. She placed her back against the wall. Her adrenaline spiked so much her legs became weak. She took a deep breath, trying to calm down. She cautiously proceeded one foot at a time toward the back of the house, her heart racing. It was dark, so she touched the wall with her hand as she went forward. She carefully crept further with every step. She was very prudent of her footing not to make any noise. She stopped when she arrived at the end of the building. She poked her head around the edge to inspect the surroundings. No one was around.

Around the bend she could see a light coming from a patio door up ahead. This was the house. She was sure of it. She didn't move for a minute, letting her vision adjust to the dark. She continued moving one step at a time, making sure she didn't kick or bump anything that would alert the people inside the house.

She was about fifteen feet from the patio when her heart started racing faster. She stopped again for a moment, her back against the brick wall of the house. She sighed. She needed courage. She was out of her mind, prowling around the backyard of strangers. She bent low and slid a little further so she could hide behind the deck of the patio. She crouched down by the stairway of the deck. She held her breath. She counted to three, raised her head just above the floor of the veranda so she could look inside. There he was! Dalton was talking to another man. He seemed to be having a good time, laughing, drinking but then ... "You bloody son of a bitch!" she said under her breath.

She couldn't move, paralyzed as she watched in horror as a woman came closer to him and kissed him on the lips, wrapping her hand around his waist and massaging his back lovingly. He was gazing into her eyes and whispering sweet nothings in her ear while she laughed. Her eyes bulged out at the scene that was developing in front of her. Hatred consumed her. *How dare she touch him?* She observed the encounter unfold for about five minutes as tears started to build in her eyes. She backed away slowly. She had seen enough. No wonder he had been so discreet about where he was going. Tears fell as she walked back to the cab. She tried to push them away.

"Business dinner, my ass!" she uttered with clenched teeth. She arrived back at the front of the alley within seconds. "Thank God!" she said when she saw the taxi was still there waiting for her. She hurried back, and with a trembling hand, opened the back door to slide into the seat.

"Could you take me back to the Ritz Carton, please?" she managed to say to the man. He just nodded and took off. She felt awful. Her stomach was stirring up bile and she wanted to vomit. She clamped her fists tight. She wanted to hit someone or something. She closed her eyes and tried to unscramble everything she had seen. Her Dalton was with another woman. *How long had this been going on? How many others were there?* How could she be so naïve and not have seen it? All the late nights that he had told her he was working ... he had probably been with someone else. She could feel her anger surfacing from being betrayed. She could not wait to see him, to confront him. She loved him so much, but at the same time she hated him for what he had done. She tried to clear her mind and relax until she got back to the hotel.

She finally arrived back in her room. She barely made it to the bed before she collapsed. Her stomach groaned with pain, but what was worst was her head. She could barely open her eyes from the throbbing ache in her head. She rubbed her temples with her hands. She closed her eyes. She didn't move a muscle for ten long minutes. Finally, she pulled her strength together and wobbled to the bathroom. She took the bottle of Advil from her cosmetic bag and popped three in her mouth. She swallowed them with water. She returned to the bed to lie down. Tears streamed down her face from the discovery of his unfaithfulness. She would wait up and see what he had to say once he arrived back at their room.

Chapter 12

Annette had never been happier. Her dinner party with Dalton and her friends had gone nicely. They all seemed to get along. And now how could she complain? She was in the arms of the man she was falling in love with. She was on cloud nine, but she had never approached the question that had haunted her night after night since she had met him. *What would happen when he returned to London? The most pressing question was when was he going back?* Her head was resting on his shoulder as she played with his chest, making circles in his chest hair with her fingers, when Dalton said, "A penny for your thoughts. You seem so distant." She lifted her head up and looked at him, debating if she should tell him what was really on her mind.

"I was thinking how handsome you are," she told him. He grinned at her, showing her his precious dimples that she loved so much.

"That was not what you were thinking," he told her as he pulled and held her closer.

"No, you're right. I was wondering when you were going back home to London and what was to become of our relationship." She watched his face. He didn't give anything away, so she kept quiet and waited for his response. He held her even more tightly.

"To tell you the truth, it's kind of complicated. I am a new partner in a law firm and I live in London. My plane ticket says I have to leave next Sunday, but I was thinking that if you want, I could extend my time here. I know I have to return sooner or later, but right now I'm content just where I am," he said as he pulled her body upwards then kissed the top of her head.

"I would love for you to stay as long as possible. Don't you already know that? But what about us ... later?" Annette questioned. She turned her head away from him, afraid of his answer. He still had not mentioned where she stood with him, so she waited.

"Annette, I want to know everything about you, but I don't dare say anything because my life is so far from here. It would be difficult for me to stay here, but I absolutely do not want to lose touch with you. I want us to be together. It will work out. When I'm with you, I'm alive. You bring life to me. Nothing else matters but you," he replied seriously turning her head and looking into her eyes.

"Does that help?" he continued. She dragged her body forward until she was inches from his face. She smiled, as she brought her lips to his and kissed him passionately. A sexual electrifying sensation consumed her and she knew exactly how to appease it. She pulled away from his lips just to say, "Yes, that does help." There still was hope and Annette believed they would work out the problem of the long distance romance. Tonight he was hers and she was going to take advantage of all that he had to give her. She knew in her heart that even though it hadn't been long since they had first met, she loved him. He was her destiny and her soul mate.

* * *

Sidney was sulking on the sofa in their hotel room for the last three hours, staring at nothing in the dark, was not able to move. All kinds of emotions happened, from rage to sadness. She felt numb. Her eyes were red and swollen from all the crying. Tears had stained her face, but she had no more tears to cry. Her hair was disheveled. She was still wearing the same clothes from this morning, even though they were all wrinkled and dirty. She could smell the sweat that had permeated them, but she didn't care. She was heartbroken, but mostly she was infuriated from the shock of the discovery of Dalton and that woman. *Who was she? What did she mean to him? Where had he met her?* He had only been here in America for two weeks and already he had another woman under his arm. Now she knew why he had kept delaying her trip. He didn't want her here. *So what happens now?* Her mind was a maelstrom. She had many questions without answers.

She was trying to decipher what she had seen and what she was going to do about it. Tears had welled for hours, but now she was done crying. She was exasperated. She cast her eyes toward the clock on the wall. It was now midnight and Dalton still had not returned. She knew in her heart where he was and what was going on, but she wanted to deny it. She decided that she had to be mature about this situation. She would have to talk to him tomorrow. He would tell her it was all a misunderstanding, that he loved her, and that he was sorry. He would tell her that she had it all wrong. Who was she kidding? She knew better.

She rose. Her whole body ached from not moving. She rubbed her lower back and stretched her arms as she walked to the bedroom. She shed her clothes and slipped into bed. She was exhausted by what she had discovered about her man. She needed to sleep so that she could think straight. Recurring questions about the identity of this woman and her relationship with Dalton kept tormenting Sidney. She tossed and turned many times.

Sidney had to have a clear head when she spoke to Dalton, otherwise she might say or do something she would regret for the rest of her life. This man belonged to her and she would be damned if this bitch would take him from her. She shut her eyes, turned on her side, and tried to clear her mind so she could sleep. Sleep was her only refuge.

Within an hour she was sound asleep dreaming of her beloved fiancé. It wasn't long before the dreams turned into nightmares.

* * *

Annette heard the music of her alarm clock. It woke her up at the break of dawn. She had to get ready to go to work, but she didn't really feel like it. She extended her arm to reach for Dalton, but all she felt was a cold bed. She opened her eyes. There was not a trace of him. Where had he gone? She swung her legs over the side of the bed. She grabbed her bathrobe in her hand and slipped it on as she headed for the kitchen. She swept the area with her eyes, but Dalton was nowhere to be found. She hoped she hadn't scared him away with all her personal questions last night. On the counter to her right she noticed a note addressed to her. She picked it up with trembling hands. She was afraid of the contents, but a smile came to her lips instantly. It read:

Good morning, Gorgeous.
Sorry, but I had to leave. I will see you soon. Loved the evening.
Give me a call.
Dalton

She would call him later in the day. She headed towards the bathroom to get ready for her job. She walked to her closet and stood in front of her wardrobe. She took out a pair of blue dress pants and a white shirt. She laid the outfit nicely on her bed. She still had to work. She couldn't just stay in bed with her man ... or could she? She giggled a bit at the thought of spending a whole day in bed with Dalton. "Mmmm! ... Stop it," she told herself as she entered the bathroom and turned on the hot water faucet. She let her robe fall to the floor as she jumped into the tub. The water warmed her body and as she soaked, she reminisced about the time she had spent with Dalton the previous night.

* * *

Dalton snuck out of Annette's house around three o'clock in the morning when she was sound asleep. He had stood over her by the foot of the bed for a brief minute, just admiring her as she slept. He had to get back to his hotel room. While he had been lying in bed holding Annette close, he decided that he never wanted to leave her side again. She was the one he truly desired to spend the rest of his life with, not Sidney. How was he going to tell Sidney he didn't love her anymore, but he did love another woman? He knew he had to make things right with Sidney as soon as possible, but he still felt sad. He really didn't want to break her heart and cause her pain. He had no other course of action but to tell her the truth.

He quietly let himself into the suite. He noticed Sidney was sound asleep in the bedroom. He opened the hallway closet without a sound. He took out the blanket and a pillow. He threw them on the sofa. He peeled his clothes off. It was his turn to be on the couch. He lay down and sighed. Relaxing, he thought about his reunion with John at the dinner party. Dalton knew exactly who he was. He had been in a number of his classes and they had met briefly at parties on campus, but they had never been close. They only thing that bothered him was that John knew Annette and he might remember Dalton had always hung out with—her husband Mark.

He couldn't dwell on it. He was going to break up with Sidney so he could be free, and it would be fine. He had to tell Sidney that his feelings for her had changed. He wanted to be with another woman– Annette. That was not going to go well. He flinched as he thought about the confrontation he had ahead of him. He could not lead her on anymore. She was a good woman, but she was not for him. He hoped she would understand, but just the same, he would have to be prepared for a battle. She would find someone else one day. He had to send her back to London as soon as possible. Tomorrow he would face Sidney and put her on the next plane back to London.

He closed his eyes, pulled the blanket up over his shoulders, and fell sound asleep immediately. He woke up a few hours later from the sound of a truck honking outside his hotel window. He turned on his side, trying to fall asleep again, when he had a strange feeling come over him. He opened his eyes slightly and saw Sidney sitting in the chair across from him. Her arms were folded in front of her. The scowl on her face told him she definitely was infuriated. She was fully dressed in pants and a sweater, and she even had her hiking boots on. Strange!

"What time is it?" Dalton asked her, still drowsy as he sat up on the edge of the couch and stretched his arms. Sidney didn't answer him. She just stared at him. Her eyes were slanted and she was not smiling. *What was the matter with her?*

"How was your business dinner?" she finally asked him. He knew by the tone of her voice she was upset. He would have to be careful about what he said to her.

"It went well, thank you. You were sleeping when I came home and I didn't want to wake you, so I bunked here," Dalton answered her calmly, but he could tell from her demeanor she still was not a happy camper. He could swear she had been crying.

"Where was the dinner?" she asked without moving, her arms still tucked across her chest. Her leg twitched. He noticed her hands were slightly shaking, and he saw her make two fists. *What was going on with her?* Had he missed something?

"It doesn't matter where dinner was. What's the matter? You seemed angry and I don't like the tone of your voice." Dalton was trying to calm her. He reached to touch her knee with his hand, but she pulled away. She slapped his hand away.

"Don't touch me! Answer my question," she yelled at him. Dalton was surprised by her reaction. Usually she was so subdued around him.

"I had dinner at a colleague's house. Why?" he replied, unfazed. He watched as she stood, walked to the window, and looked outside at the Boston Commons. He got up from the sofa and put his pants on. He walked to the closet and grabbed a t-shirt to slip on. She was quiet.

"Who was the woman?" she asked him without looking at him or moving from her spot. He couldn't see her face. His heart skipped a beat. *Did she know about Annette?*

"What woman?" Dalton inquired, shocked by the question. *How could she know? Why would she ask that?*

"The woman that was all over you at dinner last night," he heard her say. He froze. He turned around from the closet to look up at her again—this time more closely. She still hadn't budged from her spot. He couldn't see her expression. Maybe she was testing him to see how he would answer.

"What are you talking about, Sidney?" he asked again, waiting patiently to find out what she thought she knew. He scratched his head and cautiously took a few steps toward her.

"Last night when you left to go to dinner, I followed you to the North End and I saw you with her," she told him. Dalton was outraged by what she had just divulged to him. He couldn't believe it. He bit his lower lip and placed his hands on his hips.

"You followed me?" he whispered. A million things went through his mind at once. *She had seen him with Annette? What had she seen? How was he going to explain her?*

"I saw you with that woman. You were kissing her. I thought you loved me. We are supposed to get married this summer and that's what you do? WHO IS SHE?" Sidney screamed at him as she turned to face him. Her face was turning red from rage or distress.

"Sidney, please calm down. I never meant for you to find out this way or to hurt you," he said, watching her closely. He had never seen her with this much anger in all the years he had known her. She was breathing heavy and he noticed her fists. They were in balls. She took a step forward.

"It just happened. I'm so sorry," he said to her sympathetically. He looked away from her. Guilt was written all over his face that he had been caught cheating. His stomach felt tight, like he was going to be sick. He placed his hand on his abdomen. He might as well get it over with. It was what he had wanted all along, wasn't it?

"What are you saying? That you don't want to marry me anymore? That you don't love me any longer? You're wrong. I don't believe you," she said. He could see her lips start to quiver and her eyes fill with tears.

"I don't know what I want right now, but I have to go find out." Dalton was so sorry she had come to find out about Annette this way. He rubbed his hands together and closed his eyes, waiting for her wrath.

"And when will you know? Am I supposed to just wait around until you make up your mind? You want to throw away everything we have built together for a roll in the hay? Is that it?"

"Sidney, you have to give me time. I didn't plan this," he said. She moved closer to him. In three long strides she was standing in front of him. He noticed tears streaming down her face. She raised her right hand and in one swift blow she hit him across the face. He felt the sting of her hand against his cheek. He deserved it. He bowed his head in silence.

"You bastard. You have to decide what you want. Decide now or get out of my sight!" she said as she searched for an answer that never came. She walked away into the bathroom. He heard the door slam. Dalton bent down, retrieved his jacket off the chair, and put it on. He needed fresh air to clear his mind. He was confused. Or was he? He had a decision to make and he was not prepared for this outburst. Sidney knew. He opened the room door and sauntered out in the hallway with no answers to his dilemma.

* * *

Sidney sat on the toilet seat, crying her eyes out once again. She buried her face in her hands. She heard the door of the suite close, so she knew Dalton left. She could feel a major headache coming on. Her whole head throbbed with pain. Unable to catch her breath, she was trying to control her emotions, but having a hard time. She was broken, but most of all she was angry. Furious! Disgusted! She examined her hands. They trembled uncontrollably. She stood up in front of the mirror and turned on the cold-water faucet. She cupped water in her hands then splashed it on her face to wash her tears away. She seized a towel off the rack and dried her face. She walked out to the living room. She noticed his briefcase resting by the table on the ground. She ran to it and kicked it with all her might. The case went flying in the air and hit the wall. It opened and papers scattered everywhere. She felt better. Calmness came over her.

She slumped to her knees, prepared to pick up the contents of his briefcase, when she spotted a picture of a woman sticking out of a yellow envelope. She reached over with a shaking hand and scooped it up. She gasped. Her right hand went straight to cover her mouth. She inhaled and held her breath. It was a photograph of the woman she had seen Dalton with last night. *Who was she?* She took out the rest of the articles out of the sleeve. There was a letter addressed to Dalton. She picked it up and she read it. Her eyes bulged out. What the hell was this? She reread the letter a second time. "Oh my Lord!" was all she could say.

 He had come here to meet this woman. He had lied to her. He had not traveled here for business, but to meet her. She wanted to rip it up, but she didn't want him to know what she had discovered. She put the photo back in the envelope. She just sat there on the floor, dumbfounded, with the note in her hands. Minutes passed by without her moving. Her mind was all over the place ... then she had a question.

Did this woman named Annette know how Dalton had deceived her? Did she know about this letter from her dead husband? Did she know about the agreement between them? She bet her life she didn't, but she was soon going to inform her about it. Sidney was going to confront her. She might not know her phone number, but she knew where Annette lived. That was all she needed. She was going to get her man back one way or another. She snatched her coat out of the closet and walked out of the hotel, determined to enlighten Annette on a few facts.

Chapter 13

Annette was filing briefs. It was the end of the day when her phone rang. She reached over and picked the receiver up.

"Hello, Mr. Paige's office," she said casually while writing a notes in a file, trying to finish so she could get home early.

"Hi, Annette, this is Helen. How are you doing?" she heard her friend say but she sensed she sounded nervous.

"Great. It was nice seeing you last night. We have to do it again soon. What's up?" Annette said, still writing while listening to her friend.

"Yes, yes, we had a fabulous time, but that's not why I called. I'm not sure if it's my place to tell you this, but here it goes. John was telling me that Dalton looked familiar last night, but he couldn't pin it down. Well, he did," Helen informed her. Annette stopped writing to concentrate on the conversation. She put her pen down and sat back in her chair. Something in Helen's voice really alarmed her.

"Okay, what did he remember?" Annette asked intrigued by what Helen had to say.

"John told me they all had graduated the same year from Harvard Law, right?" she said.

"Right. So ...?" Annette was trying to be patient. Her foot was drumming against the floor. She really wanted to get back to her work so she could go meet Dalton.

"John found his Harvard yearbook this morning and figured it out. Did you know Dalton was Mark's roommate in college?" Helen told her. Annette dropped the papers she was holding. She didn't believe what she had heard for a second.

"What?" she questioned her friend, unable to utter anything else.

"John remembered this morning. They were always together at the parties, but John didn't hang out with them. He had forgotten because Dalton was younger, had longer hair and a beard. He had returned to London after graduation. John hadn't seen him in ten years," Helen said. There was silence on the other end of the phone.

"Annette, are you still there? You didn't know did you?" she asked concerned.

"Yes, I am. He told me he knew Mark, but he never mentioned he was Mark's roommate. Are you positive?" Annette inquired further. She couldn't understand why he would hide such a thing from her.

"I'm sorry, but yes, John is sure. We thought you should know," she replied.

"Thanks, Helen. I'll talk to you soon. Bye." Annette was confused as she put the phone back. She just sat there, thinking, *why had Dalton not told her that he had been Mark's roommate? What else was he hiding? Why hadn't he said anything?* There had to be a reasonable explanation and she was going to find out when she met up with him for dinner later on. She was going to get to the bottom of this mystery. Maybe there was a simple answer. She tried to focus and return to her work, but she couldn't concentrate. A half hour later she gave up. She gathered her coat and pocketbook from where they had been hanging in the lunchroom. She walked out of the building, her mind spinning with questions about Dalton. She decided to go home to change her clothes before she met up with Dalton. He was the only one who had the answers to all her questions.

* * *

Sidney tucked the letter in her jacket pocket. She was riding in the back seat of a cab on her way to Annette house. She checked the time. It was five-thirty in the afternoon, so hopefully this woman would be home from work by now. The only thing that was making her a bit nervous was that she had not heard from Dalton since their argument this morning. Where could he have gone all day? He didn't know too many people in Boston. She hoped he wasn't at Annette's house otherwise all hell was going to break loose. The car stopped in front of the bitch's house. "Could you wait for me? I shouldn't be too long," she told the cabbie, and proceeded to open the door. She stepped out and walked right up to the front door. Her legs felt heavy, but she had to go through with what she had come here to do. She took a long breath and exhaled. She was ready. She wanted her man back and this was the solution. She took the letter out of her pocket and held it in her hand. She reached over and rang the doorbell with her index finger.

She heard the bell ring inside and someone yelled, "I'm coming." Sidney waited patiently. Though her legs were still feeble, nothing was going to stop her from confronting this woman. The door swung open. She was facing the woman who'd had her hands all over her fiancé the previous night. Sidney just stood and stared at her. She was even prettier in person. The picture didn't do her justice.

"Can I help you?" Annette asked politely. She was dressed up in a purple dress with matching shoes. She looked ready to go out.

"Are you Annette Russell?" Sidney asked her while looking her over from head to toe.

"Yes, I am. What can I do for you?" she asked again, still holding onto the frame of the door, as she looked impatient.

"My name is Sidney Moore. I'm Dalton's fiancée," she told Annette immediately. She waited a few seconds to let the information sink in. Sidney watched Annette as she opened her mouth and then closed it. Nothing was coming out of her mouth.

"What did you say? You are ... Dalton's, Dalton Rivers, fiancée?" she finally asked with her eyebrows knit. She looked stunned.

Good! Sidney wanted this woman to suffer.

"Yes, I am. Could I have a minute of your time to talk?" Sidney said to her. Annette was still holding the door half closed, not budging from her spot.

"Can I come in?" Sidney asked again. She watched as the door moved backward and Annette took two steps back. Sidney closed the door behind them. They were both standing in the small entryway of Annette's house, staring at each other.

"I'm not here to fight with you or cause you any problems, but I wanted to meet you so I could see for myself what Dalton saw in you, and let you know he was engaged to me," Sidney said. She was trying not to get mad that Dalton was having an affair with this ... this ... But she could feel rage building.

"What do you want?" Annette asked again as Sidney noticed her lips quaking from the rude awakening. But Sidney was not done yet.

"I came here to give you this letter. This is the only reason Dalton befriended you. He felt obligated to your husband. That's all." Sidney passed her the letter. Annette took it from her and unfolded it. Annette started reading it. Suddenly her hands were shaking uncontrollably and tears swam in her eyes.

"Where did you get this letter?" Annette whispered to her, her eyes glue to the letter.

"I found it in Dalton briefcase. He left it in our hotel room. He doesn't love you. I'm his fiancée, so keep your hands off him, bitch! Do you understand?" Sidney told her. She narrowed her eyes, turned around, and started to open the door. She glanced back at Annette who was still standing there. Annette could not move. She was white as a sheet. Sidney thought she might faint any minute, but she didn't care what she did. Sidney just leered at her.

"Dalton is mine and will always be mine," Sidney said then laughed out loud.

"Get out of my house! Now," Annette shouted at her angrily as she crushed the note.

"You can keep the letter," Sidney told her calmly as she slammed the door behind her.

Sidney felt as if a heavy load had been lifted off her shoulders as she walked back to the cab to head back to the hotel. She grinned to herself, having accomplished what she had come to do, which was to put a wedge between Annette and Dalton. Dalton was her man and she was going to fight for him. She didn't care who she hurt along the way.

* * *

Annette couldn't breathe. She was feeling light headed. Her world was spinning. She had to hold on to the wall. She tried to get to a chair in the living room before she fainted. She dropped into the nearest chair. She looked down at her trembling hands. Her whole body was shivering as a chill passed down her back. She was still holding the note in her hand. She laid her head against the back of the chair and tried to regain control of her senses. This was a nightmare. She couldn't be part of this. She had to relax. She placed her hand on her heart as she felt tightness through her chest. "Calm down, Annette. Breathe for God's sake!" she told herself. Time ticked away and before she knew it an hour had passed her by and she hadn't budged from her seat.

She brought the note up to her eyes once more and read it. Mark had sent this. He had wanted her to move on and he had asked Dalton to take care of her. *Why hadn't Dalton said anything to her? Why had he misled her all this time? Had he come to Boston just to meet her? Had he ever planned to tell her about the letter? And the most important question was why hadn't he told her about Sidney? He was engaged to another woman.*

She looked at the clock in her kitchen. She was supposed to meet him in fifteen minutes at The Daily Catch, a restaurant in the North End. She told him that it was one of her favorite restaurants. She couldn't fathom seeing him tonight, though. She had too many things to think about—the lies, the letter, and their relationship. Had it ever been real for him or had he just been helping a friend? Or worse, had he just done it to have sex with her. She was heartbroken. A river of tears started flowing down her cheeks she couldn't control.

She missed too many pieces to the puzzle. For such a long time she kept her heart locked up, trying to keep all her memories of Mark to herself. She had just begun to trust someone, to believe she might have a future with someone and now ... She needed to have a clear head next time she spoke to him. But did she want to see him again? The answer was no. Her world had been shattered and destroyed. No more hope, no more Dalton.

Tears plummeted down her cheeks and she was unable to control them. She placed the letter on the coffee table in front of her and walked towards the bathroom. She turned on the water and undressed. She just wanted to sink into a hot bath and try to erase the pain she felt. She just needed time to sort things out. Tomorrow she would face the problem, but not tonight. This evening she desired to be alone with her thoughts so she could try to find a solution to her misery.

* * *

Dalton spent the day walking around town. He browsed the stores at Copley Place to pass the time away, not buying anything. He wandered from store to store all afternoon. He stopped at one of the bistros to get a bite to eat, but he barely touched his food. He kept checking the time. He still had about an hour and a half before he was to meet

Annette at The Daily Catch restaurant. He made the decision to return to the hotel to shower and get ready to go see Annette. Hopefully Sidney would be more rational now.

He unlocked his hotel room and peered inside. All was quiet. Sidney must have gone out. He hurried in and jumped into the shower, all the while listening for Sidney to return. Fortunately she didn't show. He really didn't want another argument like the one they had this morning. He marched to the closet and quickly took out a white button-down Burberry shirt, buttoned it, and then pulled on a pair of dark trousers. He slipped on his black Louis Vuitton shoes. He examined himself in the mirror and decided he looked good. He snatched his jacket and walked out as fast as he could, hoping he wouldn't run into Sidney in the hallway.

He wasn't going to let Sidney ruin his evening. He was almost running down to the lobby. He still had half hour before dinner, so he stopped at the hotel bar next to the entrance and ordered vodka on the rocks. He swallowed it in two gulps and was on his way. He felt better. His nerves were on edge. He wasn't sure where he stood with Sidney. The doorman flagged him a car and the driver drove him to the restaurant even though he was early. He arrived at the establishment, hoping that Annette might already be there.

It was a small restaurant, but he was lucky and was seated right away at a window table. He liked the spot because he would be able to see Annette when she arrived at the bistro. He sat down and ordered another vodka on the rocks. He discreetly listened to the conversation of the older couple next to him, debating what to have for dinner. Forty-five minutes later, Annette still hadn't shown up to meet him. Maybe she had gotten delayed at work. He ordered another drink. He occupied his time by twirling the straw from his drink or munching on a plate of cheese and olives that the waiter had placed on the table.

He checked his watch one more time, sensing something was wrong. She was rarely late. He gave up and dialed her number. He popped another olive in his mouth as he chewed on his straw. He listened as the phone rang and then went to voicemail.

"Hi, Gorgeous. I hope you are on your way to the restaurant. I'm getting worried. Give me a call," Dalton said, a little concerned. This wasn't the first time she had stood him up, though ... Another twenty minutes went by. He picked up his phone and punched in her cell number, but the only thing he got was her voicemail.

Something was not right. He stood up, took his wallet out of his back pocket, and threw a ten-dollar bill and a twenty-dollar bill on the table for the drinks. He walked out of the place. He decided to go to her house to check if she was all right. Something must have happened. He could feel it in his heart. He flagged a taxi and gave him the address.

Within minutes, he was at her residence. It was a short drive to her door. He ran down the walkway and up the steps of her porch. He reached over and rang the doorbell several times, but she never answered. He cupped his hand to peek inside her home from the side window. He noticed a few lights were on inside. He took his phone out of his pocket and dialed her number, but again he was connected to the voicemail. He peered inside again and finally saw her in a bathrobe with a towel wrapped around her head. He made a fist and knocked loudly on her front door.

"Annette, it's me, Dalton. Open the door. Are you okay?" he yelled at the door, troubled. He knew something was wrong, but he could not imagine what.

"Go away. Leave me alone. I don't want to see or speak to you ever again," Annette shouted through the wood door. Dalton was taken aback by her comment. He didn't know what was going on unless ... *Sidney*. No, that was not possible.

"Annette, darling, open the door. Talk to me. I don't understand. Did I do anything wrong?" he pleaded to her. There was complete silence on the other side of the door. He knew she was standing on the other side, only a foot away. He bowed his head as he placed his hand flat on the door, waiting.

"Annette, please open the door. I'm begging you. Tell me what the matter is," he said in a soft voice. "I love you. I would never do anything to hurt you." He blurted out the words without thinking. He didn't fully register what he had said until a few moments later. It was at that instant he realized that he couldn't bear to be separated from her. He did love her.

He heard the bolt lock being unfastened, and the door opened a crack, though a chain was separating them. He took a step toward her. He could see she had been crying. Her eyes were puffy and her nose was red. He stretched out his hand to push the door a little, but the chain held fast. He pulled away. He felt a chill from the cold weather.

"Please, Annette, talk to me. Let me in," Dalton pleaded once more. He wondered what had upset her so much that she didn't want to see him. He was terrified. He didn't want it to be the end of their relationship. He had to fix whatever was wrong.

"Please ..." he tried. She shut the door for a moment. He heard her finally unhook the chain. She reopened the door and backed away. He slowly stepped inside. He closed the door behind him. The house was completely still. He saw she was sitting at the counter in the kitchen, looking at her hands. He took three paces forward and was beside her. He reached out to touch her arm, but the instant he made contact with her, she quickly pulled away from him as if he had burned her.

"Don't touch me!" she said angrily, staring straight in his eyes. Dalton pulled his hand away. He dragged the stool next to her and sat down. His heart ached with pain. What happened to make her so irate and so distant from him? He looked down at the floor and sighed. He crisscrossed his fingers tightly and placed them on his lap.

"Annette, what's the matter?" he said in a low voice. He saw a tear fall down her cheek. It was unbearable to see her so distraught. She turned her head away from him as she wiped the tears.

"You lied to me all along. I feel like a fool. You made me believe I had a chance with you. You ... deceived me," she snapped at him. Her eyes looked like daggers.

"What are you talking about? I would never intentionally lie to you. I care for you more than anyone I ever have in my life. I just told you that I love you." Dalton was confused and he didn't know what was going on until she spat out her next words.

"Do you love me as much as your fiancée Sidney?" It was as if someone had dug a knife through his heart. He didn't know what to say or do. The pain he felt was unbearable.

Chapter 14

Annette sat on her seat, still in a daze and bewildered. She waited for him to explain, but he wasn't talking or moving. She saw his mouth twist into a grimace. She knew he was hurting, but it was probably because he had gotten caught. His expressions and his mannerism told her that everything Sidney had told her was the truth. She turned her head to face him. He sat there looking at his shoes as he twiddled his fingers. He seemed so nervous and unsure of himself. His foot was jerking up and down. Not a word had escaped from his mouth since she had mentioned Sidney. She wondered, *does he know that I have the letter. Probably not!* She might as well get it over with. He would find out sooner or later. She took the folded letter resting on the countertop in her hand. Her blood was boiling. She passed him the letter.

"And could you explain this?" she demanded in a flat tone, watching his every move. He hadn't spoken to her yet, but he took the letter from her. He unfolded the paper and gasped. His jaw dropped and he looked as if a train had struck him. The blood drained from his face. He was white.

"I can explain this. Where did you get this?" Dalton said to her immediately, his eyes focused on her. She noticed he had started to extend his hand for hers again, but decided to pull back.

"Where else but from your fiancée, Sidney," Annette shot back his way like a venomous snake. She wanted him to feel her pain.

"If you'll give me a chance, I'll tell you exactly what happened. I'm really sorry you had to find out everything like this." He was trying to make her understand, but she was not in the mood to let him manipulate her. She did not trust much of what he could say at this second. He had lied to her, misled her, and betrayed her trust. That in itself was unforgiving. How had she let this happened? She glared straight ahead. She couldn't look him in the eye, petrified she might scream at him, or worse, punch him in the face for being so disloyal to her.

"Annette, please look at me, I'm going to explain the whole story." She didn't move an inch or say anything. She waited for his answers.

"I'm listening," she told him, stone-faced.

"This is the whole truth, and you can believe it or not. I knew your husband. I was his roommate in college. We had kind of made this stupid ... promise with each other, but I never thought he had been serious until I received this letter a few weeks ago. I dismissed it. I just dropped it in my briefcase. Then I came to Boston for a business closing. I didn't know you were Robert's assistant until I met you. I was stunned. But it was then I fell in love with you." He leaned toward her and reached out to touch her shoulder, but she rebuffed him and stood. She walked around the counter. Grasping the bottle of Chardonnay from the cabinet, she poured herself a large glass of white wine. She didn't even offer him a glass. She gulped a big mouthful. She wasn't sure if she believed him. Still ... She refilled her glass.

"And your fiancée, when were you going to tell me about her?" she asked as she looked down at her wine glass and rapped her finger against the glass. She would not look his way. She brought her glass up to her lips, taking another gulp of wine, trying to calm her nerves. She was desperately trying to stop her tears from falling. She shut her eyes then blinked several times, pushing them away.

"I tried to keep her away. I don't love her. She came here on her own from London. I didn't want her here. I love you, not her. I never meant to hurt you, Annette, I didn't plan any of this. Since I met you, you are all I can think of. You are the one I love. Please, Annette, don't push me away. Give me another chance," he begged her. Annette glanced up. She watched as he got up from his stool to start pacing in her kitchen from one end of the island to the other while pushing his dark hair from his face with his hand.

"Why didn't you tell me anything about her or the letter before now?" she snarled at him. He approached her one step at a time. He extended his hand again toward her to touch her arm, but she moved away, rebuffing him. She did not want him to touch her. It would kill her.

"Don't do this ... I never meant to harm you. I was afraid you would think I was crazy to agree to such an agreement, and you wouldn't have anything to do with me," he answered. He was trying to smooth the situation over, but he was not going to get off so easily.

"Is that all?" Annette barked, hoping that was all he had to say.

"No, it's not. Can you ever forgive me? I want us to be together. Like I said, I do love you," he pleaded with her. She saw a tear escape the corner of his eye, but she didn't care.

"I want you to leave ... now," she told him sternly as she walked toward the front door, gripped the doorknob, turned it, and swung the door open. A cold breeze swooped in and hit her. He just stood there with his hands in his pockets of his jacket. He closed his eyes as if he was thinking. He finally came toward the entrance.

"I won't give up on you. I will be back tomorrow. Good night," he told her, then his hand went up to stroke her cheek, but again she turned her face away from him. She saw the hurt in his eyes, but she paid him no heed. He had injured her badly. The glimmer in her eyes was gone and she would have to move a mountain to pardon him for his indiscretions and his deception.

* * *

Dalton was heartbroken, but he also was furious. He was angry with himself for leaving Mark's letter in his case for Sidney to find, and for losing the only woman he truly loved. He should have been honest with her from the beginning. What had he been thinking? The cold wind stung his face as he trudged back to his hotel, but he didn't feel anything. He tried to hold back tears, but it was fruitless. They escaped and he let them fall.

As he plodded wearily down the streets he realized he had clamped his hands into fists. Sidney tried to destroy the only relationship he really needed in his life. He understood that because she loved him. His love for Annette gave him strength, and with her by his side he could overcome whatever was thrown his way. He had faith she would come around; otherwise he might crumble to pieces. How could he have such passion and love for a woman he had just met a few weeks ago? She made him feel whole; like he could conquer the world and that he was the only one in her eyes. But now with every step he took, hatred was building in his soul toward Sidney. He needed to control this loathing or it might cloud his judgment.

He slowly came upon the hotel. Not even the chill in the air bothered him. He tried to clear his head before he confronted Sidney. At last, he stood in front of his hotel room door. He reached into his side pocket and pulled out his keycard. He inserted it and he slowly opened the door. He was ready to face Sidney. He strode inside with determination. He knew what he had to do. She was sitting in a chair watching the television. As soon as she saw him, she stood up and came running toward him with open arms.

"Darling, you came back. I've been waiting all day for you. I was so worried about you," Sidney told him as she tried to embrace him, but Dalton gripped both her hands tightly, pushed them away from him, and placed them gently at her sides. Her touch was now repulsive to him. He bypassed her and went to the closet. He gripped his suitcase, unzipped it, and threw his clothes inside, one by one.

"What are you doing?" she asked him with concern on her face. She grabbed the clothes as she tried to stop him from putting any more in the suitcase. He stopped, stood straight, and turned toward her. The glare he gave her made Sidney take a step backwards.

"Sidney, I want you to listen carefully to what I'm going to tell you. I'm leaving you. I don't wish to marry you. I no longer have feelings for you. Go home to London, because I don't want you near me right now. This situation happened and I can't change it. I want to be with Annette, not you. Now leave me alone to pack," he told her in a cold, harsh tone. He didn't even glance her way. He continued to put his belongings in his suitcase.

"You don't mean that. I'm the one you love. We have been together for years. Don't throw it all away for that bitch. I love you, Dalton. I'd do anything for you. I've even forgiven you for your infidelity." She touched his arm lightly and smiled at him, but he gave her the cold shoulder, trying not to blow up but ...

"Oh! Yes, I mean it. I'm leaving. Don't come near me right now. I never thought you could be so underhanded and conniving. I wish I had never met you, I will never forgive you for this," he said as he placed his toiletries in the bag.

"I did it so we could stay together. She's not good for you like I am. I love you," she kept saying, but it did not deter Dalton from his task at hand. He shut the suitcase, zipped it, and grabbed the handle in his right hand.

"You can't leave. I can't live without you. Dalton." She stood in his path with her arm stretched out but he stepped to his left and went around her. He walked to the living room. He bent down shoved the last few items in the front pocket of his bag and picked up his briefcase with the other hand. He shot another wicked look at Sidney and told her, "Go home. We are done."

"No, I won't let you go. Dalton, please stay!" she yelled at him. She had her hands covering her mouth as tears welled in her eyes. "I love you. Don't go. Do you hear me? Don't ruin our lives because of that bitch."

Dalton opened the door and marched out of the suite, leaving Sidney standing alone in the room with her demons. He carried his suitcase to the front entrance, hailed a taxi, and disappeared. Within fifteen minutes he was in a reception area of a new hotel, ready to check into another room. He was at the Boston Harbor Hotel located on the historical Rowes Wharf Harbor in Boston. His accommodations had the sweeping views of Boston's cityscape. He dropped his belongings at the entry of his suite. He was exhausted from all the drama and the sorrow Sidney had caused him this evening, but he didn't feel like sleeping. He decided to go roam around the lobby area since he couldn't be with Annette.

He wandered into the hotel bar. He really didn't need a drink, but he wanted to drown his misery away—at least for a brief spell. The lounge had mahogany walls and attractive lighting with small tables that surrounded the outside perimeter. The ambiance of the bar was friendly and inviting. This hotel bar room was the home to the city's most extensive selection of fine scotches. Dalton felt right at home. He drifted in and collapsed into one of the chairs at the counter. He immediately ordered a double Chivas Regal neat. The instant the bartender placed it in front of him; he gulped it down and then ordered another. He snatched his second round of scotch in his hand and walked to sit by himself at a corner table in the dark area of the bar. Not long after he had sat down, he lifted his hand toward the waitress to order another double.

He observed the people as they delighted in their conversations, but all he felt was sorrow. He heard his cellphone ring. He awkwardly snatched it out of his pocket and looked at the caller ID. "Damn you,

Sidney. Leave me alone." He clicked the button to silent mode and placed it next to his scotch.

For once in his life he felt alone even though the room was full of people laughing and having a marvelous time. He was lonely. The only person he longed to talk to or be with was Annette. He felt empty inside.

He looked at the bartender and he lifted his glass up again and mumbled, "Another one, please." The alcohol was beginning to affect his speech and his movements. He was drunk. He had lost his love and he was trying to forget or replace his torments with alcohol. In less than an hour he had indulged in several more scotches without any source of food. He determined the solution was not going to be found in the alcoholic beverages he had consumed, but maybe if he were lucky it would make him forget his problems for a short amount of time.

Tomorrow he would be able to find his way out of this mess. Another hour passed before he asked the barman for his tab. He took the bill and signed the invoice to his room. He stood up. He wobbled and his vision was foggy. He proceeded to his room, but the alcohol had caught up with him. He concentrated on walking away from his spot. He leaned his hand against the chairs because his equilibrium was being tested. He tried to regain his composure, straighten his posture, and let go of the chairs. As steadily as he could, he treaded his way back to his room.

He could only think of how he screwed up the only relationship he had ever really yearned to keep. Obsessed! He needed a clear head if he was to recapture Annette's heart. When he arrived at his suite he stripped his clothes off and threw them wherever they fell. He tried to keep his balance until he slumped on top of his bed, face down. He rolled onto his back and rested his head on the pillow. The room spun and his head pounded. He shut his eyes and placed an arm over his forehead. He couldn't think anymore. He needed to forget at least for a small period of time. He prayed for sleep and within minutes he was sound asleep.

* * *

Sidney was beyond herself with torments. She hoped Dalton would not do anything rash or harm himself. *No, he was okay.* He had her standing in an empty room, alone and devastated. She had bawled her eyes out until there were no more tears to shed. She had even screamed until she didn't have any energy left. She collapsed into a chair in the living room of the suite. She didn't want to leave the suite because he would come back to her when he realized she was the one he loved. She called Dalton several times during the evening, but he never answered or replied to her texts. She kept looking at her phone for a sign, but unfortunately ... nothing!

She didn't know his whereabouts or how he was doing. He was alone in a large city. She sat in an overstuffed chair in her room for four hours, covered with a brown blanket as she stared at the wall. Thinking! She couldn't understand or believed what Dalton had told her. He was upset and hadn't meant what he had told her. It was understanable. He was a bitter man at this time, but it would pass. She had broken up his affair. He would return to her. She was the only one who knew this man—how he thought and how he did things. As she sat motionless she could hear him utter the words that had broken her heart: "I no longer have feelings for you, and I don't want to marry you."

A shooting pain ran down her lower back and her legs from not moving around from her spot. She was in extreme pain from sitting so long in one position, yet she had tolerated it until now. She couldn't endure the discomfort anymore. She bent down and she rubbed her legs. She had had a serious car accident three years previously and she had been trapped behind the wheel. She had injured her legs at the time and ever since then she had suffered from the incident. The only thing that relieved some of her pain was to lie flat on her back, but she hadn't done that because she didn't want to miss him when he returned.

She needed to take pain medication for her agonizing discomfort. She found her drugs in her make-up bag. She unsnapped the childproof covers off the bottles that held her prescription drugs. She took two pills out: a Valium, which was a muscle relaxer, and one Oxycodone, which was a narcotic for the pain. She popped both pills in her mouth. She poured water into a glass. She swallowed them as she walked to her bed to lie flat on her back to try to ease her torture. She could feel her mind drifting away as the pills took their full effect. She felt deprived of physical and emotional feelings.

Now that her suffering was being taken care of she would be able to sleep. One thing she was sure about was that she was going to win her fiancé back. She was going to keep calling him until he answered her calls. Her eyelids became heavy and she could barely keep them open. She tried to stay awake, but her thoughts and her pain were drowned away by the medication she had taken until she woke up the next morning.

* * *

The following morning Dalton woke up with a new agenda. He turned his head to check the alarm clock time. It was seven o'clock. He now regretted the drinks. The first thing he did was pick up the phone to call room service for a bottle of Tylenol for his head, which was throbbing, and a hearty breakfast to settle his stomach from all the alcohol of last night. He was going to get Annette back at any cost. He called Annette several times at home, but she did not answer him. He showered to invigorate his senses. By then his room service order had arrived. He ate his two eggs, bacon, home fries, toasts, and tea. He felt much better. He pushed away from the table. Now he could face the world. His headache had diminished and he was ready.

He went directly down to the concierge desk in the lobby. He sat down in the seat across from the woman behind the desk. She smiled at him.

"Good morning. How may I be of assistance?" the lady asked him very professionally.

"I would like you to order flowers and have them delivered to this address," he told her as he searched in his pocket for the note with Annette's address.

"Certainly, sir. What kind of bouquet would you like me to order for you?" she asked pleasantly. She picked up a pen and paper from the drawer to write down the instructions.

"Could you get two-dozen, no, make it three-dozen red roses, please," he told her confidently. He wrote down the address on the hotel stationary and passed it to the woman. "And could you charge it to the credit card I have on file? I'm in room 544," he continued and smiled at her.

"Did you want anything written on the card, sir?" she inquired politely as she passed him another piece of paper and her pen. He looked at the paper for a second before he wrote:

>Annette, I am so sorry.
>Give me another chance.
>Please, forgive me.
>I love you, Dalton.

He gave her back the piece of paper, feeling a bit embarrassed when she read it.

"Thank you. I will make sure the flowers get there this morning," she told him. She gave him a shy smile. "Is there anything else I can help you with, sir?" she asked as she laid her hand on the phone.

Dalton shook his head. He stood up from his chair and he walked away with no destination in mind. He knew he loved this woman with all his heart and that he had been a fool to think he could get away with not telling her the truth.

He flagged a cab at the entrance of the hotel and told the driver to drop him off on Newbury Street. He didn't want to end up at another bar, so he decided to go browse the street for a few hours. He was lost, unable to concentrate on anything but Annette.

The hours flew by as he explored one store after another without buying anything. He stopped for lunch at Legal Seafood at Copley Place. He sat at a table by the floor-to-ceiling windows that overlooked Boston's historical South End. He ordered the sea scallop, but when it arrived he wasn't hungry. He picked at it with his fork, but he barely touched it. He was not in the mood for food. All he could think of was how to fix his situation with Annette. He looked outside at the beautiful sights, but he saw absolutely nothing. He had enough of his meal, so he placed his napkin on the table and asked the waiter for the check. He left the restaurant without eating or feeling any better.

It was late afternoon, so he made the decision to go see Annette and try to explain himself to her once again. He never meant to hurt her in any way and he would never cause her pain ever again. It had just happened. He walked to the front of the Marriot Hotel which was adjacent to the Copley Square stores. He took a taxi to her house in the North End. He would not leave until she forgave him for his indiscretions. He was determined.

* * *

Annette was exhausted from crying all night. She had not slept a wink since she had found out the truth about Dalton. She had dawdled from room to another. She was lost unable to find a solution to her dilemma. She had called Robert in the morning to excuse herself and explain the situation to him. He had been surprised by her admissions, but he had been very understanding. She was in no shape to concentrate on any kind of work, so Robert told her to take the rest of the week off. He would check in with her in a few days. He told her not to worry about anything concerning work. He would manage without her.

She was settled under the covers in her bed where she had been residing since the night before. She had seen Dalton's calls, but didn't want to talk to him. It hurt her too much. How could he deceive her so badly? She was so confused and she couldn't think straight. She was in love with him, but would she ever be able to fully trust him if she forgave him? That was a question she could not answer at the present time. It was haunting her.

She heard the doorbell ring. She slowly rolled out of her bed. She snatched her robe from the bench at the end of her bed and slipped it on. She tied the belt tight around her waist as she dragged her feet to the front door. She checked who it was through the peephole. She opened the door when she saw it was a deliveryman. "Annette Russell?" he asked her.

"Yes," she replied uninterested.

"These are for you," he told her, then passed her a bouquet of roses. She kicked the door shut with her foot. The vase and the flowers were so heavy it took both her hands to hold them. She walked to the kitchen as fast as she could manage and placed the vase of flowers on the island counter.

She unclipped the card from the fastener, opened the envelope and read the message. She tossed the card besides the roses. She felt tears sting her eyes. She went back to her original place, not caring about the flowers. She pulled the covers up to her chin and held onto the blankets with a tight fist. She brought her knees up to her belly and wrapped her arms around them. She didn't want to deal with this problem. She just wanted to sleep the pain she felt in her heart away.

She had been dozing off and on for a few hours when the doorbell rang once more. She hauled herself out of bed and she went to answer the door. As she passed the kitchen, she could smell the aroma of the roses. She checked who it was. It was Dalton. She rested her head and the palms of her hands against wooden door. She heard him knock on the door, and he shouted, "Annette, I know you are in there. Please let me in. I love you and I never meant to hurt you."

"Dalton, please leave me alone. I don't want to talk or see you right now," she answered him through the door, her suffering unbearable. She placed her hands over her ears, not wanting to hear what he had to say, and pressed her back against the door. She tried to muffle his voice out, but to no avail.

"Annette, please forgive me. I'm so sorry for how it turned out. Please give me a second chance. I promise I'll never ever lie to you again, God help me!" he yelled, begging for her to let him. "I truly love you," he said. She couldn't take it anymore. She turned the lock and unfastened the chain. She opened the door just enough so that she could see him. His hands were resting on the door and his black hair was being blown around by the wind. She could see he was cold, but she still was not going to let him in.

"What do you want from me?" she asked him quietly. She couldn't look him in the eye, so she bowed her head, but she kept her hand on the handle of the door.

"Please, let me in. We need to resolve this. I don't want to be without you. I can't function ... I don't want to live without you," he told her almost in a whisper. She lifted her head and glanced up at him. His eyes were swimming with tears. He deserved to feel pain. She couldn't bear to see him so tormented, even though she was angry with him.

She took two steps back to let him in. The chill of the winter wind came bearing down on her as she closed her robe tighter. He closed the door. She left him standing by himself as she wandered to the kitchen and flopped down on one of the stools near the roses he had sent her. He slipped off his coat and threw it on the railing in the living room. He leisurely dragged himself to sit beside her. He reached over and tenderly cupped her hands in his. He massaged them gently with his thumbs. It sent a shudder through her body when he came in contact with her. She immediately pulled her hands back and placed them on her knees. He placed his hand over hers, but this time she yanked them away and she crossed her arms over her chest.

"Please, look at me. Show me your baby blues that I adore so much," he said to her, but she wouldn't lift or turn her head. She totally avoided his eyes by looking away. "I swear to you, I never meant to cause you any pain. I love you so much and that was why I was so afraid to tell you the truth. I want this relationship to blossom. I'll do whatever you tell me to. I am no longer with Sidney. I broke up with her and I moved to another hotel," he appealed to her.

"You broke my heart. How can I ever trust you again? You betrayed me," she told him as a tear broke free. He gently reached over and wiped the droplet away with his thumb.

"Do you love me? Answer me this question," he begged her. She didn't want to play that card, but she couldn't stop herself. "Yes," she murmured to him, still not gazing his way.

The next thing she knew his arms were wrapped around her shoulders and he was pulling her onto his knees. She stiffened her muscles, but she couldn't resist him anymore. He held her tight on his lap and just rocked her. He lifted her chin up to meet his eyes and he kissed her lightly on the lips. "Please forgive me. I need you in my life. I'll never hurt you again. I swear," he said in a low voice. She nodded slightly as she saw the corner of his mouth turn upward. His lips converged on hers. Another kiss followed that was as passionate as the first time they had kissed. She could feel his hands caressing her thighs.

She pulled away from him and said, "You'd better mean what you are saying, otherwise—" He didn't let her finish her sentence before his mouth was on top of hers again. She heard him growl as he scooped her off his knees and he carried her toward the bedroom. She never objected.

Chapter 15

Sidney was consumed with winning back Dalton's heart. She was not going to sit around anymore and cry over spilled milk. The past was in the past and she had to think toward the future. She had a plan. The first thing she needed was transportation. She found a National Car Rental agency on Atlantic Avenue, walked over and rented a blue 2013 Toyota Corolla. It was perfect to execute her objective. It was a very popular car, so she could blend in easily with other cars on the streets.

Next, she drove around town looking for a beauty salon that sold wigs. She spotted one on Broadway Avenue and parked her car nearby. She walked into a store called Wig World in Temple Place, located downtown Boston. She examined the short human hairpieces and the mustaches that were on display. She purchased a short auburn wig and a mustache. She paid cash because she didn't want to leave a credit card trail. She marched out of the store with an evil grin on her face.

Her next stop was Target, where she bought a black cap, gloves, and a pair of men's hiking boots one size larger than her own foot, and a man's oversized black hoody jacket. She also found a mom and pop hardware store in the South end of Boston where she bought a small metal hammer and a screwdriver.

She took all her purchases and threw them in the trunk of her rental. Sidney smirked as she drove back to the hotel with her new disguise. Now she was ready. All she had to do was be patient until dawn came. Then she could carry out her plan. The next morning she rose early. She dressed up in her men's clothing. She meticulously glued her mustache under her nose, adjusted her auburn wig, and stuffed her boots with newspaper so they would fit better, then tied her boots in place. She stepped back from the mirror to admire her masterpiece. It was time. She was ready. She locked her room. She took the elevator down to the garage, hopped in her rental car, and drove to Annette's address. The sun was just coming up when she parked her blue Toyota up the block from Annette's.

She adjusted her rearview mirror so she could watch Annette's home. An hour went by when she observed Annette coming out of her house. She watched as she bolted her front door and walked to the bus stop down the street. She was probably headed to her job. Sidney waited until Annette boarded the vehicle. Sidney was excited when she disappeared into the bus. *Good, she was gone.* Now it was her chance to explore Annette's home to try to determine what would motivate Dalton to fall for this woman and what he saw in her.

She casually strolled down the street until she arrived in the alleyway that separated Annette's house from the neighbor's house. She scanned the area with her eyes to make sure there was no one watching her. She didn't see anyone, so she raced down the alley all the way to the end. She stopped to catch her breath by placing her back against the brick wall. She was breathing heavy, her nerves taking the best of her. She felt a tremor in her legs. *Control!* She poked her head around the back of the building where Annette's veranda was located. The coast was clear.

She sprinted to the porch and crouched next to it. She waited a minute, listening to her surroundings, then rose and took the steps up two at a time straight to the patio door. She reached into her pocket and took out her screwdriver and the tiny hammer. She wasn't sure if what she wanted to do would work, but she decided to try. She placed the screwdriver next to the lock and hit the top of it with the hammer. She heard a click and the glass door opened slightly on the third strike. She slid the patio door to the side so she could squeeze inside. She didn't move once she was inside. She listened for an alarm, but it never came. She took a breather.

She walked a few paces toward the hallway, which she hoped would be in the direction her bedroom. She stopped in the doorway of her bedroom and gawked at what she saw in front of her. The whole room was decorated in yellow and white, from the bedspread to the wallpaper. *How tacky!* She crossed the room and approached her dresser. She placed her hand on the handle and hesitated for just a moment, wondering what this bitch had inside. *The hell with it,* she thought. She pulled every drawer out, throwing all her personal things on the ground—from her underwear to her socks. She laughed hysterically at the chaos.

The more she touched Annette's stuff the angrier and more disgusted Sidney became. *How dare she come near her man?* This bitch was going to regret having ever laid her eyes on him. She smashed the pictures off the walls with her hammer. She stomped on them with her boots. She hooked her arm across her shelves then dragged all her perfumes and toiletries off the ledge. Sidney watched as they tumbled down and crashed on the floor. They all broke to pieces. She laughed loudly.

The next project she tackled was the kitchen. She hurled everything out of the drawers and cupboards to the ground. She opened the refrigerator door, picked up the condiments, eggs, and yogurts, and threw them all against the walls. Her rage flared up. She removed a knife from the butcher's block and decided to keep it. She held it tightly in her hand until her knuckles were white. She headed for the living room. She was breathing hard. She lifted her arm high and brought it down in the fabric of the sofa. She punctured and ripped every single piece of furniture apart. *What a beautiful sight!* She laughed again. It was a loud, villainous sound. She was done.

This would keep her busy for days. This would keep Annette away from her Dalton. Her last act was to pound the tip of the knife into Annette's wood island in the kitchen. She walked to the front door, turned, and admired her work. She unlocked the door and leisurely walked back to her car. She looked at the time. She had only been inside for thirty minutes. She didn't have a care in the world. She chuckled as she drove back to the hotel, reflected on her masterpiece. She hated this woman and she would make her pay the price for touching her man.

* * *

What a hectic day at work! Annette was exhausted, her feet hurt, and she couldn't wait to soak in a hot bath before she met up with Dalton. She had to catch up on the last two days she had missed at work. Annette walked the short distance from the bus stop to her home. She finally arrived at her front door. She took her keys from her purse to unlock the door. She gasped at what she saw. Her shaking hands went to her mouth as she dropped her bag in the entryway. She noticed the front door was ajar. Had she not locked the door this morning? She slowly pushed the door with her fingertips. It moved smoothly, but what she saw horrified her. Her eyes bulged out. Someone had invaded her domain, her home.

She was paralyzed on the spot with fear and she could barely breathe. She took a step back to hold on to the porch railing before she fell backwards onto the veranda. Her head was reeling from the sight. Her world had been violated and destroyed. She didn't want to enter; afraid the intruder might still be inside. She grabbed her cellphone with a shaking hand and immediately dialed the police.

"911. What's your emergency?" the lady asked her politely.

"My name is ... Annette Russell. I'm standing outside my house at 245 Laneway Street. Someone broke into my home and ... and," she told her as her voice broke. She couldn't speak as she started to sob.

"Miss, are you hurt?" the operator questioned her.

"No, I'm fine, but my home is ... destroyed," Annette managed to say between sobs, still leaning against the railing of the entrance.

"Miss, I need you to stay on the line. I've dispatched a police unit to your address. Do not go inside. Do you understand?" the woman told her.

"Yes, I understand," Annette answered her as she tried to get her emotions in line. Within two minutes she could hear sirens approaching toward her. An unmarked car parked by the curb in front of her house. An older gentleman in his late fifties jumped out and came towards her. He was dressed in a blue suit with a black overcoat. He ran up to her, taking the steps two at a time, and stood beside her in seconds.

"My name is Detective Turner. Are you alright?" he asked her as she noticed his badge, which hung from his neck by a chain.

"I'm fine but my home ..." Annette couldn't even talk anymore. She started to cry.

"I was up the street when the call came in. Have you gone inside the premise yet?" he asked her with his eyes on the interior of her home. He placed a hand on his revolver then unfastened it.

"No, I haven't," she whispered and shook her head.

"Could you stand back? Do not come in. I'm going to check inside. Wait for the patrolmen to arrive and tell them I'm in here, okay?" he told her as he took his 9mm gun out of his holster and moved inside the house. "Boston Police," he yelled as he slowly marched forward into her house.

She waited patiently on her porch until he came back, not budging from her spot. She was frightened. She felt a wave of nausea come over her. She was nervous. She lifted her trembling hands up to her stomach. She rubbed her hands together, trying to control them. All she could think was who would do this? *Somebody had invaded her home.* It was where she felt the most secure. Her security had been stolen from her. Her inner peace was gone. It was as if they had violated her.

"It's all clear, Miss, but I must warn you, there's a huge mess inside. You can go in now," he told her as he motioned for her to go ahead. He followed close behind her. She hesitated, but continued forward through the entrance.

"Oh! My God! No! Who would do such a thing? Why?" She was outraged at what someone had done to her place. Her eyes watered up instantly and she could not hold the tears back any longer. Both her hands came up to cover her face. She couldn't move. She bawled her eyes out and she began to hyperventilate.

"Miss, I need you to calm down. I'm sorry, but I have to ask you a few questions. Please have a seat." He went and got her a stool to sit down on from the kitchen. In spite of her efforts, she couldn't stop crying. He found an unbroken glass on the floor, picked it up, and filled it with water before offering it to her. She grasped it in her hands. She brought the drink up to her mouth and sipped it.

"Please sit," he ordered as he pointed at the stool. She sat down and surveyed what had been her palace. Her hideaway retreat was now a disastrous room. "Now, tell me who might hate you this much to do such a thing!" He said while Annette was trying to gain control of her emotions. He took out a notepad and pen from his coat pocket and examined the damages around him.

"I don't know anyone who would do such a thing," she answered him in disbelief as she shook her head.

"When did you leave the house today and who else has a key to your home?" he inquired as he continued to look around the room.

"I left this morning for work around six-thirty. No one else has a key," she answered, wiping away the tears from her cheeks with a tissue. She saw a patrolman had arrived outside and was coming up the walkway.

"All right, I'll have the crime scene investigators see if they might be able to lift fingerprints, and I'll have the patrolmen knock on the neighbors' doors. Maybe someone saw something unusual in the neighborhood this morning," he told her. She could only nod at him.

"But for now, I'll write you a police report for insurance purposes. That's all I can do for now. You need to find out as soon as you can if there is anything missing, like jewelry or electronics." He reached into his inside jacket pocket and offered her his card. She took it and thanked him. Detective Turner turned and gave instructions to the patrolmen. They went to canvas the neighborhood for information.

"I suggest that if you have another place where you could spend the night, or probably a few days, you should make plans. At least until you get this house cleaned and the CSI people are finished. I also need a number where I can get ahold of you if we find anything," he told her as he wrote down her cell phone number in his notepad.

"I'll call you later and let you know where I will be," she told him, uncertain where she was going to go just yet.

"Sure, no problem. You have my number," he replied. He exited the house and he left her alone with her mayhem and the patrolmen.

She looked at her phone in her hand and dialed Dalton's number. She didn't want anyone else near her. He was going to be her comfort, her protector, and she needed him now more than ever. He answered on the second ring, "Hi, Gorgeous. Can't wait to see you."

"Dalton, I ... I've been ... my house has been burglarized and destroyed," she managed to say to him, but her voice broke down as her weeping started all over again.

"Annette, where are you? Are you injured?" He demanded with concern in his voice.

"No, I'm okay. I'm home. Could you come over right away? Please?" she asked him in between breaths as she sobbed.

"I'll be there as soon as I can. I'm coming, Annette," he told her and she heard the click of his phone.

Dalton threw on his jacket as he ran out the door and down the hall. He couldn't think straight, but at least Annette was not hurt and that was all he cared about. Anything else money could buy. He had the doorman flag him a cab as fast as possible. Within minutes he was at Annette's home.

"Please, wait for me. I won't be long," he informed the driver he paid the cabbie quickly and dashed out of the car toward the front entrance. He noticed all the police vehicles parked in front of her house. A patrol officer stopped him in the yard by raising his hand, "Can I help you, sir?" he asked him as he held hid ground.

"I'm a friend of Annette Russell, the owner of this house. I came to help her," Dalton answered. The officer moved to the side to let him by.

He rushed up the stairs and plowed into the house. He felt as if someone had punched him in the face. He needed to catch his breath when his eyes caught sight of her house. Annette's home looked like it had been gutted out. Lunatics had devastated it. When he saw Annette's expression, his heart sank. He could tell she had been crying and that she didn't know what to do. He extended his arms out to her as she rushed into them. He wrapped her up tight in his strong arms and held her close. He wanted to erase the pain written on her face. Her sadness was torturing him.

"Everything is going to be all right. I'm here," he whispered into her ear.

"Who would do such a thing?" she asked in despair as he held her near and stroked her hair with the palm with his hands.

"I don't know, but it will be okay," he told her. He let go of her to look at her again. He kissed her moist cheeks where the tears had not dried yet. "Let's get out of here. Go put some clothes in a bag. You can come and stay with me until the police are done. We will put it back together. We'll find a company that deals with this untidiness. I'll help you," he told her in a positive voice, but Annette was not moving. She just stared at the mess that was in front of her.

"Come on, let's get out of here," he repeated. "You need a break. We can come back tomorrow," he said as he took her arm and guided her towards her bedroom. He watched as she retrieved a bag from the floor and chose some clothes. She stuffed them in the tote bag. All the while tears kept streaming down her cheeks. Dalton heart sank even deeper as he felt helpless at her ordeal. He finally couldn't bear to watch her anymore. He reached over and touched her shoulder lightly.

"All set? Let's get out of here." He seized her bag. He escorted her out of the house to the awaiting taxi and headed to his hotel.

Within an hour they were cuddled close together on the couch, trying to relax in the living room of his suite while watching television. Annette had stopped crying. Dalton had ordered room service, but she had only picked at her pasta. Annette had taken a long bath and that had put her in a slightly better mood.

There was a knock on the door. Dalton stood up to see who was at the door. To his surprise it was the police.

"Good evening. Is Annette Russell here? My name is Detective Turner." He extended his hand towards Dalton to show him his badge. Dalton quickly glanced at it and then stepped back to let him in.

"My name is Dalton Rivers. I'm Annette's boyfriend. Please come in," he told him. The detective entered as Dalton followed him close behind. Annette sat up at the edge of sofa when she saw the detective.

"Hi, Annette. The patrolman told me I could find you here. I hope you are feeling better. I came over because I had a few more questions for you," he told her as he sat down in the chair across from her. Dalton went to sit beside her and took her hand in his for support.

"No problem. Did you find out something?" she asked him right away.

"Well, first I wanted to ask you if know anyone that owns a blue Toyota Corolla," he questioned her as he took out his notepad to take notes, but Dalton noticed he never took his eyes off them.

"No, not that I can think of. Why?" she replied as she turned to look at Dalton. He shrugged his shoulders and shook his head.

"Your neighbor across the street said she saw a large man with red hair and mustache, dressed in dark clothing come out of your home early this morning. Would you know who that could be?" he asked her and glanced at Dalton.

"Out of my house? No, I really don't know who that could be. I was at work early," she answered as she pursed her lip while thinking.

"Unfortunately, she didn't see the license plate of the car. And did you notice if you had anything missing?" he continued to ask as he looked around the room.

"No, I didn't have a chance to really look. I know my electronics were still there, but they were destroyed or damaged," she said as she bowed her head away from the men so they didn't see her disappointment.

"Okay, let me know if you think of something else, okay? The team found several fingerprints. They are going to put them through the system. I will let you know the list of names to see if we can eliminate suspects. If we find anything suspicious, I'll give you a call," he informed her. He stood up, ready to leave. He tucked his notepad and pen back into his coat pocket. He came closer to Annette and shook her hand, then Dalton's. "Nice to meet you," he told him. He walked towards the exit. He thanked Annette as Dalton escorted him out.

* * *

The next morning Sidney decided she needed to find where Dalton was staying. *How was she going to find him?* She asked herself as she sat down on the chair at the work place in her suite. She tapped her fingers on the top of the desk as she thought. She noticed the telephone directory. She took it in her hands and opened it to search for Boston hotel names in the yellow pages. She started from the top of the list, following the numbers with her index finger. She grabbed the phone receiver and started to dial the numbers of the receptions of each establishment. She had been at it for about thirty minutes when she ended up calling The Boston Harbor Hotel.

"Good morning, The Boston Harbor Hotel. How may I direct your call?" the lady said.

"Good morning. Could you connect me to Dalton Rivers' room, please?" Sidney asked again, as she had done with all the other hotels in the city she had called.

The receptionist said, "One moment, I'll connect you." She sat at attention; excited at the prospect she had finally found him. She waited anxiously as she heard the first ring followed by the second ring.

"Hello ... hello ... Can I help you?" the man said on the other end of the line and then hung up. She heard the voice of the man she knew so well. She couldn't move or speak, elated. She had found him. She placed the receiver back in its original place and picked up a pen. She wrote down the address of the hotel down on her hotel stationary paper. She was going to go talk to him. She was confident she could persuade him to take her back now, since Annette was busy with the cleaning of her house.

She was at the hotel within an hour. She walked to the front desk and leaned against the counter. "Good afternoon. How may I help you?" the young lady said.

"Hello, could you give me Dalton Rivers' room number?" Sidney asked her politely.

"I'm sorry, but our policy does not allow us to give any room numbers. However, I can ring him for you if you would like," she answered courteously.

"No, thank you. I can call him," Sidney answered her and walked away, looking at the large room behind her. She went to sit down in one of the leather chairs in the lobby. The receptionist would not give her his room number since it was against their policy. It made her a little angry. She was content to sit and wait for him to pass by her. She would stop him to talk to him at that time. She made herself comfortable. She crossed her legs and she started to pretend to read the magazine that had been left on side table to pass the time away.

Sidney kept her eye on the prize, never wandering to far from the entrance. Two hours had ticked away when she finally saw her fiancé walking by in the foyer. But that bitch was hanging on to him, smiling and enjoying his company. Heat rose to her face as anger flared up. She tossed her magazine down on the floor next to her. She jumped to her feet and immediately moved toward him at great haste.

"Dalton, can I have a word with you?" she shouted to him as he neared her. He turned his head to look at her, surprised to see her. His attitude change right away when he saw her. He stopped laughing and his expression became very serious. He frowned at her.

"Sidney, what are you doing here? I told you to go home. We have nothing else to talk about. So please just leave me be," he told her calmly. He clutched the bitch's hand and started to walk towards the elevators, leaving her standing in the lobby. She couldn't accept the rejection, so she ran back to him and she yanked his arm just to stop him from leaving, but he became irritated with her. He pulled away from her grip. He narrowed his eyes at her.

"Let go of me. We have nothing to discuss. I am done with you. Now leave me alone," he repeated to her with determination in his eyes. She couldn't resist saying something as fury went through her.

"You would rather be with this bitch than me! You are throwing the years we have had together for a roll in the hay. She doesn't know you or love you like I do," she threw at him in a loud voice. She was standing inches from him. People were starting to gape and point their way, but it didn't bother her. Dalton put his arm around Annette's waist and pulled her close protectively.

"Stop it right now and leave me alone," he told her as he proceeded toward the elevator. He stopped and pressed the elevator button.

"Dalton, look at me," Sidney screamed. He didn't even look at her, completely ignoring her until the doors opened. "Listen to me," she continued. He guided Annette by the hand as they stepped inside without another word. Sidney watched him as he pressed his floor number. The panels closed shut and they disappeared behind the elevator doors.

She titled her head, but she was not defeated. No one took her fiancé. She was not going to give up without a fight as she touched her engagement ring with her fingers. She was determined to win or she would die trying to get him back. That bitch was not going to have him or defeat her. He was hers. She turned on her heels, held her head high, and walked toward the front door. She noticed people were still observing her, but she left the hotel without any shame or guilt. She had to get rid of her and she would soon.

Chapter 16

Annette had never been called a bitch in her life. What was she doing with a man who had a psychotic fiancée that couldn't let him go? She knew Dalton meant what he had told her, that he was finished with this woman, but for some unknown reason she didn't trust her. Should she be afraid of what Sidney might do? She was overreacting ... but Annette had seen the hatred that Sidney had projected toward her with her eyes. Her hands had turned into clenched fists when she had stared at her.

Annette was silent on the way up in the elevator, trying to get the heebie-jeebies out of her stomach. She hadn't felt good since the first confrontation with Sidney. She felt queasy. She just wanted to get away and relax. As soon as the door to their room opened, she sat down because her legs were like jelly. She had never experienced such hostility and she was scared of this woman. Dalton sat beside her and cocooned his arms around her. She rested her head on his shoulder, trying to regain her composure.

"I'm so sorry. I never thought in a million years she could do such a thing. I just want you to know that I don't love her anymore. I want us to be together," he told her, trying to smooth things over and her put her mind to rest. But she had no words for him.

"Don't worry, she is just mouthing off. She would never hurt you. It's not in her and I would never let anything happen to you. I'm so sorry," he said, once again trying to reassure her.

"I know, it just caught me off guard," she finally said to him, not wanting to worry him.

"I have to call Robert and tell him what happened at my house. I am going to need some more time off to deal with the destruction of my house," she told him, as she pulled away from him, walked to the desk, sat down, and picked up the phone to inform her boss of her misfortune.

"Hi Robert, its Annette," she said to him. She hated asking him for more time off, but she had no choice. She had to get her home in order. She decided to take a few more vacation days. He was a very understanding boss and a good friend. She explained her situation to him. He was concerned for her and allowed her to take as much time as she needed. By the time she had hung up the phone, she felt better. At least she didn't have to worry about her job. She returned to sit beside Dalton, who had heard her conversation with Robert. He placed his hand on her leg and massaged it.

"I made a decision while you were talking to Robert. I'm going to take a leave of absence from the law firm to help you out," he told her. "If there is work to be done, they can fax me the documents, email me, or call me," he continued. She was surprised, but extremely happy he was willing to do that for her. She appreciated it. She leaned forward, laid her hand on his chest, and kissed him on the lips.

"You don't have to take time off for me. I'll be fine. I don't want you to jeopardize your position just to stay with me," she told him softly.

"Don't worry about me, my love. I don't do anything I really don't want to do, and right now I want to be with you. I can afford to take the time off. I like to work, but it's not my only source of income. I'd rather be here with you," he replied, he pulled her into a hug. He lifted her chin up with the tips of his fingers. When his soft lips touched hers again, she felt a shiver go down her back and all the way down to her toes.

This man knew how to get her sexually aroused. She pressed her breasts against his upper body as their tongues began to sway together. She wanted to feel more of him as her hands caressed the back of his neck and she ran her fingers through his hair. He pulled away and grinned at her. "My, my. Aren't you a hot-blooded woman in a passionate mood? You must feel better," he whispered in her ear as he licked her earlobe. That was all she needed to hear as she pushed him down on his back on the couch. She hopped on top of him. She straddled him as she nibbled on his neck and unbuttoned his shirt.

* * *

The next morning Sidney arrived at Dalton's hotel to have breakfast in the restaurant. She had woken up at the break of dawn and she was dressed in her disguise. She had her hat down low and was wearing her auburn wig and mustache. She asked to be seated at a certain table against the wall where she had an almost perfect view of the lobby. She bought a Boston Globe newspaper at the convenience store along the way. She could hide behind it and not be noticed as she ate breakfast. She dove her fork into her eggs, took a bite, and slowly drank her tea. She was hungry. She had not been able to eat anything the night before because she had been so upset about the encounter with that bitch. But when she had gotten up this morning she'd had a new scheme on how to get Dalton back. From where she was sitting she observed the tourists going in and out the front door. She was hoping to get Annette alone. She had plans for her.

"Will there be anything else?" the waitress asked her as she placed her check beside her on the corner of the table.

THE PLEDGE

"No thank you. That will be all," Sidney replied to her. She folded her paper, then she dug her fork into her eggs again as she kept an eye on the front door.

She monitored the lobby for Annette and Dalton.

An hour went by without any sighting of them. Only her eyes were visible from the top of her newspaper. She spied in silence, pretending to finish reading her paper. But suddenly there she was. Sidney spotted her alone and here was her chance. Sidney paid her check and she was ready to move. She stood up from her table and moved swiftly out of the restaurant. She started follow her from afar. She discreetly hid in the shadows behind the pillars in the lobby. Annette was by herself. Where was Dalton? Annette was dressed in gray sweat pants and a pink hoody. Sidney hurried out of the entrance of the hotel to catch up with her with long strides. She trailed her, just as she planned earlier.

* * *

Annette woke up early as she did every morning for work, but today she had a free day. She opened her eyes and listened to Dalton's soft snoring beside her. She'd had a good night's sleep nuzzled next to Dalton. He had been so kind and concerned for her well-being. She wanted to do something special for him this morning. She gently turned and rolled out of bed without disturbing him. She stood by the bed and watched as Dalton slept soundly. He looked so appetizing in the dim light of daybreak, with his ruffled black hair and the shadow of whiskers on his face.

Quiet as a mouse, she dressed in sweats and brushed her hair quickly. She picked up her hotel key, as well as fifty dollars in cash, which she stuffed in her pocket. She carefully paid attention to each step she took until she closed the room door behind her. She headed down the hall toward the exit of the hotel.

She knew of a small family-owned Italian bakery called Modern Pastries. It was not too far from the hotel on Hanover Street in the North End. They made the most delicious cannoli. The baker made them using only the finest ingredients. Her mouth watered at the thought of the taste and the aroma of the baked goods when she entered the store. It was one of her favorite places for sweets. She frequented it often with her husband when he had been alive. She remembered how they would walk hand in hand to the store on Sunday afternoons and just sit at one of the tables in the bakery and indulge in numerous desserts while having a cup of coffee.

Annette wandered down Atlantic Avenue with her hands tucked in her front sweatshirt pocket until she arrived at the end of the street and turned right. She enjoyed the cool fresh air of the morning on her face as she strolled down the streets while humming her favorite song. She was excited at the prospect of seeing Dalton devour the pastries. Her mind drifted to Dalton as she walked. She thought about how good Dalton was to her. She loved how understanding and compassionate he had been with her, especially after the break in at her home. She was ecstatic he had decided to take a leave of absence from his work to be with her. It had meant a lot to her. She couldn't believe she was getting a second chance at love. It showed her he cared for her wellbeing and that he wanted to be near her. She still wondered who could have caused such damage to her home and why. It had probably been a random burglary that had gone terribly wrong.

She couldn't even breathe as she thought of how someone had gone through her most personal items and had just discarded them without a second thought. She abruptly stopped and placed her hand against the building next to her. She could feel a panic attack coming on from all the recent events. She bent down, placed her hands on her knees, and inhaled the fresh, crisp air. She straightened up, exhaled, and marched ahead, one step after another. She felt like she had been violated and she didn't feel safe in her own home anymore. Would she ever feel secure and carefree in her home again? She wasn't sure. She had to believe that yes, one day she would. That was all she could do, otherwise she might lose her mind.

Tears burned her eyes by just revisiting the disaster she had on her hands. She would not let the tears spill out, so she blinked them away. She would be fine. She was a strong woman and she would persevere. She had a man that loved her by her side for support. That made all the difference in the world. She didn't have to do it by herself. She was thankful that he didn't have to return to London right away.

She stopped at the red light at the corner of Richmond Street. She waited as the cars passed by her until it was clear. She crossed the street swiftly and continued her journey down the avenue. She admired the old brick buildings along the way that featured many restaurants and boutiques that had been there since she was a little girl. Many people hurried down the sidewalks, probably going to work, not even taking a second look at her. She was approaching the bakery. She made her final turn onto Hanover Street. Only a few more blocks and she would arrive at her destination. She accelerated her pace. She could see the sign up above the storefront. She licked her lips and her mouth watered as she thought about devouring those cannolis.

Finally Annette stood in the front of the bakery storefront, peeking through the window at the marvelous pastries that awaited her. She pushed the door and stepped inside. She loved the mahogany wood cases displaying the variety of sweets, especially the assortments of small cakes. She stooped down to get a better look at the desserts. She smelled the scent of cakes being cooked in the back room. It made her think of when her grandmother baked cookies for her. She was trying to make up her mind when she heard her name.

"Miss Russell, how nice to see you again. How are you? It's been a while. How may I be of service this fine morning?" An older Italian woman in her sixties with gray hair smiled at her. She had a white chef's apron wrapped around her waist. She waited for Annette to make her choice as she leaned her elbows on the counter in front of Annette.

"Good morning, Mrs. Lucy. I'm trying to decide which cannoli to order," Annette answered cheerfully as she kept admiring the pastries in the showcase.

"You should have one of each. This way you can taste every one of them or you can eat them later on," she answered as she prepared a box for her.

"You are absolutely right, as always. I'll take one of each," she told her, happy to have made her selection.

"Very good. Here, have an Italian cookie while you wait and I'll go prepare your cannolis," the older Italian lady told her, then passed her an Italian cookie in a wrapper over the counter. She nodded at Annette, who gladly took it.

"Thank you, Mrs. Lucy."

"It won't be long. Would you like a cup of coffee with that while you wait?" she asked her, but Annette shook her head to decline. She took her cookie in her hand and went to sit down at one of the tiny wood tables by the window. She munched on her Italian cookie. She wanted to have her coffee with Dalton when she got back to the hotel. Fifteen minutes later she heard the familiar, loving voice of Mrs. Lucy coming from behind the counter.

"We are all set. Here we go," she said as she gave her a white square box that was roped up with a string. Annette took it and brought it to the cash register to pay. She thanked her one more time and departed from the bakery, on her way back to their room to surprise Dalton.

* * *

Sidney stalked the bitch down the streets to Hanover Street. She watched as Annette entered an Italian bakery. Sidney slid into one of the alcoves of a flower shop down the block that hadn't opened for business yet. She waited patiently as she kept an eye out for Annette. She scuffed the heels of her boots on the pavement as she admired the arrangements of flowers in the window. The more she shadowed Annette, the more she realized how much she despised the woman. She detested this woman! She was probably buying pastries for her man, and that infuriated her even more. She tapped her boots on the concrete floor as she rubbed her hands together to keep them warm.

She had to do something; otherwise she was going to lose Dalton forever. But what? She discreetly watched people go by in front of her. They didn't even glance her way. This was one of the busiest streets in the city. Most people were going to work or were in a hurry to get to their destinations. They didn't care or look twice at someone standing in an entrance of a store. She felt like a ghost just lingering around to scare someone. She giggled out loud. It was a funny thought. She felt invisible. It gave her a sense of power that made her feel as though she were invincible.

She saw that bitch come out of the bakery. She was holding a white pastry box. Sidney turned her face toward the window when Annette passed by the entryway of the flower shop. She didn't want to attract any attention. As soon as she was clear, Sidney stepped down from the platform and started to follow her down the street. She could see her box bobbing up and down as she walked. She was going to feed sweets to her Dalton for breakfast and he would probably lick her fingers. She would probably kiss his mouth while he was devoured the baked goods. "Over my dead body," she murmured to herself as jealousy invaded her.

The more she reflected about it, the more her rage mounted inside her. She should not be with her man. She was the chosen one. She quickened her pace to be near her. She was now three feet from her back. She kept an eye on the white box. Sidney clenched her fists and narrowed her stare at the back of Annette's head. Her heartbeat accelerated while she pursued her. She imagined she could almost detect the scent of the lovemaking on her from the previous night. She clamped her teeth together, trying to keep herself from lunging at her. Not yet, she told herself. *Not yet!*

They were moving toward a major intersection. Sidney halted right in behind her, inches from her. No one was near them except a couple next to Annette. They had to let the traffic go by and wait for the light to turn so they could cross the street. *Annette had her man.* How dare she take her fiancé? Dalton was the one Sidney loved and would die for. Sidney looked down the avenue to her right and noticed a taxi driver racing down the street to make the yellow light before it turned red.

Annette stood at the edge of the sidewalk. No other person was in the front of her. Without thinking any further, rage consumed her. Sidney raised her arms and with a strength she hadn't thought she had, she pushed Annette in the back into the oncoming traffic. She heard Annette scream from surprise or fright. Sidney watched as she went stumbling into the road just as the taxi driver was upon her. Her pastry box went flying in the air. Sidney heard the screeching of tires and she could smell the burnt rubber of the taxi's wheels.

The cab hit her with the front quarter of the car. Annette was thrown upon the hood of the car. Her head smashed into the windshield, and she tumbled to the other side of the car. She saw Annette roll around on the ground a few times as she stopped in the middle of the road on her belly.

"Oh! My God, she tripped into the traffic. Call 911. The cab just hit this lady," Sidney yelled as she placed her hands to cover her mouth, while walking in the opposite direction of the accident and then around the corner. "Someone call 911. I'll get help," she shouted once more. She turned to check on the accident from afar as two people ran toward Annette. They gathered around Annette, attempting to help her. She saw the cabdriver get out of his car to check on her. He ran back to his car and was on his radio, trying to get help.

THE PLEDGE

Sidney just kept on walking away from the scene. A few blocks away she heard sirens blaring, but she just casually wandered away and back to her hotel with a sinful expression upon her face. She kept laughing. *Annette could not have survived the accident.* Now she had an opportunity to get her Dalton back and she was happy.

Chapter 17

Dalton rolled over in the king size bed, his eyes still closed. He spread his arm over to the other side of the bed, but only felt the cold bed sheets and a pillow. Annette was no longer beside him. He opened his eyes and scanned the bedroom, then the living area. He was disappointed. She had sneaked out of the bed without him being aware of it. She let him sleep in, though. *How thoughtful!* He rose up on his elbows to get a better look at his alarm clock. It was ten after nine. He flopped back onto his pillow. He shut his eyes, but he could no longer fall asleep.

He got out of bed and walked, fully naked, to the other rooms in search of his sweatpants that were still sitting on the floor. He picked them up off the ground and put them on. He laid on the couch, enjoying the fact that he didn't have to go to work. He had inherited an extensive trust fund worth millions of euros when his father died a couple of years back. He did like to work. It kept his mind occupied. His inheritance was a secret that not too many people knew. Not even Sidney was aware of it. He picked up his phone and texted Annette to tell her he was up and missed her. She never answered back to him.

He made himself comfortable by fluffing the pillow underneath his head just right and crossing his feet. He clicked on the television to occupy his time. He found the sports' channel ESPN. He was at home watching a soccer game. During one of the commercials he remembered Annette had not returned or called. He checked his watch. She had been gone almost an hour. He decided to call her cell phone, but it was fruitless. He heard her phone ring in the other room. *Why hadn't she taken it with her?* That indicated that she couldn't have gone far. She should return soon. Another hour went by without any contact from her. Now he was troubled. He walked to the window and stared outside. He retraced his steps as he sat at the edge of the sofa for the last minutes of the game. *Where could she have gone this early in the morning?* It was starting to weigh heavy on his mind.

He jumped into the shower, trying not to fret over where Annette could be, all the while trying to figure out where she could have gone. It wasn't like her to not let him know where she was going, but he really had not known her habits that long. Maybe she had gone downstairs to have breakfast. Or maybe she had gone for a walk, not wanting to wake him ... but she should have been back by now. He would go check downstairs after he was dressed if she had not returned. He dried his body, dressed with a pair of Burberry jeans with a Hugo Boss black shirt. He slipped on a pair of black loafers. Annette hadn't returned. He took his key from the desk and headed to the hotel restaurant.

Within minutes he was standing in front of the desk of the bistro, waiting. A young woman came toward him and smiled. "Good morning, sir. How many?" she said joyfully to him as she looked down at her sheet of reservations.

"Good morning. Could you tell me if a petite blonde woman came in for breakfast? Or better yet, could I take a peek around to see if she is here?" he asked her as he took a step toward the entrance of the dining area.

"Sure, no problem. Go ahead," she answered with a smile. She turned her attention to the people next in line. He swept the dining area looking for Annette. The room wasn't too packed, so he surveyed the area quickly. He backtracked back to the entrance of the bistro without any clue if she had been there. He searched around the lobby and reception area. Still he did not find her. He would have to wait. Maybe she'd had errands to run and had gone to finish them. But it seemed like she would have left him a note or said something the previous evening. He was baffled. He walked back to the room at a slow pace. He raked his hand through his black hair and sighed. He was perturbed. He was also getting concerned, but what else could he do but wait? *Where could she be?*

* * *

It was now late afternoon and Sidney was back in her room. She had walked the streets after the accident as if nothing had happened. She succeeded in getting Annette out of her life. She never looked back. She had a clear conscience in spite of what she just had done. She didn't even feel any remorse. She took her auburn wig out of her jacket pocket, then took off the men's clothes and folded them neatly. The boots were the last item that she shoved into a black leather bag before she pushed it under the bed.

She walked into her bathroom, started running a hot bath with a few drops of lilac perfumed bath oils so she could smell good when she met up with Dalton. She didn't have a date yet, but she would when she called him. She laid out Dalton favorite blue dress on her bed. She pulled her heels out of the closet, and last but not least, she matched a necklace and earrings. She wanted to look flawless when they finally reconciled. She would make him forget Annette. There wasn't anyone in her way now. He would come back to her. She took a step back to admire her outfit on the bed. She bent down to smooth her dress out with her hand. It was perfect.

She walked into the bathroom and tested the water in the tub with her hand. She turned the faucets off. She hopped into the tub to soak

THE PLEDGE

all her worries away. She felt beautiful as she examined her body in the bathtub. She could face anything now. Forty-five minutes later she was ready. Everything was as it should be. She looked and felt magnificent. How could he refuse her now? She locked the door behind her. She set out to find Dalton at his hotel. She was self-assured and confident he would take her back.

She arrived at The Boston Harbor Hotel within fifteen minutes. She took a seat in the bar area. She ordered a Cosmopolitan drink for herself and a whiskey on the rocks for Dalton. She didn't usually drink, but this was a special occasion. She was ready. She crossed her legs, adjusted the hem of her dress by pulling the edge of the dress up above her knees.

She took her phone out of her bag and texted Dalton a message that read: **I'm in the bar area downstairs in your hotel. Why don't you come join me for a drink?**

She put her phone down on the countertop of the bar and waited for his answer. She sipped her drink, anticipating the meeting. Her phone pinged. She smiled, but his answer was: **I do not want to meet you. I don't have time right now. What do you want?**

She was surprised at his response. Why would he not want to meet with her now that Annette was gone? He had to come down. Her fingers moved quickly she texted: **It's urgent. I need to talk to you. Please come meet me.**

He answered: **I'll be right down.**

Great, she knew he would come. She sat up straight and took out her portable mirror from her bag and checked her lipstick. She grinned. *Perfect!*

Five minutes later she heard his sensual voice. "What is so urgent, Sidney?" he asked her, standing by the stool beside her, he seemed preoccupied as he scanned the area.

She pushed the stool out and said, "Have a seat and I'll tell you. I ordered you a drink." She watched as he pulled the seat back and reluctantly sat beside her. He didn't even touch his whiskey. She placed her hand on his knee and started to stroke his leg, but he covered her hand with his to stop her. He gripped her hand and placed it on her knee. She ignored the gesture.

"I'm here for you. We are going to be together. I need you in my life," she told him as she leaned toward him. But he discreetly withdrew from her.

"Sidney, listen to me. I don't want to hurt you anymore, but you have to pay attention to what I'm going to tell you. There will never be a 'we' again," he told her as he glanced away from her. He sighed irritated.

"No, no. We can be together now, I forgave you," she replied as she shook her head at him. She reached to touch his arm, but he jerked away and then stood up as if she had burned him. He just looked at her. He bent down and kissed her on the cheek.

"Sidney, we are no longer a couple. You need to return to London. Your life is there, not here with me. Goodbye," he informed her in a whisper as he started to turn away.

"I'm not leaving without you. I'll die without you. I love you too much and I know you love me, too," she shot back, but he was already walking away from her. He didn't even turn around at the sound of her voice. He kept a steady pace. She watched him as he turned the corner and disappeared down the hall. What had gone wrong? She realized other guests sitting at the bar were eyeing her. "What are you looking at? Mind your own business," she shouted in their direction. She guzzled her drink down, stood up, and left the bar.

Sidney was confused about how their meeting had gone so wrong. She frowned. Maybe he didn't know that Annette was dead. Should she go back to London? She no longer felt wanted or loved, but she would make him change his mind. She needed to clear her head, and find a solution to get her love back.

* * *

THE PLEDGE

Detective Turner was dispatched to a pedestrian car accident that occurred early in the morning because the crash seemed suspicious. They had not been able to identify the victim who had been hit by the cab driver. He interviewed a witness who said that he wasn't sure she had tripped. He thought that someone might have pushed her into the oncoming traffic. They mentioned seeing a red haired man with a mustache who was about 5 feet 10 inches in height. He was wearing a black hoody jacket with jeans. He was yelling for someone to call 911 while he was rushing away from the scene. Now, why would he walk away?

The woman who had been hit was in bad shape, but hopefully would survive. She was now in surgery. He hoped to identify her when she woke up. She had a bad concussion and was unconscious upon her arrival at the hospital.

Turner stood at the nurse's station in the ER at Brigham and Women's Hospital. He was waiting to get the person's belongings because she had no ID on her person. The nurse greeted him. "Good evening, Detective Turner. I don't have much for you, but this might help you." She gave him a plastic bag that contained a hotel card and some money.

"Thanks, Denise. Is that it? Nothing else?" he asked her as he inspected the clear bag.

"Her clothes were cut off when she arrived. The card and money were in her pockets, but the paramedics mentioned she had been carrying a box of pastries from Modern Pastries if that helps," Denise told him. She smiled and then returned to her work.

"Thanks." Turner examined the key card. It was from the Boston Harbor Hotel. He needed to go check if the hotel could identify the holder of the card. If that didn't work out, he would go to the bakery to see if they might remember her. But right now he only had a description of a woman who was in her early thirties and had blonde, blue eyes, and a petite frame.

He had no photos because they had wheeled her straight to surgery. He drove his squad car to the hotel and parked it in the underground garage. He pushed the elevator button to the receptionist area of the hotel. He walked directly to the front desk. The young lady smiled at him. "Good evening. How may I help you?" she asked him.

"My name is Detective Turner from the Boston Police Department." He took out his shield from his jacket pocket and showed it to her.

"I would like to speak to your supervisor, please," he informed her. He put his shield away in his coat pocket.

"One moment. I'll get him for you," she told him, then dialed a number on her phone.

"There's a police detective at the front desk. He would like to speak to you, sir," she told her supervisor. She listened to his response and then hung up the phone.

"Mr. Simon will be right out," she told Turner. He took the card out of the baggie. He leaned his elbow on the front desk while waiting for the manager. He noticed an older gentleman in his late forties dressed in a blue suit approaching him behind the desk.

"My name is Larry Simon. How may I assist you?" he asked Turner as he came around the desk and stood beside him.

"I'm Detective Turner. I'm investigating a recent car accident involving a pedestrian. She didn't have any identification on her, but she did have one of your room keys. I was wondering if you could help me identify her." Turner showed him the card. Mr. Simon took it in his hand and examined it.

"I can tell you who it is registered to and their room number if that would help," he told Turner as he went to the other side of the counter.

"That would be most helpful," Turner answered him as his eyes were on the supervisor.

"If you'll follow me over here, I'll get the information for you," he motioned him to the station next to the woman. Turner watched as he placed the card in a machine. It scanned the card and information appeared on his computer screen.

"It is registered to a Mr. Dalton Rivers. He is in room 524 on the fifth floor." He picked up a pen and wrote the details on a piece of paper for the detective. He passed the card and note to Turner. The name didn't immediately dawn on him.

"Is there anything else I can do for you, sir?" the supervisor asked him. "The elevators are down the hall to your right," he added as he pointed the way.

"No thank you. That will be all," Turner told him as he placed the card back in the baggie and proceeded towards the elevators. When the elevator doors opened on the fifth floor, he searched right then left to find the hallway where 524 was located. He marched down the alleyway, examining each number on the doors until he was standing in front of the correct door. He knocked hard on it. He heard movement from the inside.

"Who is it?" someone said through the door.

"I'm Detective Turner from the Boston Police Department. Could you open the door, sir?" Turner replied to him. The door flew opened instantly and Dalton stood in the doorway.

"Turner, what are you doing here?" Dalton asked him, still holding the handle of the door with a concern look on his face.

"Can I come in? It might be easier to explain it in there than in the hallway." Turner recognized him from the other night. He watched Dalton take a couple of steps back to let him enter. He closed the door behind him.

"I'm investigating a car accident that happened earlier this morning. The person who was hit had your room key in her pocket. Who else would have access to this room?" Turner questioned him. He noticed the man turned white as a sheet and didn't look steady on his feet. He had a blank expression on his face.

"Sir, are you feeling alright? Do you need to sit down?" Turner asked, as he touched his arm. The man felt moist and clammy. Dalton opened his mouth to speak. His eyes perturbing out, but nothing was said. Turner thought the man was going to pass out or was in shock.

"Is she ... ?" He couldn't even finish his sentence.

"No, no. She was hurt, but she didn't die. Now come here and sit down," Turner told him as he escorted him by the arm to the nearest chair. He seemed to relax and catch his breath once he sat down. Color gradually came back to his face.

"I gather the woman is Annette?" Turner asked him as he took out his notepad to write the information. He looked up at Dalton and raised his eyebrows while waiting patiently.

"It is Annette. She's staying here with me. Since her house was broken into and ransacked, she's been staying with me," Dalton said, having regained his senses and color in his cheeks.

"I know who she is. I investigated that incident—" But before Turner could finish, Dalton cut him off. He was now standing in front of him and was very alert.

"What hospital is she in? How badly hurt is she? I need to go find her." He was throwing questions so quickly that Turner didn't have time to answer them. He grabbed his jacket and put it on, ready to leave.

"Hold on. First, she's at Brigham and Women's Hospital. And I don't know the extent of her injuries yet. She was brought up for surgery. That's all I know. When was the last time you saw her?" he continued to interrogate him, but the man seemed too preoccupied to answer his questions. *This woman was not lucky. Someone was out to get her,* Turner thought.

"Oh! Dear Lord. I have to go to her," Dalton said to himself.

Turner was not going to get answers this way, so he said, "What if I drove you to the hospital? You can answer my questions along the way."

"Fine. Yes, let's go now." Dalton left the suite and started to walk towards the elevators as Turner followed him close behind.

"Where's your car?" Dalton demanded as he repeatedly pressed the elevator button.

"It's parked in the lower garage. When did you say you last saw her?" Turner asked him again as the elevator doors opened and they stepped inside. Dalton quickly pressed the garage button.

"She was gone before I woke up this morning. I tried calling her but she hadn't taken her phone with her. I went downstairs to look for her, but never found her. I thought she might have gone to do errands around town. I knew something had happened. It's not like her to disappear without telling me where she had gone. I hope she's okay," he said, a bit distressed. He was sweating, but it wasn't hot. Turner observed him. He kept shifting his weight from one leg to another nervously.

"She was carrying a box from an Italian bakery down the street when she got hit. Oh! And do you know a red-haired man who would want to hurt her? " The detective asked him.

"No. Why?" Dalton asked as he watched the number on the panel decrease as they headed toward the garage.

"We received a report from one of her neighbors that when her house burglarized, a red-haired man was seen leaving her house. The same was reported at the accident," he informed Dalton. Dalton whipped his head to look at him.

"I don't know anything about a red-haired man or who would want to hurt her. Are you sure you don't know how she's doing?" Dalton inquired once more as he pushed his hair from his forehead.

"I'm sorry, but I don't. You are British, right?" The detective noticed, then patted his chin with his finger as he glanced Dalton's way.

"Yes. What does that have to do with anything?" Dalton wanted to know. The door opened and Dalton ran out into the garage. He stopped abruptly looking from left to right.

"Just wondering. One of the witnesses mentioned that the person yelling to call 911 had some kind of accent," Turner said. It eliminated

Dalton from being a suspect. The red-haired man had an accent, but Dalton was a much bigger man. Turner figured he was at least six foot three and had a larger frame than the culprit.

"Where's your car?" Dalton screamed at the officer as he waited impatiently for a response. Dalton kept looking everywhere.

"Over here. Have a seat. I'll drive you." Turner pointed at the dark sedan to his left as Dalton quickly opened the door and sat in the passenger seat without another word. Turner started the car and took the ramp toward the exit. Turner figured he could continue questioning him after he found out how Annette was doing. Maybe Dalton would be a little more receptive to his inquiries. Not much more was said along the way.

Chapter 18

Dalton could barely breathe. He was insane with worry. Here he was sitting in a police car with a detective who had just told him a taxi had hit Annette and that she was in surgery with unknown injuries. *What the hell had happened? And who was this red-haired man who was after her?* He looked out the window of the vehicle watching the people pass by on the sidewalk. He turned toward Turner and asked him, "Can't you drive faster?"

"Sure, I can. Watch this!" Turner answered. He reached over and pushed a button. Immediately the car's sirens began to blare and its blue lights flashed. The noise of the sirens told the people in the cars ahead of them to move out of the way. The drivers parted, allowing Dalton and Turner to travel much more quickly. *This was a splendid idea,* Dalton thought.

They arrived at the ER Trauma entrance in record time. Dalton opened his door before the car had even made a complete stop. He ran into the building, searching for the nurse's station or an information desk, anyone who would give him facts about Annette's condition. He stopped in front of the main desk and asked, "Could you tell me how Annette Russell is doing? She was brought here this morning. Do you have an update on her condition?" he asked urgently. The nurse raised her head from her charts and looked up at him, "Are you family, sir?" she asked.

"I'm her ... Yes, I am," he answered with confidence. He noticed she was glancing over his shoulder at Detective Turner, who was nodding his head her way. Dalton was grateful Turner was helping him.

"She's in surgery. You can have a seat in the waiting room to the left and I will have the doctor talk to you as soon as he is finished. That's all I can tell you," the nurse answered before she returned to her paperwork.

"Excuse me, but could you tell me what her condition is? Why is she in surgery? Please?" Dalton pleaded. His heart skipped a beat as he stood in front of her. He hoped it wasn't too grave. The nurse took a look at her chart as her eyes went directly to Turner afterwards. Dalton glared at him. The detective nodded at her.

"She was brought in with a severe broken leg which is presently being repaired. She probably will be in the operating room for at least another hour. She also has a bad concussion, as well as minor cuts and bruises. It's nothing that won't heal in time. She should be okay," she answered him. She turned around to go attend one of the doctors who was waiting for her.

"Thank you," he said, but she didn't hear him. She was already gone.

He walked to the waiting room, his head bent low. He slumped into a chair, his elbows on his knees and his hands on his face. He dragged his fingers over his face and through his hair.

"You love her, don't you?" he heard the detective's voice say as he sat beside him in the empty chair.

"Yes, I do," he replied to him, but kept his head bowed low. A million things had gone through his mind when he had first heard she had been hurt. He couldn't have endured losing her again. Even the brief separation from her had taken a toll on him. He had never been so terrified in his life. He needed to have her in his arms again.

"How did you two meet?" the detective asked him. Dalton smirked at him as he raised his head to look his way and laughed.

"You wouldn't believe me if I told you. Anyway it's a long story," he replied to him as he grabbed the remote control for the television that was resting next to him. After a few minutes he couldn't concentrate on anything but Annette, so he threw it back on the seat.

"Try me. We certainly have time to waste here, so you might as well entertain me," Turner told him as he looked his way, waiting for Dalton to open up. Dalton began telling Turner about the letter, and how he had met Annette at the law office a few weeks ago and they had hit it off right away. He left out the part about Sidney. Turner was very attentive to his every word.

Another hour crawled by. He still had not heard from nor seen a doctor. Dalton had gotten up several times to stretch his legs in the hall. He seemed to float from one end of the room to the other, his hands in his pockets. He kept poking his head out in the corridor. Minutes later he would sit back down. Dalton rubbed his temples with his fingers as a headache had developed from the stress. He could barely open his eyes his head hurt so much. His knee shook up and down when he was sitting and he couldn't stay still. His patience was wearing thin.

"Where is the bloody surgeon? I have to get more information on Annette's condition because I'm going crazy just sitting here doing nothing," he told Turner. He stood up again, but Turner stopped him by holding onto his arm.

"The nurses won't give you any information. You are not family. Let me try. I know them," he told Dalton as he turned toward the exit of the waiting room.

"Thanks," Dalton sat back down to wait. He watched as Turner left the room.

Finally, ten minutes later, Turner returned. A man dressed in scrubs accompanied him. He came forward, so Dalton stood and shook his hand, "Mr. Rivers, my name is Doctor White. I'm the trauma surgeon who has been taking care of Annette Russell. She is out of surgery and she is in the recovery wing," he told him.

"What's the matter with her? Why was she in surgery? Can I see her?" he shot at him. Doctor White raised his hand up to kindly silence him and motioned him toward the chair. Dalton went and sat down. The doctor took a seat beside him as Dalton stared at him.

"Now, Mr. Rivers, she was brought in to the trauma ward this morning and her injuries were assessed. She has a really bad concussion. She has two fractured ribs that caused her right lung to partially collapse. We immediately installed a chest tube to remove the air in her lung and we put her on oxygen. The tube will be removed in a few days if everything goes well. Now, she also has a bone fracture of the tibia bone. It's the large lower bone of her right leg. It was protruding through her leg when she was wheeled into the unit. We had to take her into surgery to fix her leg. The bone was fused with two plates and screws to keep it immobilized," Doctor White explained to him quietly.

"Oh! My dear Lord! I want to see her. Will she be okay?" Dalton asked him as he rubbed his hands on the top of his jeans. His eyes were swimming with tears.

"I suppose you can see her. Her lung and her leg should heal with time if there are no complications. Follow me and I will take you to her. But Turner, I don't want you to ask her any questions today. Can you wait until tomorrow when she feels better?" the surgeon said as he got up and started to walk down the hallway with Dalton on his heels.

"Sure, no problem. She's probably all doped up anyway. She wouldn't be any help. I'll leave you alone for now. Thanks doc. Dalton, I'll see you later," he answered, then cut around the corner and disappeared down another hallway.

* * *

Annette tried to open her heavy eyes, but it took too much effort. Her mouth was dry like sand and she was in extreme pain from her head all the way down her legs. She didn't dare moved, afraid it would hurt more. Her hooded eyes tried to focus. She felt someone touch her hand and squeeze it then she heard Dalton's voice. She concentrated on his voice. She wouldn't move her head in fear of more pain.

"Hi, Gorgeous. You're in the hospital. You had an accident, but it's going to be all right. If you understand what I'm saying, squeeze my hand or nod." She closed her eyes and she gave him a slight nod. "That's great. Now the nurse said that when you woke up from surgery you might have pain. Do you have any?" he asked softly while massaging her hand. She grasped his hand tightly. "Okay, hold on. I'll go tell the nurse you're awake and have pain so she can give you medication." He patted her hand then left her alone. He was gone.

No, don't leave me. I need you, she thought. *I'm scared.* She could hear footsteps coming in her directions. A woman's voice started talking to her. "Hi, Annette, my name is Molly. I'm going to check your vitals. How are you feeling?" she said to her. Annette nodded, still trying to wake up. She partially opened her eyes. She could feel her hand touching her arm as she checked her blood pressure and her pulse. "You must be thirsty. I brought you ice chips. If you open your mouth, I'll give you some," Molly told her. She parted her lips. She felt a cold, wet sensation in her mouth. It relieved some of the dryness. She reopened her mouth. She wanted more. "Now, I'll give you something for the pain if you need it," she said as she wrote her vitals down in her chart.

"Yes," Annette whispered. She partially opened her eyes to watch the nurse put a needle with medication in her IV. Within seconds she felt the drug take effect.

"Now, don't worry. Just sleep for now. You have a good-looking man here who I'm sure will be here when you wake up." Those were the last words she heard as she dozed off into a deep sleep.

* * *

Sidney arrived back at her hotel room. She felt devastated. Her mind was broken with an unbelievable sorrow. The man she loved so much had once again pushed her away. She dropped into the chair and popped her heels off. The alcohol had taken effect, but she wanted more so she could ease the pain away. She walked to the mini bar, swung the door opened, and grasped two bottles of vodka and a bottle of orange juice. *Excellent!* She mixed the liquids together then chugged it down. It burned her insides. She grimaced as she returned to the sofa. She made another drink while sitting and guzzled it down. She lifted her feet and placed them on the coffee table. She just gazed at nothing in particular. She was trying to solve her problem.

Well, Dalton didn't yet know that Annette was gone. There's no way she survived that hit by the taxi, but Dalton did not know what had happened yet. She kept repeating this in her mind. He would need her for comfort and understanding when he found out. He would know soon enough. She had to give him time. Maybe she had gone after him too soon. That was what had happened. It was too soon. She smiled then laughed out loud.

She would give Dalton a couple more days. When he found out she was dead, he would come crawling back to her. She was sure of it. She would take him back with open arms. She would be loving and sympathetic. She chuckled as she put her heels back on and decided to go out to have a drink downstairs instead of staying in her room by herself. She was all dressed up for a night on the town, so why waste it? She might as well go have a little fun and maybe dance. She was not going to cry for this man any longer. He would eventually come back to her once he was alone and Annette was dead. She picked up her purse from the chair, opened the door of her room, and strutted her stuff down the hall toward the elevators for an evening of fanfare.

* * *

Two days later Dalton felt helpless just sitting in the Intensive Care Unit while watching Annette sleep. She had improved a lot since the first day. She would murmur words to him briefly when she would wake up, but he hadn't seen her smile yet. He just wanted to hold her in his arms and take all her suffering away. She still had an oxygen mask, as well an IV, which was attached to her arm. The chest tube that had been connected to her torso had been removed the previous day. She had a cast on her right leg that went all the way up to her thigh. Her leg was propped up on pillows.

All kinds of monitors beeped, keeping track of her breathing, her heart, and her pulse. She looked so pale and powerless to him. Her small, fragile hand was limp, but he would not let go of it. He had kept a vigil next to her for the last two days. She only woke up a few times, but she had fallen asleep shortly thereafter. The doctor had come to check on her and reported she was in stable condition. He was optimistic about her progress. He said that she would probably be moved out of the ICU within a day or so.

His head was leaning against the bed while he sat close to her bed. Suddenly he heard Annette moan. He lifted his head and he stood up near her bed to be able to hear her if she spoke. Her eyes fluttered then opened. She seemed to be more alert today than the other times she had awake.

"Hi, Beautiful," he told her as he touched her cheek with the palm of his hand. He noticed she looked at the cup of water that was on the table next to her. Dalton grabbed it and asked, "Are you thirsty?" She nodded slightly. "I'll be right back. I'll get you fresh water," he told her and left the room in a hurry. He was almost running down the hall to the hospital kitchenette to get her ice water. He did and walked back as fast as he could. He took the straw between two of his fingers and placed it near her mouth.

She gave him a weak smile and said, "Thanks." She sipped a bit.

"Do you want more?" he asked as he offered it again. She nodded, and then drank another sip. "How are you feeling?" he asked as he showed her his dimples in a broad smile. "The doctor said you were going to be good as new. Do you remember what happened?" he questioned her as she looked up at him.

"I think ... someone pushed me into the street," she answered him.

"What do you mean someone pushed you? You must be mistaken. You need to rest and get better. We can talk about this later," he told her as he frowned, wondering if the medication combined with the concussion were affecting her memory.

"You should go home. You look awful ... Take a shower," she managed to say between breaths. He passed his hand over his chin. He could feel his whiskers. He needed a shave.

"I'm fine. Even better now that you're awake. I'll go later," he replied and took her hand. She shook her head and squeezed his hand.

"No, go. Please. I'll be okay," she told him. He didn't want to argue with her, but at the same time didn't want to leave her. What if she needed something?

"She's right, you know. You should go home for a while so you can shower and change your clothes. She'll be all right. I'll keep an eye on her. Don't worry," a nurse said as she walked in and heard the conversation. She went to the other side of the bed to check her vitals.

"I suppose I could use a shower," he said, a little embarrassed at the way he looked. His clothes were all wrinkled, he needed a shave, and he didn't smell too appetizing either. He glanced at the nurse one more time for reassurance. She nodded at him.

"Take a break. She's awake and she isn't going anywhere," the nurse said with a tilt of her head toward the door.

"Okay, I'll go and be back in about an hour," he said, he leaned down to kiss her cheek.

THE PLEDGE

"Good," he heard Annette say. He picked up his jacket off the chair and walked away, but by the time he arrived at the elevators, he looked back down the hallway, feeling shocked. He couldn't stop thinking about the possibility that someone might have pushed her. *Who would do such a thing?*

Chapter 19

Two days had gone by since she had shoved and eliminated Annette from her life. She was happier than she had been since she had arrived in Boston. She felt calm, unthreatened. She wasn't going to lose Dalton. Her man was free again and she would win him back. She had not heard from Dalton, so she decided to give him a call. Maybe they could meet for lunch.

"Hello," Dalton said in a dull tone when he answered his phone. She was surprised he had answered her call.

"Hi, Dalton. Please don't hang up," she pleaded as she crossed her fingers, hoping that her cheerful tone would make him listen to what she had to say.

"What do you want?" he asked her flatly. Just the fact he was willing to hear what she had to say was encouraging. She paced back and forth in her room while she spoke to him.

"I wanted to apologize for my behavior the other night. I don't want to lose your friendship. I want us to stay friends even though we are not together anymore," she lied. She really did not mean a word she was saying. She bit her fingernail, waiting for him to speak.

"It's okay. I understand," he told her.

"I was wondering if I could take you to lunch to make amends for everything I put you through. I'm really sorry." She would say anything he wanted to hear just to be near him.

"I suppose I could meet you for a quick lunch. I have a lot to do this afternoon," he answered her. It brought a smile to her face. She was right. He still loved her. She jumped around her room with joy. Thank God Dalton couldn't see her.

"How about I meet you at your hotel in the Rowes Wharf Sea Grill restaurant? I hear they have a good selection for lunch and it's quick," she said to him, her heart starting to race at the prospect of seeing him again.

"I'll be there in about a half hour," he told her.

"Very well. See you then. Bye," she said and clicked off her phone. She jumped up again. She had done it. Her plan was working. She cracked up laughing. She was so happy. *He's going to have lunch with me!* That was a start. At least he hadn't pushed her away like he had the other night. Maybe she had been too forward. She probably had scared him away, but now he had no one. She was his love. She ran to her closet and swung the door open. She was going to wear something sexy.

She hustled around the hotel room. She picked a green, low-cut shirt and a pair of black designer pants by Sarah Burton. They fit her like a glove. She pinned her hair up in a bun, then applied a touch of blush and lipstick. She grabbed her coat and scurried out the door.

She was the first to arrive at the bistro. She sat at a table by the window that over looked the harbor where she could see the boats on the waterfront. She loved the atmosphere of this place, with its oak wood tables and wicker chairs. The high, ornate ceilings and the large windows let the warmth of the sunshine into the room.

A long mahogany bar stood to her left. It was lined with leather stools and it had a huge mirror behind it. It hosted an array of distinct alcohol bottles. She thanked the waiter as he gave her the menu and she ordered a glass of white Pinot Grigio wine to try to ease her nerves.

She had a good view of the entrance of the restaurant and her eyes were glued to it. She asked to be seated at the same table where she sat two days previously. She had missed Dalton these last few days and she couldn't wait to see him again. She had to return to London soon for work and she hoped he would be sitting beside her when she departed for England.

The waiter brought her glass of wine. He placed it in front of her. She reached for it right away and took a sip. Finally she spotted him as he strolled her way. She raised her hand to attract his attention, but he didn't wave to her. He looked so elegant with his dark hair and broad shoulders, which she loved so much. He was wearing her favorite Burberry checkered shirt that she had bought him for his last birthday and black trousers. He stopped at the table and nodded. When he showed her his dimples she instantly became sexually aroused. The urge to take him upstairs to his room and do unspeakable things was tempting. She needed to relax so she wouldn't scare him away.

"Nice to see you, Dalton," she told him as she patted the seat next to her for him to sit down. Instead, he went around the table and sat across from her.

"How are you doing?" he asked pleasantly as he took the menu in his hands and started to read the selections for lunch.

"I'm good. Would you like a glass of wine or a whiskey?" she offered him as she took another drink of her wine. She was in no hurry. She hadn't even opened her menu.

"No thanks. But I'm starving. I think I'll have the ground tenderloin burger and a beer. What about you?" he asked her as he placed his menu on the other side of the table.

"I'll probably just have a chopped salad. That looks pretty appetizing," she replied. She handed her menu to him to put it aside with the other one. The waiter took their order and went to get a Budweiser beer for Dalton.

"So tell me, did you finish all your work for the firm?" She was trying to make conversation while they waited for their food. She would take any morsel of information about him he had to offer. She had missed him so much.

"Yes, pretty much. I took a leave of absence from the firm, but I'll still work on a few contracts through emails," he told her as he admired the view outside, while buttering a bun the waiter had placed in front of them.

"Wow! You deserve some time off. You have been working so hard. How long do you think you'll take?" she asked, surprised he was taking time off.

"I'm not sure just yet. I'll decide as I go along," he answered her and chewed his bread. Then he asked her, "How have you been spending your time?" She could feel tension in the air. He wouldn't look directly at her. He kept glancing out the window.

"I've been shopping up a storm, and I went to the theater the other night. I've been keeping busy," she told him, glad he was interested in what she had been doing with her time. The waiter delivered their meal and they both ordered another drink. Sidney picked up her fork and took a mouthful of her salad as Dalton sank his teeth into his burger.

She was enjoying her meal and just being near him until he asked, "When do you think you'll return back to London?"

"I will probably go back next Sunday. I have to get back to work soon. What about you?" she inquired as she took another bite of her salad, keeping her eyes on him.

"Oh! I don't know. It all depends how things go," he answered vaguely, so she decided to pursue the subject as she chewed on a tomato.

"What things?" she continued and looked at him in wonder. *What would keep him here?*

"Well, if you really want to know, Annette was injured in a car accident. I have been caring for her in the hospital," he answered her as he munched on his burger. Sidney dropped her fork on top of the table.

It hit the side of her plate. He looked up at her. She had a hard time swallowing, but she did. Her appetite vanished. She grabbed her glass of wine and took a mouthful of it.

"What do you mean ... she's in the hospital?" she asked, horrified by his revelation. She wiped her mouth with her napkin. She couldn't believe she was alive. She must have misunderstood him. Her stomach became upset at the news.

"A couple of days ago a car hit her. She has a concussion, a broken leg, and a few broken ribs. But she's a fighter and she's going to make it," he told her as he continued eating his hamburger.

"She's not dead?" she mumbled. Thank God he didn't hear her! He looked up at her, but didn't stop eating. "She was lucky she survived such a hit. What hospital is she at?" she asked while trying to figure out her next move to get rid of her.

"She's at Brigham and Women's Hospital. I have been there since the accident occurred," he answered. "Are you okay?" He asked as he glanced her way.

"Yes, yes. I was just thinking. I hope she ... she'll be fine," she answered him. She was quiet the rest of the lunch. She had to find another way to dispose of her. She bit the inside of her cheek, trying not to scream her head off. Their conversation was at a standstill. She smiled as he spoke, but she was feeling hatred enter her soul as jealousy was creeping in.

"I have to get going. Thanks for lunch," she heard him say. He hugged her at the end of lunch and they parted ways. Her eyes were fixated on him until he disappeared.

She was infuriated her plan had not worked. It had only brought them closer. "Damn you, bitch," she said under her breath. She returned to her hotel room after lunch. She was so mad that her anger showed on her face. She tightened her lips and clenched her teeth. Her nails dug into her fists. They were hurting from being clamped together so tight. She slammed the door hard when she entered her suite. Her face was pink and her mind was in a whirlwind. She had to find another way to get rid of her.

She moved towards her bed and dropped to her knees. She bent down, reached under the bed, and dragged her black leather bag out. She put it on top of her bed and unzipped it. She stared at what was inside the bag: her auburn wig, her mustache, and her men's clothing. She touched the hair of the wig with her hand. She had been successful at harming her once, but this time she would not make the same mistake. She would make sure she was dead. Totally out of their lives.

* * *

Dalton was back where he belonged—near his love—by late afternoon. He was glad he had gone to lunch with Sidney. He believed she was adjusting well to the break up and she was moving on. The best thing was that she was returning to London.

He stopped at the nurse's station to see how Annette was doing. He was told she was doing much better and if by the morning she kept improving, she would be moved to a regular room. He thanked them and he went to find Annette. He was delighted when he arrived in the room and she was sitting up in bed. Some of her color had reappeared on her face. He advanced toward her with a smile. He leaned down and kissed her on the cheek.

"You look so much better. How's it going?" he asked her as he searched the room for a chair. He pulled the chair next to her. He noted she no longer had the oxygen mask, but only a small tube like that was attached under her nose. He stretched out his hands to take her free hand in his and stroked it lightly.

"I feel much better. The pain has diminished, but only because of all the medication they have been giving me. I am getting stronger," she slowly said to him. He could see she was still feeling pain with every breath she took because of her broken ribs and the tube that had been removed. Her face twisted into a grimace and she blinked the tears away.

"Don't talk if it hurts. You don't have to. Just rest," he told her. She nodded then laid her head back on her pillow. They heard a knock on the door. Dalton turned his head and saw Detective Turner standing in the entrance.

"Am I interrupting anything? I see you are feeling much better since the last time I saw you. Do you remember me? My name is Detective Turner from the Boston Police Department. I wanted to ask you a few questions concerning the accident if you feel up to it," he told them as he took a step forward toward the bed.

"Can't it wait another day or so? She still has a lot of pain," Dalton told him. Turner shook his head slightly and moved forward. She briefly glanced at him and nodded.

"It's okay, Dalton," Annette said in a whisper. She grasped the side of the bed to try to lift herself up into a sitting position, but was unsuccessful. Dalton rose to help her by fixing her pillows further upright. He took her hand in his and stood beside her protectively.

"I'll be as brief as I can be. A witness thought you tripped and fell into the road. Is that correct?" he asked as he looked her way.

"No, no," she shook her head. "I didn't stumble ... I was pushed," she managed to say.

Dalton's was caught off guard as he took a step closer to her bed. Shocked, he said, "Are you sure you were shoved?" She nodded, closing her eyes and squeezing his hand.

"Did you see who pushed you forward?" the detective asked as he took notes. Annette shook her head and grimaced.

"A witness said she saw a red-haired man leave the scene. If I remember correctly, he was also seen at your house when you got burglarized. Does that ring a bell?" he asked. Annette shook her head once more. Dalton could see it was tiring and upsetting her by the frown on her face.

"Can we do this another day when she feels better?" Dalton mentioned to Turner again.

But he replied as he glanced from his notebook at Annette, "Just one more question and I'll leave you alone. Someone also indicated that the red-haired man had an accent. Can you think of anyone you know who might have an accent?" Annette just shook her head again. It was Dalton's turn to ask a question.

"What kind of accent are you talking about?"

The detective closed his pad and placed it in his pocket. He momentarily looked at Annette and Dalton said, "A British accent. At least, that was what the witness thought. I hope you feel better, Miss Russell. If you think of something, here's my card. Have a good day," he said, taking out one of his business cards from a folder and placing it on the side table.

Dalton watched as the detective turned and walked away without another word. He looked at Annette and patted her hand, "Why don't you try to sleep a bit. I'll be right here when you wake up," he told her. He saw a slight nod as she closed her eyes. *What a coincidence that he was British! Did she know many people who had accents?* A chill ran down his back. *Probably no one. But he did ... Sidney. Would she try to kill Annette? No, that was wrong. He had said a man, not a woman, had pushed her. That eliminated her.*

The day flew by. The only good news was when Doctor White came in the evening to check on Annette. He stepped into the room. He was studying her medical chart. He lifted his gaze and smiled at both of them as he closed the chart.

"Well, you seem to have improved. I'll have your oxygen taken off tonight. I don't think it is necessary anymore. The x-ray of your partially collapsed lung looks good and your leg will just need time to heal. I know you are still in a lot of pain because of your ribs, but that will get better as the days go by. I'm going to order that you be moved into a regular room tomorrow morning," he told Annette and Dalton.

"How long will she have to be in the hospital?" Dalton inquired, concerned.

"The antibiotics are taking care of the infections. If all goes well and there are no more problems, she should be able to go home day after tomorrow. Have a nice day," Doctor White answered with confidence. He turned to leave to attend to other patients.

"Thank you," Annette whispered to him as her eyes followed him out the door. Dalton noticed her eyes had filled with tears. He could tell she didn't want him to see them as she moved her head away. She was looking toward the opposite wall.

"What's the matter, Annette? Everything is going to be okay," Dalton said to her. He leaned above her. He gently turned her face with his hand so she was looking straight at him. A tear rolled down her cheek. He wiped it away with his fingers. His heart melted at her pain. "Tell me what the matter is? Are you in pain?" he encouraged. He touched her cheek with the palm of his hand.

"It's just; I don't have a home to return to. It was destroyed remember? And I can't fix it...." she said as another tear fell down her cheek.

"Why don't you let me worry about that? I am not going to leave you stranded in the streets. Tomorrow I'll check with the police. They should be done with the investigation. I will hire a company to clean and repair the house. You won't even know anything ever happened. You will have a place to return to. How does that sound?" Dalton said and winked at her. She nodded. A smiled appeared through her tears.

"Thank you. You are too good to me. How am I going to repay you?"

"That's easy. I'm going to move in with you so I know you are well taken care of until you are back on your feet. I'll get the best of both worlds—a place to stay and you. Anyway, I'm sick and tired of the suite at the hotel. I would much rather be with you," Dalton told her as he kissed her lightly on the lips. He couldn't wait until he could have her naked body next to his and make love to her. But right now he would have to be patient. It brought another smile to her lips. With all the bad luck she had endured in the last few days, it made his heart melt to know she was such a trooper.

"You have a deal, mister, but I can be a very demanding patient," she said and laughed, and winced from the pain in her chest. It was the first time he had seen her untroubled and that was a good sign. He would make sure he was with her so no one would ever hurt her again.

"Now, stop crying," he told her as he settled in his chair by her bed.

Chapter 20

Turner sat at his desk at the Boston Police Department, leaning back in his chair while going over his notes of the Russell case. He scowled at the pattern he was seeing. Someone was out to kill this woman. It was evident that the same red-haired man had been at both incidents. He was trying to figure out why, but he had no answers. One thing he was sure was that it was somehow linked to the British boyfriend, but he couldn't pin it down. He grabbed the criminal report that had been writing up by the investigators. No known fingerprints or fibers had been found, but a few red hairs had been analyzed and processed. The hair was synthetic. It was from a wig.

He shuffled the reports around on his desk, comparing statements from the witnesses who had seen this man. In both cases it was said he was about five-foot eight to five-foot ten in height and was of medium built. A footprint had been found in the snow in the back of Annette's house of a size ten boot. The print led from the back alley to the street. The size of the boot print eliminated her boyfriend, because he wore a size twelve shoe and was at least six-foot two. He definitely had a larger built. He also noted that nothing had been stolen from the house. The house had been ransacked and ruined with a knife. This incident was personal. Why else would someone dig a knife into the kitchen island?

He threw the papers back on the desk, and scratched his head with his hand. *There had to be a connection, but what?*

He picked up the phone to call the detective who had been first on the scene at Annette's car accident.

"Hi, Darrell, this is Detective Turner. I have a question for you. Did anyone check the area of the surrounding street of the Russell car incident to see if a store in the vicinity might have a video of a red-haired man leaving the area?" he asked him as he looked at the mound of files in front of him.

"I don't think so, because it was considered a car accident at the time. Why?" Darrell replied.

"Well, I'm investigating a break-in that happened at the victim's home a few days previously, and one piece of evidence we have was a red-haired man with a moustache," he explained to him as hope invaded his mind. Maybe he could get a picture of this man.

"I'll check the nearby stores in the neighborhood and get back to you. You believe that there's a connection?" he asked Turner.

"Something is fishy here. Let me know if you find anything. The victim is still in the hospital, but I have a funny feeling that when she gets out, the offender might try to hurt her again," Turner told him as he drank his cold coffee. He made a face and looked at his cup then replaced it on his desk.

"No problem. I'll get on it right away. I'll give you a call if I find anything. How about I call you later in the day?" he told Turner. He was elated this kid might locate a connection.

"Very good. I'll await your findings," Turner said and hung up the phone. He was worried for the woman. Someone did not like her. He didn't know why, though. He hoped he wasn't too late to save her because his instinct told him that this criminal would try again, sooner or later.

***

The next morning Dalton called a cleaning company to scrub down the house and bring it back its pristine look. He had gone furniture shopping the previous evening and had replaced pieces of the living room and bedroom that had been ripped and broken. The walls had been freshly painted and the patio door locks replaced. He even installed a high-tech alarm system, as well as cameras on the front and back doors. He never wanted Annette to be afraid again or lack anything. His love for her had exceeded all of his expectations. He had paid extra money to have everything done in minimum amount of time.

He even ventured into a women's department store to buy her lingerie and an assortment of clothes that ranged from casual to dressy. He wasn't sure if she would like them, but he had tried to please her. He knew she would appreciate the time and effort he put into it. He knew this because of her kindness.

Time flew by. The next thing he knew, Annette was being released from the hospital. He hired a town car and driver to bring her back from the hospital to her house. He rolled her wheelchair to the entrance of the hospital. She was happy to leave, but he sensed sadness in her heart. He stopped pushing the chair and put the brakes on when he was almost at the main entrance. He parked it next to the door. He kneeled in front of her. He took her hands in his and said, "I have a surprise for you. We are not going back to the hotel. We are going to your house," She gasped, bringing her hand up to cover her mouth.

"I can't go back now. It's a total mess. How am I going to ...?"

He could see she was getting perturbed, so he said "Shh!" and placed his index finger on her lips.

"Listen, I had the house restored. Don't worry; it is all taken care of." She bowed her head. He could see concern written on her face as she wrinkled her forehead.

"You are too good to me. I won't be able to repay you right away, but I will as soon as I'm back at work," she told him with determination.

"I don't want you to repay me because I'm going to consider it my rental fee. If you'll have me, that is," he replied to her as he stood up and continued to wheel her out to the car.

She glanced up and reached for him with her hand. "You are welcome to stay as long as you want...." Her voice broke. "Thank you." He helped her get into the backseat of the car. He reached over and buckled her seatbelt. He ran around the back of the car and slid in beside her. He told the driver the address then took her hand in his and held it tight all the way back to the North End of town where her house awaited her.

When they arrived, he assisted her get out of the car with her crutches. He opened the new front door lock. Dalton placed the key in her coat pocket. "Welcome back. I hope you like it." She hobbled forward into the house as he held her bag. She halted in the entranceway to examine her home. She turned toward him.

"Oh My God! It's ... perfect." She told him as she checked her habitat.

"Great. Now let me carry you to our bedroom." She nodded and smiled at him. He scooped her up in his arms as she enveloped his neck with her hands. He carefully carried her, doing his best not to cause her any more discomfort. Within seconds he laid her gently on top of her bed. He propped a pillow under her leg, grabbed a light blanket from the edge of the bed and covered her and took a step backward.

"I am here to serve you, my lady. Just tell me and I shall fetch, cook, or do whatever else is needed," he told her and bowed in front of her with his hands spread out. He heard her snicker and it brought joy to him to see her cheerful once again.

"Well, your lady would like you to come nearer so she may thank you with a kiss," she told him and outstretched her arms toward him.

"It would be my pleasure to assist you, my lady," he responded as he moved nearer to her in bed. Dalton cupped his hands around her face. Her fingers stroked through his hair down to his shoulders. He gazed deep into her eyes and kissed her, showing her how much he had missed her. When his lips touched hers, his body burned all way down to his groin area, but he knew he had to wait until she became stronger and healthy again. He pulled back from her and just said, "I love you."

* * *

Sidney's hopes had been shattered by the news that Annette was still alive. But what caused her more distress was the fact that Dalton was still with that bitch. She now had to be smart about her next move if she was to get back her man. She would not give up that easily. She needed information and the only way she could acquire it was through Dalton. She had been scheming a new strategy for three days. Now she was ready. She sat alone in her suite, transferring her phone from one hand to the other as she thought about her next step. She made the decision to text him instead of calling him. That way she would have time to think about her responses.

She texted him: **Hi, Dalton, I was hoping to see you again before I returned to London. I know you are busy with Annette in the hospital. Let me know.** She pushed the send button. She placed the phone on her coffee table. She watched the screen attentively and waited for him to answer her. Minutes ticked away. She stared at her iPhone.

Finally, a ping! She snatched the phone off the table and read the message. **Sidney, I'm really busy taking care of Annette at home. I don't think I'll be able to meet you before you leave. Sorry.** That son of a bitch was telling her that he couldn't come meet her. And it was all because of Annette. *Calm down*, she thought. She took a deep breath and let it out. She did this several times before she looked at her phone again. She stood for a couple of minutes, thinking hard about what she was going to reply. Then it came to her. She typed: **Don't worry about it Dalton. I'm fine. I'll text you later.**

She had the information she wanted. Annette was recovering at home and Sidney knew where she lived. She would get to her in time. The only thing she needed now was a way to get Dalton out of the house.

* * *

Annette knew how blessed and lucky she was to have such an attentive man by her side to care for her. She watched as Dalton prepared breakfast for her as she laid on the new sofa in the living room. She had a good view of the kitchen from where she was lying, since the house was so open. She laughed, her eyes sparkling with joy as she observed him scramble eggs in a bowl and cook bacon at the same time. He was trying to put bread in the toaster and was having difficulty. She looked away, trying not to laugh as he ran from one corner to another, trying not to burn breakfast. She was so grateful for all he had done. He had brought her home and was trying to help her adjust. She still had pain, but it seemed to be getting better. The doctor had given her a prescription for medication for her discomfort. She was taking them faithfully, but the problem was that they made her sleepy. So for most of the day she kept dozing off.

She heard the ping of the text on Dalton's phone and observed him answer it, but she didn't ask him about it. She had a feeling it was from his ex-fiancée. *Who else would he text?* Dalton didn't know many people in Boston who would be sending him a message on a Saturday morning. He finally finished her scrambled eggs, bacon, and toast. She could smell the coffee brewing on the counter. She wished she could assist with the chores, but right now it was not going to happen. She could barely stand without pain shooting down her leg or her chest hurting from the broken ribs or the chest tube incision. She watched him set the food and her coffee on tray. He walked towards her with it. She scowled as she pushed herself up into a sitting position to accommodate the tray.

"That looks delicious," she giggled as she took the platter and rested it on her lap. She noticed the bacon was undercooked and the toast was a little burnt, but who was she to say anything? She picked up the fork to spoon a mouthful of eggs. She ate it. She didn't want to hurt his feelings after he had worked so hard. Dalton turned and went back to the kitchen to retrieve his plate. He sat on the chair next to her and attacked his breakfast. Annette was picking at her food, moving it around in her plate with her fork.

She thought of his recent text. *Why had he not mentioned it? Who had texted him?* She took another bite. She had to ask. She couldn't take the uncertainty. *Had it been his ex-fiancée?* She took a fleeting glance at Dalton. She didn't mean to be the jealous type, but it was eating her up. So, as casually as she could, she asked, "I heard your phone. Did you receive a text?" Dalton looked up from his plate, still chewing. She gripped her coffee cup and took a sip, her sight on him pretending not to be too concerned.

"Yes, I did. It was ... umm ... Sidney. She wanted me to meet her to say goodbye. She is returning to London. But I told I couldn't make it," he replied, then bit into a piece of dry toast and continued eating his breakfast.

"If you want to go, you can. I don't want to stop you. I'm a big girl. I can take care of myself for a few hours," she said, not really meaning any of it. She was relieved Sidney was going home to London. She did trust Dalton, but he had lied to her so many times before that she felt like she still had to keep her guard up when it came to Sidney. She didn't want to get hurt again by losing him to his ex, even though he had declared his love for her.

"No, I don't want to see her again. I would rather be here with you," he answered. Relief swept over her. She was pleased he had made the decision to refuse to see her off.

* * *

Turner had been filling out criminal reports all afternoon at the precinct. His eyes were tired from looking at the computer screen. He pushed away from his desk as his chair rolled backward. He got up and walked to the coffee station. He poured himself another cup of coffee, hoping it would rejuvenate him. His day had been slow and he was trying to catch up on his paperwork. He hated filing reports. He'd rather be on the road catching criminals. He sipped his mug of coffee on his way back to his desk. He glanced at his cup with distaste. He sat down again at his desk on his metal chair. He had to get himself a more comfortable chair. His back was aching from being rooted to this spot. He opened the drawer of his desk and tossed two Tylenol into his mouth. He swallowed them with another drink of coffee. He was getting too old for this type of work. His phone rang and he quickly picked it up, glad to have a distraction from the reports.

"Detective Turner," he answered as he stretched his legs under the desk.

"Turner, it's Darrell. I went back to the area of that taxi accident and guess what? I found us two store videos," he told the detective with excitement.

"You just made my day. Now, tell me you got a shot of the red-haired man," he said, hoping for a break. He doodled a picture while waiting for his answer.

"I haven't had time to look at the CDs just yet. I'll bring them up to your office and we can watch them together," Darrell offered.

"Move your butt. I'll meet you in the video room. How long are you going to be?" Turner asked him, anxious to look at those tapes.

"Give me ten minutes. I'm on my way. How's that?" he answered.

"I'm still waiting. Ten minutes!" Turner had a good feeling and hoped for the best, but in this type of business sometimes you win and other times you got nothing. He picked up his coat and walked up the stairs to the third floor to the viewing room. Within minutes he spotted Darrell coming down the hall with a paper bag. He sprinted into the room, and when he saw Turner, he lifted his paper bag in the air.

"Here I am," he said as he gave the CDs to Turner.

He took them from him, opened the case, and popped in one of CDs. He fast-forwarded it to the approximate time of the event. They were both peering at the screen intensely. Turner crossed his arms on his chest and fixed his eyes on the screen as it unfolded.

"Right there. But we don't have a clear image of the face, just his backside. It's not a very big man, that's for sure." Turner reviewed it several times then pushed the eject button. He carefully discharged it. He took out the other CD and dropped it in the machine. He pushed the button to forward it to the timeframe, and folded his arms in front of him again. He watched as the scene developed. The man was walking fairly fast, but they did get a pretty good look at him. He smiled as he lightly punched Darrell in the arm.

"Good job. Now let's get it on paper and pass it around to the patrolmen." Turner felt much better. Now all he had to do was identify this person. He had an idea of someone who would be able to help him.

Chapter 21

Sidney marched back and forth from one room to another, trying to come up with plan on how to get Dalton to visit her. She needed to get him away from Annette. Her mind was blank. Nothing was surfacing. She was getting irritated and madder by the minute. She pounded her fists on the counter of her bathroom. She glanced up at her face in the mirror, her hands leaning against the counter. She looked dreadful. Her eyes were puffy with dark circles. She had lost weight since she had arrived in Boston, so her cheeks seemed concave. Her hair was matted. She had not ventured outside her room or taken a shower in days as she tried to construct her strategy to get rid of the bitch. She picked up her hairbrush to untangle her hair. She brushed forcibly. Suddenly she stopped. She noticed her prescriptions narcotic drugs that were just sitting on the counter.

"What if ... Yes, that's it. It might work," she said out loud, thrilled she had found a solution. She lightly clapped her hands together. She knew Dalton, and she had the answer. He would feel guilty and come to try to rescue her. He would feel sorry for what had happened between them and blame himself. Best of all he would be away from Annette. She chortled at her genius scheme. She walked back to the bedroom and grabbed her phone from the night table. *What was she going to tell him?* She sat down on the bed as she placed her finger against her chin, concocting. First she had to get ready, but she would have to wait until the sun went down. The darkness would give her cover and she would be able to maneuver easily without attracting too much attention.

She immediately pulled her disguise from the leather bag. She laid each piece on the bed. She checked the time on her alarm clock. It was too early to make that crucial phone call. *Be patient!* It would be her best performance yet. She would have to be convincing to pull this plan out.

First, she had to know how much time it would take Dalton to get from that bitch's house to the hotel. Then she needed a weapon. She went to the desk and searched the yellow pages for the number of a taxi company in the Boston area. She wrote down the number on a piece of paper and shoved it in her jean pocket. She grabbed her keys and headed down to the underground garage. But on her way down the hallway she saw a tray of leftover food on the floor that was waiting to be picked up by the hotel staff. Her eyes detected a shiny object on the dinner plate. She stopped in her tracks. She looked around, scanning up and down the hallway. No one. It was deserted. She quickly seized the metal object and hid it instantly under her jacket. She now had an item to inflict bodily harm. She had a large steak knife. She snickered "This will do nicely," she said as she continued her descent down to the garage with the knife in her hand.

She located her blue rental car and drove toward the North End to Annette's address. She arrived fairly quickly, but the traffic was starting to get heavier. The evening rush would begin in another hour or so. She checked the time. It was fifteen minutes after four in the afternoon. She parked her car by the curb down the block from her house. She waited a half hour, then she picked up her phone to ring the number of the cab company. She gave them an address of a few houses down the street and waited again. She needed to know how long it would take them to get here because she knew neither Dalton nor Annette had a car. Dalton would have to call a taxi.

She watched in her rearview mirror as the cab came down the street. It had taken him fifteen minutes. She didn't wait for him to find out there was no one to pick up. She turned the key to her engine and started driving back to the hotel. The traffic had gotten heavier, just as she had expected. Twenty minutes later she was back in the garage. She looked at her watch. She gave Dalton fifteen minutes to get upstairs to her room to find out she was not there. She had a little more than an hour to execute her plan.

She rushed back up to her room. She grabbed her disguise and dressed up in her cover. She adjusted her wig on her head, glued her mustache on her upper lip, and pulled her cap low. She looked unrecognizable. She was back in her car within a half hour, driving back toward the North End of town. The darkness had fallen upon the city of Boston. She was eager to carry out her master plan.

* * *

It was early evening around suppertime and Dalton was lounging with Annette on her bed watching an old movie, *The Way We Were* with Robert Redford and Barbara Streisand.

"Are you hungry yet?" he asked her as he felt his stomach rumble. He placed his hand on his belly and rubbed it. She turned her head and laughed. She paused the movie.

"Okay, I know you're starving. What do you want to have to eat? I'll have whatever you want. These painkillers the doctors gave me suppress my appetite, but I know I have to eat something. So you choose," she mentioned to him as she waited for his response.

"What about Italian? We are in the middle of the North End, so there should be a restaurant nearby that I can walk to and go pick up," he said to her, but he would agree to whatever she wanted. He twirled her hair around his fingers as she thought of a place.

"There's a small mom and pop Italian restaurant called Francisco's down the street. They have take out. It's a short walk—about a block and a half from here on your left when you leave the front door. They make homemade meatballs, and their alfredo pasta is to die for. There's a menu in the drawer in the kitchen by the stove if you want to look at it," she answered him.

"No, that sounds ideal to me. I'll get the menu so you can call it in. And order garlic bread, too," he said as he walked to the kitchen to get her the number. He came back to the bedroom and he handed it to her.

"You call and I'll go get it, okay?" he picked up his jacket from the closet, threw it on as Annette called and placed their request.

"We are all set. Just turn left and walk down to the next block. You can't miss it," she told him. He had started to walk away when he heard her say, "Where's my kiss, big boy?" He turned around, bent down over her to peck her on the lips.

"It's really a shame you are in this condition, because I would like to eat you up right now." He told her and immediately saw her blush as she gave him a small slap on the arm.

"I won't always be in this condition," she teased as he left her alone.

"I'll be right back," he yelled as he opened the front door and locked it behind him on his way to the restaurant.

* * *

As Sidney was driving down Annette's street to park her car by the curb, someone caught her eye. It was Dalton. He was walking down the sidewalk. She quickly pulled over after she passed him and ducked down in her seat. She didn't think he saw her because he kept on walking. He never turned his head to look her way. She wondered where he was going, but she couldn't follow him either. She didn't want to be recognized, even though she was wearing her wig and disguise. She would have to wait it out until he returned back to the house. She couldn't take the chance of him barging into the house while she was there.

He didn't look at her car. He didn't know she had rented it, so she was safe for the moment. She would keep an eye out for him in her rearview mirror. She unbuckled her seatbelt and settled into her seat. She took her knife out from its hiding place and touched the edge of her weapon with her fingers to see if it was sharp. She accidently slit her index finger on the blade. She felt a sharp tingling pain as a drop of blood appeared. She nonchalantly wiped the blood on her pants. She couldn't wait to get rid of that bitch. She wasn't afraid of her. She had to be eliminated. There was no other solution. All she knew was she could not live without her man. He belonged to her. She decided to wait and call him when he returned to the house. She adjusted her car mirror as she anticipated her encounter with Annette.

* * *

Annette was relaxing with her eyes closed and her head against the headboard as she waited for Dalton to return from the restaurant. She heard her phone ring. She reached over to her side table and picked it up. She looked at the caller ID, but didn't know the number.

"Hello," she answered. She felt a fierce pain in her side by the movement.

"Good evening, Miss Russell. This is Detective Turner from the Boston Police Department. I hope I'm not disturbing you," he said politely.

"No, no, not at all. What can I do for you?" she said, pondering if they had caught the intruder or at least had a lead.

"We were lucky. We have a picture of a suspect who may have pushed you in front of the taxi. It comes from a video of a store a few blocks away. I was hoping if you and your boyfriend would take a look at it to see if maybe you recognized the person," he explained to her.

"Sure, that would be fine. Dalton is not here at the moment. He went to pick up food for supper, but he should be back shortly," she told him. Hopefully they had found the person responsible for her injuries and would be put behind bars.

"Another thing is, we also found out from one of your neighbors across the street that he also saw a red-haired man leaving the area around your home when it was burglarized. We think this may be the same person and that the two crimes are related. I'll pass by in about an hour and a half or so. Will that be convenient for you?" he asked her.

"That sounds good. And Dalton should be back by then. Thank you," she replied to him.

"Very well. See you then. Goodbye," he responded and she heard the click of the phone. She replaced the phone back to its place. She wondered *who could be so cruel to destroy her home and try to kill her.*

* * *

Time passed slowly. Sidney was just sitting in her car, counting the automobiles that went by. But a half hour later Sidney sat upright. Her eyes darting at everything that moved. She noticed a man approaching down the block. He was holding a large brown bag. She would know his stride anywhere. It was her Dalton. She slid down in her seat once again as he neared her house. She hid down in the seat so he would not notice her, even though her car was up the street. She was not taking any chances of him spotting her. She poked up her head, looked in her rearview mirror just in time to see Dalton going up the steps of Annette's house. She watched as he pushed the door with his shoulder and walked in. All right, she had to give him a few minutes, and then she would call him. She wouldn't rush.

Ten minutes went by and she exhausted her patience. She dug her phone out of her pocket. It was time. But, she decided to text him instead of calling him. She typed away her message that read:

THE PLEDGE

My darling Dalton, I can't live without you. My heart is shattered. I am ending my life in hope that one day we can be reunited together. Love you always ...

Sidney reread the words and decided if this didn't get him to come find her, nothing would. She pushed the send button. All she had to do was observe and wait as the man she loved panicked. He would run to her hotel to try save his love.

* * *

Dalton entered the kitchen and placed the Italian food on the counter. He was in the process of putting the pasta on a tray to bring it to Annette when he felt his phone ping. He had another text message. He reached into his pocket to read it. He couldn't believe what he was reading as his hand started to shake. He analyzed the text. "Oh! Dear Lord, no!" he yelled as he ran to the bedroom where Annette was lying down.

"What's the matter? You look like you saw a ghost," she said to him. He was speechless, standing in place, unable to think. He gave her the phone and she gasped. Her hand went straight to her mouth when she saw the content.

"Let me try to call her," he said as he rang her number. He heard it ring and ring, but Sidney never answered. *What now?* "I have to try to help her; otherwise I won't be able to live with myself if something happens to her." He already felt guilt come upon him for breaking the engagement with her. He felt helpless. *What should he do?* He glanced at Annette for an answer that she did not have. She was as much in shock as he was at what Sidney had done.

"I have to try to stop her. I'll ... do you think she ... call 911 and sent them to The Ritz Carlton Hotel right away. I'll call a cab and go over there right away. Maybe I can stop her from ending her life. I hope I'm not too late." He was so confused. *Why had she done this?* He had never wanted something like this to happen to Sidney.

"Go. Hurry. I'll call 911," she told him as she reached for the landline of her house.

He grabbed his jacket and slipped it on while running out the door. He called a cab company, "Please hurry. It's an emergency," he told the cab operator. He hung up and went to the front entrance to wait for the taxi. He kept fidgeting while he stood on the porch. Minutes passed, but it seemed like hours. He kept looking down the street, ready to spring down the pathway.

"I called 911. They are sending the paramedics right away. Call me when you have news," he heard Annette yell to him. He turned around and saw her on one foot with her crutches at the door. There was a grimace of pain on her face.

"I will," he shouted back. He stood waiting, hopping from on foot to the other. A cold sweat passed through him. "Where is the bloody cab?" he said as he impatiently glanced down the street for the taxi. He didn't know what he was going to do if she died. He was not prepared for this. How could she do such a thing? Finally, he noticed a white cab coming down the street.

"He's here. I'll call you," he called out to Annette. He rushed down the steps two at a time, and then ran to the middle of the street. He lifted his arm to flag the driver to his position. The car stopped. He jumped into the backseat and shut the door.

"The Ritz Carlton as fast as you can. It's a matter of life and death. Hurry!" he screamed at the driver, who examined him suspiciously in the mirror, but took off right away. Dalton sat at the edge of his seat, holding onto the armrest while wondering if he was going to be too late to save her.

Chapter 22

Sidney observed the taxi stop in front of the house and watched Dalton sprint to the car. The driver took off at rapid speed down the street. She was right about Dalton's feelings. He still loved her. Otherwise why would he try to get to her to save her life? She felt touched by how fast he had responded to her text. Now the clock was ticking away. She only had approximately an hour before Dalton figured out he had been fooled and would return to Annette. She would have to work fast and be careful not to be seen by anyone. She moved her car closer to the house and parked it in front of house so she could throw Annette in the trunk and then drive away quickly.

Darkness had covered the sky. She was ready for this mission. She stepped out of her rental and rushed toward the alley between the two buildings. As soon as she was at the end of the passageway, she laid her back flat against the structure. She took her knife out and held it next to her leg. Her heartbeat accelerated. She had to calm down. She closed her eyes and took two long breaths. She felt better. She took it one step at a time as she watched the front and back of the pathway. She crouched down to poke her head out and see if she could detect anyone in the area behind the house. The coast was clear, so she hurried up the steps to her deck. She went to the glass patio door and tried to slide it open, but it was locked. She noticed a new lock on the door. She cupped her hands upon the glass and peeked inside. The house seemed empty. Annette was nowhere to be seen. She must be in the bedroom.

What had worked the first time when she had broken in should work now. She took her screwdriver and small hammer out of her pockets. She placed the knife down on the top of the railing, but still within her reach. She hit the top of the screwdriver with her hammer near the opening of the lock, but to her astonishment, it didn't budge. She smacked it again, but this time a lot harder. She was frustrated the lock would not open. Her surprise attack was not working. Annette must have heard her by now. She picked up her knife in one hand and her hammer in the other. She lifted her arm up high. She turned her face away then struck the glass door with the heavy metal tip with all her strength. She heard the crashing of the glass as it fell upon the deck and inside the house.

She quickly pushed the blinds to the side and she carefully entered into the house. She stormed the kitchen, opening the drawers until she found a bigger and sharper knife. She found one in the butcher's block on the counter. She took a hold of it and barged toward the bedroom with her new weapon in hand to take care of that bitch. She met Annette halfway down the hall. She was on crutches. Annette was just standing there gawking at her. Fright was written all over her face. She creased her forehead and frowned deeply at Sidney. Annette tried to turn around to get away, but she stumbled and fell hard to the floor. The crutches flew from her hands. Sidney could see agony written on Annette's face as she lay on the hardwood floor. Sidney laughed out loud.

"Did you hurt yourself, bitch?" she asked as she chuckled out loud at her.

Sidney took two steps forward. She was on top of her instantly, holding her knife near her face. Annette pulled back as her hands went up to try to protect herself.

"If you move or scream, I'll gut you right where you lay, bitch," Sidney told her in an evil tone as she clenched her teeth together. Annette was resting on her elbows, not budging an inch. Her mouth opened, but not a sound escaped from her.

"It was you all along in the red wig. What do you want? Why are you doing this?" Annette cried out at her a tear rolled down her cheek from fright. Sidney noticed she was shaking. She was pleased she had caused such great fear.

"What do I want? I want my fiancé back, bitch. I want you out of our lives. That's what I want!" she shouted at her as she kneeled down next to her and pointed the knife in her face. Annette tried to pull away from her by pushing backwards, but couldn't, so she turned her head away and tightly shut her eyes.

"Please, don't hurt me," she begged as her palms went up near her face.

"Get up, bitch. Grab your crutches and let's go before I change my mind," Sidney commanded her. Annette reached for her crutches, but was struggling to get up. Sidney snickered at her.

"Are you having a problem?" Sidney asked her as she took a step back to watch Annette grimace from the pain while trying to stand. Sidney crossed her arms in front of her chest, leaned against the wall and peered at her, still chuckling. "Hurry up, bitch! And don't even think of trying to get away," Sidney told her, now getting annoyed with her because she wasn't moving fast enough. She watched her as she struggled for a minute. Sidney seized her arm tightly and yanked her up. She heard a loud moan coming from her, but it didn't faze her.

Suddenly they both heard it. The doorbell rang. Sidney's head whipped around, but it was too late. Annette was screaming loudly, "Help! Help me!" Sidney moved swiftly and punched her in the jaw so hard the crutches went flying to the ground. Annette lost her balance and tumbled backward on the floor with a loud crash. Annette wailed in pain.

"Shut the fuck up, bitch, and don't move, or I'll kill you on the spot," Sidney whispered to her sternly as she grabbed a handful of her hair and twisted it hard. She moved the knife flat to Annette's throat and pressed the blade hard against her neck. Annette became completely silent. The sound of Annette's cries were muffled immediately. Sidney gave her a dirty look as she held the knife more tightly.

A loud knock came. "Anyone in there? This is Detective Turner." Not one word was uttered this time around. Sidney pulled her hair tighter.

Tears were streaming down Annette's face, but still she made no sound. It was quiet. Sidney released her just long enough to jut her head out of the hallway to see if he was still at the entrance. *What was going on? Why was he here?* She could see the front of the house from this angle. She stooped down low and ran to the side of the window. She poked her head to see if the cop had been alerted by Annette's scream. He was leaving. He hadn't heard her. Sidney followed him with her eyes as he returned to his car. She watched as he answered his cellphone to talk to someone, then he started his car to drive down the street. He disappeared.

* * *

Dalton arrived at The Ritz Carlton within fifteen minutes. He noticed the fire department and the ambulance were parked at the front entrance as he neared the place. He threw a twenty-dollar bill on the front seat for the driver as he approached. "Let me out. Pull over," Dalton told him, unable to sit any longer. He pushed the door wide just as the taxi was about to make a stop. He leaped out and began to run toward the elevator of the hotel to get to his old room where Sidney was staying.

He stepped out in the hallway on the tenth floor and rushed to the room. He ran right into the suite, "Sidney," he shouted for her. "Are you all right?" he yelled out. The paramedics and firemen in the room all turned to look at him, surprised. They were picking up their equipment and were walking toward the exit.

One of the firemen wearing a white helmet came forward. He stopped in front of Dalton. "Did you call this in?" he asked him. He seemed a bit annoyed.

"Yes, I did. Is she okay?" Dalton asked as he tried to look past the shoulder of the fireman. But he was unable to see anything.

"She's not here. No one is. Do you have the right address?" the chief asked him. Dalton could see he seemed irritated. "Yes, I have the right address," Dalton answered, flushed. His pulse was beating hard from running.

"There's no one here. Next time get it right," he told him and started to depart the room.

"I did get it right. Look what she sent me," Dalton said as he fished his pocket for his phone. He scrolled down to find the text, and handed it to the chief. The fire chief hesitated, but then took the phone in his hand and read it.

He gave it back to Dalton then said, "Yes, it looks bad, but she is not here. Nobody's here. Would you know of any other places where she might be?" he asked him, now concerned as he took his helmet off and wiped his face with his hands.

"No, I don't," Dalton answered him as he watched them leave the room one by one. He sat down on the bed and shook his head, wondering what the text meant. He looked down at his phone once more.

"Sorry, sir, but I have to ask you to leave. This room still belongs to a guest," a man standing near him said. Dalton looked up at his uniform. It was one of the managers of the hotel.

"Yes, of course." He rose, but his eye caught a glimpse of a hairbrush on the bed beside him. He picked it up with his hand and examined it. There was red hair in the bristles of the brush. *Odd!* He rolled the hair between his fingers. *Sidney has brown hair, not red.* It looked like synthetic hair. It hit him like a train. He dropped the brush on the ground. He felt lightheaded. His stomach turned and it took all he had not to throw up.

It was Sidney. She had been the one who had destroyed Annette's house. She had been the one who pushed Annette into the street. *She was trying to kill her. Why? Why had she said that she was going to kill herself?*

"Dear Lord, Annette is in danger. She's going to kill her," he whispered. He knew. Sidney was after Annette. Sidney knew he would leave the house and rush over here. Sidney wanted Annette alone in the house. He could feel a coldness rush down his back.

Dalton bolted past the manager. He ran as fast as he could he didn't even wait for the elevator. He took the stairs down to the lobby. He searched blindly for Detective Turner's number on his phone as he tried to flag down a cab. He had to return to Annette.

* * *

Turner had driven around the block. He had a bad feeling. He felt something wasn't right. He could have sworn he had heard someone scream inside Annette's house but he wasn't sure. There was no evidence it was from Annette. He was sitting in his car when he heard his phone ring. He reached on the passenger seat to pick it up. He looked at the number. It said unknown, but answered anyway. "Detective Turner," he said as he noticed the blue Toyota a half a block up ahead. It was parked in front of Annette's house.

"Detective, this Dalton Rivers. Listen, Annette is in danger. You have to help her," he was shouting into his phone. He was very agitated.

"What are you talking about? Start from the beginning," Turner questioned him as he looked at Annette house.

"I'm at the Ritz Carlton Hotel. I'm on my way to Annette's house. I found red hair in a brush and I think it is from a wig. I think it was Sidney, my ex-fiancée, who pushed her into the oncoming traffic. She made me come here to see her under the pretense that she was suicidal, but she's not here. I think she went to Annette's home to harm her," Dalton shouted. He was breathing hard and struggling to catch his breath.

"Dalton, are you sure? I'm at the house now. I want you to meet me down the street at the corner of North and Clark. Do not go to the house. I'm calling for backup. Do you hear me? North and Clark. Do not go to the house," Turner told him with grave concerned. He started the engine and backed away from the house. He didn't want to attract any attention to himself. He also didn't want to give Sidney any indication they were aware of the situation or she was about to be apprehended. Not just yet. "Do you understand? I'm on this," Turner reassured Dalton. He just hoped he listened, otherwise it might get crazy and someone might get hurt.

"Yes, I understand. North and Clark. But—" Turner hung up the phone.

Turner contacted the SWAT team and advised them of the situation. He called in the license plate of the blue car that was parked in front of the residence. He waited patiently while the results from the motor vehicle agency popped up on the police computer. It was a rented and registered to National Rentals. It had been leased to Sidney Moore. That was the car seen in the area when Annette's home had been vandalized a week ago. He knew now who his suspect was and what her motive was. It all came down to Dalton and two women. One of them was an obsessed criminal.

He stepped out of his car to investigate the back of the property. He wanted to see if it was secured or if Sidney was inside the house. He walked around the back of the neighbor's property toward Annette's backyard. He approached cautiously. He pulled his revolver out when he arrived at the junction of both buildings. He held his gun at his side until he could determine if there was a threat or not. He thought he had heard someone scream when he had been at the front door previously, but it had been quiet afterwards, so he hadn't been sure. He took a couple more steps forward and squatted down near the back of a dumpster. He stopped. Turner knew he would be able to see the back of Annette's house as soon as he made the bend. He advanced slowly and took a quick look.

He observed that the patio glass door was shattered to pieces. He advanced a little further to see if he could see anyone inside. He couldn't, so he backed away. He retreated back to the alley next to the house. He radioed the precinct to inform them of a home invasion with a probable hostage situation. He knew Annette was inside because she had gotten out of the hospital two days ago. He decided to try to call Annette's house and negotiate with the intruder. Time was crucial. He was afraid this woman might try to kill the hostage if he didn't do something. He holstered his gun. He took out his notepad and flipped through the pages for her number as he ran back to his car. He had to call Annette's house. Without back up, he had to try to hold off on doing anything until backup arrived. He still had to meet the SWAT team at North Street. He dialed her house number, but his call was not answered. "Damn!" he said to himself.

He was sitting down in his car for ten minutes when he detected a yellow cab driving down the street towards him. He went to meet it. He knew it was Dalton. He had to stop Dalton from acting irrationally and going inside the house. Turner met him halfway down the street. "Is Sidney in there?" Dalton screamed at him. The detective didn't say anything. He just nodded as he took him under the arm firmly to lead him back to his squad car. He wanted to make sure Dalton didn't try to save Annette, because it probably would not have a good ending. They both sat in the front seat. Dalton was the first one to speak. He could tell he was having a hard time. He was nervous and he kept watching the house. His foot kept bouncing up and down and he was rapping his fingers on his knees.

"Why are we sitting here? Let's go inside to help Annette? We have to do something. This is driving me insane," he told him as he stared out the car window at the building.

"If we storm the house, the chances are that your ex-fiancée will certainly cause Annette harm," Turner tried to explain to him calmly as he looked out down the block.

"So, we are supposed to just sit here and do nothing until the cavalry arrives? I don't think so," he told him. Turner gripped his arm hard as he reached for the handle of the car door, trying to stop him from leaving his seat.

"Don't! If you interfere with this investigation, I will place you under arrest for obstruction. Is that clear Mr. Rivers?" he said, then let go of his arm. Dalton nodded and then looked away from the detective, displeased.

"But we have to do something," Dalton told him. He kept squirming in his seat.

"We are, but you have to be patient. You cannot barge in there. It won't end well. Another thing, Mr. Rivers! Hand over your cell phone until this is over. I don't want you calling inside," Turner told him and extended his hand towards him.

"Like bloody hell I will," he answered him with resistance. He didn't move a muscle to give it to him.

"Do you really want to go down that road?" Turner eyed him without moving his hand that was still outreached his way. He watched as Dalton took his phone out of his pocket and shut it off. Dalton slammed it in Turner's hand. Dalton definitely was not happy.

* * *

Annette was lying on the floor in the hallway. She was in extreme pain—first from the punch that Sidney gave her and second from the injuries she'd sustained when the cab had hit her. She had fallen backwards when she lost her balance. She rubbed her cheek with her fingers. She also had hit her leg against the wall. She still was dazed from the concussion and she felt light headed and dizzy. She could barely open her eyes from the throbbing in the back of her head. She was trying to analyze the situation. She knew she was in big trouble with this woman. This woman wanted her dead. She didn't think she would listen to common sense. She almost succeeded in getting her killed last week when she had pushed her in front of that cab, and now she had a knife to her throat. If Sidney thought that Annette was going to let her win, she was wrong.

"Get up you bitch. Pick up your crutches and walk, hop, or crawl to the living room and sit the fuck down," Sidney told her as she swung her knife back and forth in front of her. Annette grasped one of her crutches, lifted her body up, and tried desperately to stand up on one foot. She placed most of her weight on her crutch, but she was having a hard time. She moaned and groaned at the agony in her leg. Her face was red from exertion and tears appeared in her eyes, but she was not going to bow down and let them fall. She was not going to give Sidney that satisfaction. She finally managed to stand and lean against the wall. It was torture as she wobbled to the couch, but she made it. She slowly sat down, her leg outstretched in front of her. She positioned her crutches beside her and folded her hands on her lap.

"Sidney ..." Annette started to say, but she quieted down by the dirty frown that was sent her way. She watched as Sidney went to the front window, stood to the side, and scanned the street. Sidney's eyes were darting everywhere. She took two paces towards her; bent down to pull the crutches away from her side, and threw them to the other side of the room.

"You won't need those. And don't even think of doing something foolish, because you will regret it," Sidney told her and went back to the window.

How was she going to get out of this dangerous situation? How was she going to get away from this demented, psychotic person? She could barely stand, let alone run or protect herself. Annette turned her head slightly, studying her surroundings. She needed to find a weapon to defend herself with, but the only thing she could see was the metal frame of her dearly departed husband's picture. She inched her body closer to the picture when Sidney looked away. She was so afraid of getting caught. Her heart was pounding hard. Her whole being was trembling, but she decided she had to say or do something. She could feel a hard knot in her stomach. She rubbed her hands on the sofa from dampness. The hairs on the back of her neck were standing up. Her head was throbbing from being hit earlier. The light in the room was causing her to squint from the pain.

"What do you want from me?" Annette managed to ask her in a shaky voice. She was not going to go down without a fight. Let the battle commence. Sidney did not even acknowledge her or answer her. She just kept staring up and down the block. Annette noticed that Sidney's was now holding one of her knives so tightly that her knuckles were white. Her thumb was resting on the blade. She had cut her finger. It was bleeding. "Please, take whatever you want and just leave. I won't say anything. I'll say I didn't know you," Annette said to her, trying to appease her. Sidney turned to face Annette with slanted eyes.

"Shut the bloody hell up," she bawled out at her. "Take whatever I want? Ha! I want my fiancé back. Can you give me that?" she snarled as she took a step toward Annette. She raised her free hand. She took her wig from her head and threw it on the floor, and she pulled her mustache off her lip. She crushed it in her hand and tossed it at Annette. "Don't talk or even look at me, you bitch. Do you hear me?" Sidney howled at her. She approached, her eyes staring directly at her. She pointed her knife straight at her face. Annette receded as far back as she could on the sofa, petrified. She was paralyzed with fear.

* * *

Dalton was so distraught about Annette that he could barely think straight. He had been sitting in the car for the last ten minutes. Not another word had been spoken between the two men. *What was he waiting for? Someone was going to get hurt.* Two more unmarked squad cars arrived and parked behind the detective's car. "Stay in the car," Turner ordered as he opened his door and went to talk to the officers. He couldn't just sit here and not try to save Annette. He noticed a black armor truck coming towards their location. It stopped at the perimeter where the other cars were parked. A man in full protective gear, gun by his side, stepped out of the vehicle. He moved in the direction of the detectives. He had a handgun strapped to his hip and a bulletproof vest. Turner talked to the man dressed in black attire, but Dalton couldn't hear the conversation. He watched their demeanors closely. Dalton determined this man was the one in charge. *Was the situation so bad that they needed the SWAT team?*

Detective Turner finished talking to the SWAT team leader and headed back to the car. He sat down and said, "We are going to surround the house in a few minutes as soon as the negotiator is ready to go. He is going to try to call Sidney to find out what her terms are. I have to leave you, but I'll be back. It is imperative that you stay in this car for your own protection and the success of this operation. It will be okay," Turner told him. He nodded at him and left Dalton alone.

Fear hit Dalton. His head throbbed. He wiped his hands on his pants. He was petrified—not for himself, but for the women, as well. It was entirely his fault. He had cheated on Sidney with Annette, and then lied. He also had not been able to stop Sidney from injuring Annette. *How had it gotten so bad?* He watched as the officers gathered at one spot by the back of the vehicle. They were talking strategies. They kept pointing toward Annette's house. He looked at his watch. Not even twenty minutes had gone by since he had arrived back from the hotel, but it seemed like an eternity. They didn't know these women. They had to get the hostage out and apprehend the suspect. He swallowed hard. His palms were sweating again. He was frightened, but he knew if he didn't do something, one or both of these women were going to get hurt or worst get killed.

He slowly opened the door of the police car. He examined his options. He decided to play it cool, as if he were just observing them to see if they would pay attention to him. He stepped out of the car and leaned his body against the door. He folded his arms as if he were waiting for Turner. He weighed his options again. With the darkness upon them, they might not notice if he disappeared. He judged that he was about forty-five feet from the back of one of the house on North Street. If he could get to the back of the house, he should be able to get in and help Annette. He slid down the side of the car to the front of it until he was in position. He looked over at Turner. Turner still had his back to him, discussing their strategy.

It was now or never. He sprinted as fast as he could toward the back of the house. He was almost there when he heard someone shouting, "Get back here right now!" It only motivated him to run faster. He jumped the small fence in the adjoining backyard and kept jogging down the block from one home to the other. He turned his head to see if Turner was after him, but he didn't see anyone. As he arrived to the corner of the next house, he felt an unexpected blow to his stomach, and was slammed to the ground. The pain was so intense it took his breath away. His mouth opened to scream, but all that came out was a loud groan. He clutched his belly with his hands as he folded his knees upward, moaning from the hit.

Chapter 23

Sidney was standing at the front window. She had been looking at the street for the last half hour while keeping an eye on Annette. Something was not right. Dalton had not returned to the house and there was no traffic going by. She twirled her knife in her hand. What was she going to do? Should she leave? No, it was not an option. The cop had not come back to the house, either. She tilted her head, glaring at Annette, wondering if she was scared.

Suddenly, the phone rang again. It was aggravating Sidney. She couldn't tolerate the continual noise. She walked to the kitchen, lifted the receiver, and, as casually as possible, answered it. "Hello," she said as she gripped the handle of the knife tighter.

"Sidney, this is Detective Milo of the Boston Police SWAT team. Are you and Annette okay? Do you girls need anything?" he asked her in a tranquil voice. She was stunned. A cop had contacted her. *How did they know her name?* So, Turner had heard Annette's screams and had alerted the police. That was why the street was so stagnant and no cars had gone by.

"What do you want?" she asked him as she ran to the patio doors with the phone glued to her ear. She stood to the side of the frame and let her eyes scan the backyard. She didn't spot anyone. There was no movement, but ...

"I want to help you resolve the conflict that is going on. What do you need?" Milo asked. She was not interested in talking to him.

"Stay away from here or I will ... I want to talk to Dalton. Call me when you have him on the line," she said and banged the phone down. She dug her nails into the inside of her free hand, her nostrils flaring from anger. They knew she was there. She sprinted back to the front window to look outside to see if there was anyone nearby. She was frantic. She had to block the patio door, so she placed her weapon down on the counter of the kitchen. She gripped the dining room table and flipped it on its side and pushed it into the opening. She stacked the chairs of the dining set one at a time on top of each other so the police would have difficulty entering.

She rushed back to the living room where Annette hadn't moved from her spot. She could see from the expression on her face that she was frightened. She had a tremor in her jaw and her hands were shaking. She was terrified. *Good!* Annette's eyes seemed to follow Sidney wherever she went.

"What are you looking at, bitch?" Sidney smirked at her as she kept her eyes cemented on both entryways. "Let me ask you ... what do you think is going to happen here? Should I let you go? You would probably just run back to Dalton. I'm the one who is engaged to him. I'm the one who has been with him all these years. He's mine," she shouted and sneered at her. Sidney glared at her harshly. Her eyes were like daggers and she could feel a tic on her cheek.

"Oh! And if you think you are getting out of here, you are so wrong. You should have died when I pushed you into the oncoming traffic," she told her as she slowly moved toward Annette, her jaw clenched tight. She was only three feet from Annette when the telephone rang again. She gave Annette one last look before she scurried to answer the phone. "Dalton, darling," she said sweetly.

"Sidney, this is Officer Milo. I need to know that Annette is okay and that you have not harmed her before you can speak to Dalton."

Annoyed, Sidney responded to his demand. "The bitch is fine. Now, I want to talk to Dalton, or else she won't see daylight," she yelled. Sweat was dripping down her temples and her back. She took her black hoody off and threw it to the side. She was boiling hot from frustration. She opened the refrigerator door and looked for something to drink. She only saw a bottle of lemonade. She took it out, and swung the door shut. She twisted the top off and then gulped it down.

"I need proof she is not hurt before I let you speak to Dalton. Can you do that for me?" the SWAT leader told her again. She peered towards Annette, who hadn't moved from her spot. Sidney could tell she was listening to the conversation. Sidney felt powerful. She smiled at Annette. She put the drink down on the counter. She was in control of this situation. Sidney took three long strides. She stood with her feet apart in front of her. Annette glanced up at her. Sidney saw Annette's lower lip quiver as Sidney removed the throw pillows from her side and pitched them on the floor. She sat beside Annette with the knife in one hand and the phone in the other. Sidney twitched her nose, as she smelled her repugnant perfume. Annette immediately jerked backwards as she stared at her knife that was pointed at her side.

"Tell him you're okay. And don't try anything funny now," she told her in an unyielding manner. She placed the phone near her mouth and raised her knife near her neck.

"Hello, this is Annette. I'm not hurt ..." she said in a fragile voice that was almost a whisper. Then Sidney yanked the phone away from her mouth and placed it against her ear. She rose and started to pace from one end of the living room to another.

"Now, let me talk to Dalton in the next five minutes or else." She pressed the off button of the phone. She took a seat in a chair across from Annette, still holding the phone and waiting for her darling to come on the line. The minutes passed. Sidney had hoped she would get her answer sooner, but five minutes went by without the phone ringing. She stood up, her feet rooted firmly. She lifted her arm up high with the knife held securely, ready to go through with her promised. She curled her lips, ready to attack as she stared at her prey. Sidney examined Annette, who was sitting with her leg in a cast. Both of her hands were digging in the fabric of the sofa. Annette suddenly moved her arm to her right. She gripped her husband's picture frame, which was on the side table. Sidney creased her forehead at the sight of her clinging to her husband's photo. Sidney burst out laughing.

"I don't think your dead husband will help you now," she joked as she took one more step forward and held her knife up high. She felt the cold grip of the knife.

"I am not weak and I will not go down without a fight. So bring it on," Annette shot back at her.

"Bloody hell. The bitch has spunk. How interesting. But if you think you can defeat me, think again, little girl," Sidney said with a chuckled.

"Bring it on," Annette answered as she moved to the edge of her seat, ready to spring at her. Sidney spun around as she heard her name being called from the outside. She rushed to the side of the window, pulled the curtain back, and peeked at whoever had screamed her name. There were two armored black trucks stationed in front of the house. A man dressed in black military attire was talking to her in a bullhorn. She could see several other men hiding. All of them were armed and were pointing their guns at the house. She ran to the back of the house near the patio door to spy on the cops outside. She noticed two of them hiding behind the oak trees. Three more were on the corner of the neighbors' homes, watching the deck. She scampered back to the front as fast as she could, returning to the guy who was still calling her name.

"Sidney, the house is surrounded. You have to give it up. We don't want anyone to get hurt. Come out with your hands up. Let Annette go unharmed," he told her.

"I would rather die than to give her up. I will bring her down with me. I want to talk to Dalton. That's all I want. You have two minutes," she shouted at them. She scurried to the couch where Annette was seated and extended her hand toward her. She forcefully grabbed Annette by the arm with her free hand, but as she did, Annette hit her. The metal frame she was holding came crashing against the side of Sidney's face. She instinctively swung her knife at her. The blade sliced Annette's arm. She cried out in pain as blood came seeping out. Annette covered her wound with her hand. Sidney took a step back. Her head was spinning from the blow and her ears were ringing, but it was not going to stop her.

Sidney lifted her hand to touch her cheek. She could feel droplets of blood running down her face. She looked at her bloody hand. A rush of anger took her over. "You fucking bitch. You cut me," she said as she raised her arm up again and lunged toward Annette with her knife.

* * *

Dalton lay face down on the snow for a minute, trying to understand what had happened. His face was cold and wet from the snow on the ground. Someone snatched the collar of his jacket and yanked him upright. He could hardly breathe from the throbbing pain in his gut. He was coughing, trying to catch a gulp of air when his body was thrown against the wall of the house next to him. His arms and legs were still weak from the blow he had just received. His hands were forced behind his back and he felt metal on his wrist. He realized he was being handcuffed.

"Well, that was fun, wasn't it? Now, next time I tell you to stay put, you will listen. I don't like to do this, but you gave me no choice," Turner told him as he hauled him toward his original place. Dalton stumbled as he walked back to the car, but it didn't seem to bother

Turner. He was still pulling him by the arm with force. Dalton caught his breath after he had trekked halfway back to North Street.

"You didn't have to hit me that hard. I was only trying to help save them," he spat at him. Dalton tried to make light of the event, but Turner had a firm grip on him. When he arrived to the squad car, he shoved him against the back of the car. Turner held him in place. Dalton moaned as he crashed into the trunk. Turner grabbed him by the front jacket with an unyielding hand and said, "You are under arrest for obstruction." He grabbed the handle of the back door, opened it, and pushed him inside the backseat of the squad car.

"All right, all right. I promise I won't do anything. Just don't shut me out, please. Please, I swear I will listen!" Dalton pleaded with him. Dalton pouted as Turner was thinking.

He finally loosened his grip. He pivoted him around. He aimed his finger at him as if he were a child being reprimanded. "You better keep your word. God help me, I will throw you in jail and toss the key away. Do we understand each other?" he said as he pointed his finger in his face. He gave him a hard look. Dalton just nodded.

"Turn around," Turner told him and unfastened his cuffs. Dalton was relieved to be free from the cuffs. He rubbed his wrists that were sore from the being so tight.

"You have to let me talk to Sidney. I know her. I can make her let Annette go. I won't jeopardize your rescue again. Just let me talk to her. That's what she wants, right? I'll bring her around. I know her," he begged him.

"I'll think about it. Now, get in the car and stay there. I'll come to give you an update in five minutes as soon as I talk to Milo," he said. Dalton opened the back door of the vehicle and sat down, anxious, but most of all worried about what Sidney might do if he didn't talk to her. He watched from afar. The unit was getting ready to attack. They kept signaling them around the perimeter. They ran behind and in front of Annette's house.

Turner walked back to the car. He poked his head in and said, "We are going to try to talk to her again. If she doesn't listen, then we will let you talk to her. But only if you agree to only tell her what we want you to tell her. Understood?" Dalton nodded. "Come on. Follow me and be quiet," Turner told him. Dalton got out of the car and trailed behind Turner closely. They came up to one of the armored trucks. Turner held the door opened for him.

"Get in. That way you'll be close if we need you," Turner told him. Dalton hopped inside. He sat on the bench next to four other officers. They were ready to kill. They never looked at him or acknowledge his presence. Dalton's heart skipped a beat at the thought that he might lose Annette if it didn't go as planned.

Dalton jumped when the vehicle started to move. He tried not to think of what might happen as he sat beside them. The men around him had blank faces and were holding on to their guns. It seemed like they were on a hunting expedition, psyching themselves up for the kill. It made Dalton very uneasy. He might lose the love of his life. He held on the bottom of the seat for support. The four next to him were immobile as the armor truck moved forward.

They rode to their destination in complete silence. The vehicle suddenly stopped. The back doors opened. The men jumped out, one after the other, with their weapons drawn and shields in front of them for protection. After all had departed, Dalton slowly slid down to the edge of the bench. He leaped out, ready to follow, but Dalton was held back when he eyed Turner standing at the back of the truck. Turner put his hand up to stop him from going any further.

* * *

Annette had just struck Sidney with the frame, but it had only seemed to infuriate her even more. Sidney had staggered backwards, but now she was coming towards Annette with her knife raised. Annette noticed a red spot on Sidney's chest. It was from a sniper scope. *Oh! No. They were going to kill her.* She could not let them do that. *What was she going to do?* It seemed like everything was moving in slow motion. She wouldn't be able to live with herself if she didn't say anything.

"Get down they have sniper dot on you," Annette shouted as she pointed at Sidney's chest. Sidney looked down and saw the red spot. She quickly moved against the wall to avoid them. She could tell she had not expected that. Annette saw she was upset. Her hands were shaking uncontrollably. Sidney's face was pale and it looked like the blood had been drained from her.

"Bloody hell!" Sidney said as she stood by the frame of the windows. She grabbed the strings of the blinds on the side of the window and she closed the shades.

Thank God! Now they couldn't get a target on her. What had she done? Annette thought. Now she was Sidney's target again. The phone was ringing again. They both turned their heads at the same time. Sidney got down on her hands and her knees. She crawled to kitchen area where the phone was located. She extended her hand to pick it up.

"You bastards want to kill me. Get your bloody guns away from me, because next time I will not hesitate to kill her. I want to speak to Dalton!" she screamed at them uncontrollably.

"Sidney, let me ask for you. Maybe they will listen to me. Please?" Annette said to her. *Why the hell had she said that?* This lunatic was ready to kill her, but she didn't want her to die. Maybe if she could get them to understand she only wanted to talk to him, they might listen. She stretched out her hand over the back of the couch towards her.

She needed to gain her trust back. Maybe she would be able to get out of this alive. She hoped she was right. Sidney was breathing hard. She eyed Annette for a moment, and slowly passed the phone to her.

"Hello, this is Annette. Who am I speaking with?" she asked, keeping her eyes fixed on Sidney, who was sitting not far from her with her knife still in her hand, aimed at Annette's body. *One wrong move and she might plunge her knife into her.*

"Annette, this Officer Milo. Are you okay?" he asked her with concern in his voice.

"Yes, I'm fine. Please, all she wants is to speak to Dalton Rivers. Could you find him and let her talk to him? She said she would release me afterwards," she lied as she kept her eyes fixed on Sidney.

"I'm sorry, but I can't give in to that demand anymore. She would have to give me something and she only has you. Is she willing to do that?" he told her.

Annette interrupted him before he could finish. "You are willing to gamble my life on your stupid protocols? Damn you. Get Dalton on the line right now!" Annette yelled at him so loudly that she even shocked herself. The other end of the phone became dead silent.

"I'll see what I can do. Hold on," he finally answered. He was talking to someone else, but the sound was muffled. She couldn't hear what they were saying. She raised her finger to indicate that Sidney should wait.

"Is he coming?" Sidney questioned while her eyes darted from the front door to the back of the house. She poked her knife into Annette's side when she didn't answer. Annette cried out in pain at the jab to her side. She looked down. Her shirt was ripped and a small amount of blood was trickling through her clothing. She could feel the blood dribble down her ribs. Annette was terrified. If he didn't come back on the line soon, she might die.

* * *

Milo walked toward Dalton. He didn't seem very happy. His facial expression was stoic. Turner was trailing by his side. He was holding a phone. His hand covered the receiver.

"Talk to Sidney. Tell her what she wants to hear. You need to convince her to let Annette go otherwise we are going to storm the house. Do you understand? Can you do that?" Milo instructed him, unsmiling. Dalton nodded. Milo went to give him the phone, but Turner delayed him by tapping Dalton's arm.

"We'll be listening to every word. If we see you can't handle her, we are going in. Understood?" he told him

"Yes, I completely understand. I can do it." Dalton fully comprehended the responsibility laid on his shoulders. He took the phone from Milo. He held it to his ear. He had butterflies flying in his stomach. He wanted to throw up, but he had to calm himself and concentrate if he was to save Annette from Sidney. "Hello," he said with a trembling voice. It was not what he wanted to say but ... no one answered. He said it again. "Hello?"

"Dalton is that you?" he heard the voice say. It was Sidney.

"Hi, Sidney. Are you okay?" he asked, though what he really wanted to know was how Annette was doing. Was she hurt?

"Dalton, darling, I knew you cared and that you would come back to me. We can be together again," she said to him enthusiastically.

"Yes, we can be together again. But you have to let Annette go and not harm her," he lied to her as he looked at the detectives. They were both nodding their heads at him. Turner gave him thumbs up.

"I don't want her to interfere in our relationship. She has to die. That's the only way," she snapped at him angrily.

"Sidney, darling, calm down and listen to me. I love you and we are going to return to London. She does not need to die. We will be far away from her." He hoped she believed what he was telling her. He shut his eyes, trying to concentrate on this conversation without getting her mad. She wasn't responding. It was quiet at the other end of the line.

"Sidney are you there?" He tried to get her attention again. Turner was making motions signs for him to keep talking to her. "Darling, I love you. We belong together. Can you ever forgive me? I'm sorry. We don't need her. You are a much more sensual woman that her. I realize that now." He misled her even more.

"I can forgive you anything. I love you so much," she told him softly. Dalton received another thumbs up from Turner, then Milo gave him a piece of paper, which read: *Sidney must come out and let Annette go.*

"Sidney, I can't go to you. You have to come out to me." He was stressed about what she might answer him. He wanted her to recognize that what she was doing was wrong. He wanted her to believe that he hadn't duped her.

"I can't go out there. The officers will arrest me or kill me," she said to him. He could tell she was going to cry. Dalton noticed her voice had become shaky and unsteady. He had to try to convince her. Otherwise she might hurt Annette.

"Yes, I suppose they will arrest you, but I'm a damn good attorney. I can take care of you. I won't leave you," he said confidently. "It will be okay. Just come out to me," he said again as he glanced at Turner and Milo.

"No, I want you to come inside and get me," he heard her say.

"Hold on, Sidney. Let me ask if I can come to you," he told her. He placed his fingers over the receiver, but before he could ask Turner and Milo, they were shaking their heads no.

"We can't let you go in. Too many liability problems. Sorry," Turner told him. He placed the phone back to his ear with an idea on how to save Annette. He said, "They will allow me in if you let Annette out first."

"No, I won't let her go. She needs to be stopped and punished so she won't come between the two of us again," she said and the phone went dead.

"All units move in. Suspect is armed and dangerous," Milo said in his radio to his team. At the same time Dalton propelled himself toward Milo. His hand grabbed the radio from Milo.

THE PLEDGE

He shouted into it, "Nooo, do not storm the house. She—" He didn't get a chance to finish his sentence. Someone had him by the waist and thrust him forward. He lost his balance. Turner had Dalton down on the ground and on his belly, his face in the snow again. Turner pressed his knee on his lower back, holding Dalton down. Dalton tried to get up with his arm, but wasn't successful because Turner had a hold of one of his arms. He had twisted it backwards and was bending his wrist.

"Are you fucking crazy? I am trying very hard to be tolerant, but my patience has just run out. Don't you get it? They know what they are doing, you don't. If you go in there, she will have not just one but two hostages. Now, I like you, but I can't trust you anymore. You have a hard head and you are one of the most obstinate men I know. Now listen," Turner told him between clenched teeth as he leaned close to his ear to talk to him.

"I'm sorry, really I am. Please let go of me," Dalton winced, but Turner was not going to take a chance. His captain would shit all over him if something else went wrong.

"Dalton you are a civilian and are not allowed to be here in the first place without authorization from higher up." Turner reached into his back pocket, he unsnapped and retrieved his handcuffs. He brought them down and clicked them on Dalton's wrists. He then looped his arm in his to help him get on his feet. He gripped his cuffs and led him to the squad car, which was parked down the alley, all the while ignoring Dalton's pleas to let him go. Turner opened the door and directed him into the backseat. "Watch your head," he told him as Dalton was seated in the squad car. Turner slammed the door shut and casually walked away toward the commander's station with no guilt and without even turning around to look at Dalton.

"We are going into the house in less than two minutes," Milo informed Turner. He spoke into his radio ordering his men to get in position to attack, apprehend the suspect, and free the hostage.

Chapter 24

Sidney hung up the phone. She was still sitting on the floor. The phone dropped from her hand as she lowered her head. The last sentence she had heard Dalton say still resonated in her ear. He loved Annette, not her.

"They will allow me in if you let Annette go first," she whispered to herself. It had given her the answer she really didn't want to hear. Tears were swimming in her eyes and as soon as she blinked, the tears came running down her cheeks.

This time she really didn't care if she lived or died. But she knew one thing; she would not be the only one to die today. She fixed her sight on Annette, who was just sitting there on the sofa watching her.

"What are you looking at bitch? You won. He doesn't love me anymore. He loves you. Yes, I know this for a fact. He just told me everything I wanted to know when he said 'let Annette out, then I'll come in,'" she shouted at her as the tears fell down her cheeks. Sidney didn't care anymore.

All of a sudden it became quiet outside. Sidney got up from the floor and took a step forward. She raised the knife over her head, getting ready to strike. She heard Annette scream loudly. She tried to move away from her, but there was nowhere to go. It all seemed like she was watching a movie, but she was in it. She took another step forward, tilted her head to the right, analyzing what to do with Annette. Sidney was only two feet away. She watched as Annette lifted her hands up in front of herself defensively, her eyes peering at her, her mouth twisted in horror as she kept shrieking.

***

Turner ran toward the house in between the squad cars. He positioned himself behind one of the men dressed in black. He drew his gun, ready to fire. They heard a loud cry coming from the house. He watched as one of the SWAT team members unhooked a stun grenade from his belt. He pulled the pin. He projected it in the front window of the residence. He heard the glass break as the flash bomb exploded with a large bang in the living room.

It was meant to distract Sidney and disorient her. Turner advanced toward the front door where a SWAT team member had a battering ram in his hand. The officer swung it once. It hit the doorknob of the front door as the door flew opened within seconds. The team entered in a row, running like soldiers while yelling "Boston SWAT." They held their assault rifles up, aiming for any danger and their suspect. They were ready for anything, but realistically the only dangerous person in there was a heartbroken woman who was lost without her man. But this woman was willing to kill and that made it risky and dangerous.

Turner followed them as he heard, "Go, go." As he approached one of the rooms, he saw Sidney trying to get up from the floor. She staggered, trying to walk, but what caught his attention was that she was still holding her butcher's knife in her right hand. Her other hand was on her left ear. One of the officers had his gun pointed directly at her. He was screaming at her to drop the knife, but she was resisting. Annette laid sideways, her face in the sofa. She was unable to move away from Sidney. Her hands were covering her ears.

The sergeant of the SWAT team advanced cautiously one step at a time and shouted, "Drop the knife now." Sidney seemed disoriented, but she looked up at him. She held on to her weapon. She leaned her arm on the side of the couch for support. Her arm swung sideway at Annette's torso, but missed her by inches. The next thing that happened made Turner hold his breath and pray it wasn't happening. He heard gunfire. There was one shot, followed by a wail of anguish from a female.

* * *

Annette tried to get away when she had hit Sidney on the head with the metal frame, but it had been fruitless. It had only made her madder. Thank God Dalton had come on the line at that precise moment, because she wasn't sure she would have survived otherwise. Annette held her arm and examined it when Sidney wasn't watching. She had a two-inch cut on the lower part of her arm, but it wasn't too deep. It was bleeding and probably would need stitches, but she would survive. She looked up to watch Sidney.

Sidney was now talking on the phone with Dalton and she had hoped that he could bring her around, but couldn't. She had listened to the one-way conversation, and when it ended, Annette knew it wasn't good news by the expression on Sidney's face. She studied as Sidney looked at her knife in her hand. She rolled it several times in her hand. Annette knew when she gripped the knife that she was going finish her off. Sidney stood up and directed a dark look at Annette. She came toward her with her blade. Sidney raised it over her head, ready to strike.

Annette's adrenaline pumped. She had no defense except screaming. Annette's eyes fixed on her. She was paralyzed from fear. She could not believe she was going to die by the hand of this woman. She could barely move with her cast, but suddenly she heard the window shatter and something came flying through the living room window in front of her then exploded. The SWAT team was coming in. A huge flash of light impaired her vision. A loud bang occurred afterwards and made her disoriented. She saw Sidney being thrown backwards. Maybe she had fallen from the noise or maybe the enormous flash had confused her. She wasn't sure of anything anymore. She lost her bearings and her head hurt from the blaring sound. Her vision was blurred and her ears rung.

Then she saw them, the men dressed in black in body armor coming forward and toward them with their rifles aimed at Sidney. She was more terrified of them than being alone with this crazy woman. She shook her head, trying to refocus. She noticed a red dot aimed at Sidney's chest from a riflescope. She had to do something. She couldn't let them kill Sidney, even though she knew Sidney would not hesitate to eliminate her if she had the opportunity. Annette could not live with that guilt. She would never forgive herself. She heard them shouting at Sidney to drop the knife, but suddenly Sidney took a step forward, lunging towards the cops with her knife.

She could not let them kill Sidney. That was all she repeated over in her mind. She never thought about her own safety. Annette screamed, she found inner strength, lifted her arms up to try and stop them. She pushed herself up on her good leg and propelled herself in front of Sidney. She didn't care about her life. At that moment she just had to save Sidney. It was because of her that she had found herself in this predicament. She leaped in front of Sidney, waving her arms. Something hit her. She felt incredible burning pain go through her body as she fell to the ground. She collapsed on top of Sidney.

* * *

Dalton was wild with concern, and every possible scenario of events went through his mind. He tried to open the door. He kicked the door and the windows with his boots, but it would not open. He howled his head off at Turner, but to no avail. His ears were out of reach.

"Turner, let me out. I can help. I swear ... I won't run. Please, don't harm them. Let me out," he shouted in the direction of Annette's house.

He watched as the SWAT team shot a projectile into the house. He observed as they broke down the door from afar. He had never felt so powerless in his life. His eyes did not believe what was happening. He sat immobile with his jaw open. Dread passed through him. He was helpless in trying to rescue Annette or Sidney. And even though he did not love Sidney anymore, he wished her no harm in any way.

There had to be a way out of this car. He lay on his back under his handcuffed hands and lifted his legs and feet up. He struck the window of the car with his boots with all his strength, but without success. The window had bars across that would not break. He sat up again, distraught and sweating profusely. Droplets of sweat were running down his face. He heard sirens as the ambulance pulled up the driveway of Annette's house. He was shocked and horrified at the developing events.

"What the bloody hell is happening? Let me out," he screamed louder at the cops who were nearer to him. He feared the worst. His life was not worth living if Annette was killed. He saw the paramedics grab their gear, and run inside. A fireman followed with a stretcher.

"Who is hurt? Let me out this instant, please ..." he continued. His head was pounding so hard from howling that he thought it would explode from the pain. His eyes were anchored on the people coming and going from the home. He watched as most of the SWAT team exited and Turner trailed behind them. He stepped down from the front porch, his head bowed low. He was shaking his head. His arms were resting by his sides. Dalton vision went straight to the front of his shirt and his jacket. They were covered in what looked like blood. "Oh Lord! No!" he uttered. His eyes watered when it hit him. *What had happened in there? One of the girls was hurt, maybe dead but which one?*

THE PLEDGE

"Get me out of here, Turner, let me out, what happened in there?" he shouted at him as he approached the car. He reached over and opened the door to let Dalton out. "Take these fucking bloody cuffs off me," he ordered him. He turned around and offered him his hands. "What happened?" Dalton asked, unable to think straight, but Turner hadn't even said a word.

Dalton could smell the blood off his shirt. Turner took the handcuff key out of his pant pocket and undid the restraints. He set his hands free. Dalton turned toward Turner, rubbing his wrists, then grabbed Turner's front jacket and asked, "Are the girls okay? Whose blood is on your clothes?" Dalton pointed at his garments, not really wanting to know the answer as a cold chill passed through him. Turner just glanced at him. He shook his head. "What happened? Who is hurt? Answer me, Turner." Dalton held out both his arms, gripped Turner's shoulders, and shook him hard to try to get an answer.

"Annette is injured," he whispered as his face paled and he looked away.

Dalton let him go and rushed with long strides toward the house. By the time he reached the steps, the paramedics were wheeling a stretcher out. It was Annette. Her upper body was covered with blood, her clothes were ripped, and a huge bandage was on the upper left side of her body. Her eyes were closed; she was unconscious. She had an IV connected to her arm and an oxygen mask on her mouth.

"Sir, we need to get her to the hospital immediately. Could you move aside?" the paramedic told him as Dalton took a step to the side to let them get by, but stayed beside the stretcher.

"What's the matter with her? What happened?" Dalton questioned them.

"She's been shot," he heard the medic say. He froze. He knew he was going to faint. He held on to the metal poles of her stretcher. His legs almost gave out. He recuperated within seconds. She needed him now more than ever.

"I'm here, Annette. It's going to be all right," he told her as he walked beside the medics. When he arrived at the ambulance, he stepped up to get into the back of the vehicle, but the technician said, "I'm sorry, sir, but you cannot come with us. We will need the room to care for her," he told him.

"Where are you taking her?" he asked him as he raked his fingers through his disarranged hair from worry. He backed away a bit so the attendant could close one door.

"Boston General Hospital," he answered him as he shut the other door. Dalton stood on his spot. He said a small prayer under his breath as he watched the ambulance leave the area. He heard himself say, "Move, Dalton, Annette needs you." He started running back to the car to find Turner. He was sitting with his hands on the wheel of his police car, his head resting on it. The engine was on and he seemed to be waiting for him to get into the automobile. He didn't even wait for Dalton to shut the car door. He was already was rolling forward.

"Tell me what the bloody hell happened in that house," he demanded with a firm voice as he buckled his seatbelt in place. Dalton was furious. He scowled at Turner. He pounded the dashboard with his fist. "Tell me. What happened? What about Sidney?" Dalton asked Turner.

"It wasn't our fault. It was an accident. We entered without incident and we spotted Sidney right away. She was dazed and trying to stand, but she still had the knife in her hand. Our sight was on Sidney. The SWAT leader had his scope aimed at her. He yelled for her to drop the knife, but she ..." A choked sound came from the back of his throat. Dalton hadn't taken his eyes off him while he spoke.

"What transpired?" Dalton yelled, irritated he had stopped talking. Turner took a quick peek at him and continued.

"Sidney lunged at the cops. Annette was sitting on the couch, so the leader who was in close proximity fired his gun at Sidney, but Annette unexpectedly threw herself in front of the bullet. She was shot in the

THE PLEDGE

upper shoulder. I saw it all. I ran to her, lifted her head, and applied pressure to her wound right away. It looked like a through and through, meaning the bullet went out her back. It was so quick." He paused to take a breath.

"And Sidney? How is she?" Dalton inquired, never taking his eyes off him. Turner pursed his lips together as he hesitated for a moment, and sighed, "When Annette was shot, the bullet came out her back, but since she was in front of Sidney, they think it probably deflected off Annette's bone and ended up hitting Sidney in the heart. The paramedics pronounced her dead on arrival. She had no heartbeat. She did not have a chance, but she didn't suffer. I'm sorry. It was a freak accident." Silence invaded the car for a minute.

"Sidney is dead. She's gone," Dalton heard himself say quietly as he stared at the road in front of him. He turned his face away from Turner and just peered out his window. He felt horrible that things had turned out the way they had. Sidney was a good person who had been dealt a bad deal. She hadn't known how to deal with rejection. His main concerned now was Annette.

Chapter 24

Turner dropped Dalton at the front entrance of Boston General Hospital Emergency Ward. "I'll go park the car. I'll find you as soon as I can. Now go," Turner told him. "I just want to change this bloody shirt," he told Dalton. This was the second time in three weeks that Dalton had been to the hospital with Annette. He hoped this would be his last time for a very long time. Dalton raced inside to try to find Annette. His first stop was at the nurse's station for information to try to locate Annette. He was told she had just been taken to up the operating room again.

A nurse told him to have a seat. He slumped into the chair in the corner of the waiting area. It was a square room that had six chairs and a table with magazines. It was painted in a light beige color. A small television stood in one corner. The room was no bigger than twenty feet by twenty feet. He leaned forward to place his elbows on his knees. He massaged his face and his temple area. His head rested in his hands. He tried to think positively, but he was scared she might not survive the gunshot wound. He couldn't lose both women in one day. This incident was his fault. He should have known better. He should have broken up with Sidney right away. If he had, then she might have been

THE PLEDGE

saved. It was something he would have to live with. It was a done deal. He would mourn her later. What was important right now was Annette.

Time crawled by as he looked at his Rolex watch again. It was now nine o'clock, but he still hadn't heard anything. He heard footsteps coming towards him in the hallway. He lifted his head and saw Detective Turner entering the room. He sat down in the chair next to him. Dalton noticed he had changed shirts. Dalton focused his eyes on the TV. It was in the corner, but he wasn't assessing what was being said on the tube. He just wanted to hear news of his love. He was kneading his hands together without realizing it. "How are you doing? Did you hear any news?" Turner asked him. Dalton's worry turned to anger as he looked at him with ice in his eyes. He pressed his lips together.

"I wouldn't be here if you had let me go into the house and talk to Sidney. It's your fault Sidney is dead and that Annette is injured. It's all on you. I have nothing to say to you. Leave me alone," Dalton told him. He blamed Turner for this conflict, as well as the outcome. He hadn't given him a chance to save Annette or Sidney. Dalton stood and walked to the opposite side of the room. He sat as far as he could from the detective.

"Dalton, I'm sorry you feel that way, but this was my investigation. I know you think it's closed and done with, but we still need answers to certain questions. I spoke to other detectives before I came to find you and we believe Sidney was the one who had tried to kill Annette. We also think that she was responsible for the break-in. We found a red wig and mustache at the scene," the detective said. Dalton did not say a word as his anger turned to guilt again. He should have tried harder to fix things earlier, but he couldn't go back. He turned to look at Turner with his arms folded on his chest.

"It's not your fault. You can't blame yourself. Do you hear me? I see this type of crime often. You're not responsible. Now, calm down and I will try to get some information on Annette," he said softly. Dalton nodded at the officer. Turner stepped out of the room as Dalton closed his eyes to say another silent prayer.

Turner returned ten minutes later and went to sit near Dalton. Dalton glanced up at him.

"Do you have any news?" Dalton asked him right away as he crossed his leg away from the detective. He was irritated with him. He held the side arms of his chair tightly, waiting for Turner to give him news.

"Annette is out of surgery and she is doing just fine. The bullet that hit her didn't pierce any vital organs, nor did it hit any major blood vessels, like arteries. It did hit the top of her collarbone. I was told that an orthopedic surgeon repaired her bone by inserting a plate and screws like they did on her leg. She was very fortunate," Turner explained to him, he got up to leave. He took two steps toward the exit of the waiting room, but stopped, pivoted on his heel, then said, "Oh! I forgot." Dalton waited patiently for any bits of information he could get. "She's not awake yet. I told them to come get you the minute she wakes up," he told him. He smiled at Dalton.

"Thank you for letting me know. I appreciate it," Dalton answered and stood extending his hand to him. Turner gripped it and shook his hand. He sighed at the good news. He was relieved she was going to be okay. He managed to give Turner a small smile.

"I'll see you around. Good luck," Turner replied and walked out of the room, leaving Dalton alone with his thoughts.

* * *

Annette was back in a hospital bed when she opened her eyes. She looked around and realized she was back in a hospital room. The nurse told her where she was and why she was in the emergency ward. She told her not to worry because she was going to be all right. Her whole body was in excruciating pain from her broken leg to her entire upper right shoulder.

"Could I have something for the pain?" she murmured to her. The nurse nodded, smiled at her. She left the room and she was back within minutes. She administered a pain medication into one of her IVs with the syringe. Annette could feel some of the pain disappear within a few minutes as the medicine took effect. She closed her eyes, unable to stay awake.

All she remembered was trying to push Sidney out of the way when she had felt something hit her. She had felt a burning sensation, and then, extreme pain. She now knew from the doctor's report that she had been accidently been shot in her upper shoulder. Her eyelids were heavy. She also felt groggy and unstable. She fell asleep immediately.

The next few hours were a blur, but when she awoke again, she sensed someone holding her left hand. She slowly turned her head, opened her eyes halfway, and saw the most beautiful man watching her every move. "Hi," she managed to say with her parched mouth.

He smiled at her with those gorgeous dimples. He stood up, leaned forward to kiss her so ever gently on the lips. Dalton was beside her. Now she could survive anything. She heard him say, "Hi there, Gorgeous."

ABOUT THE AUTHOR

ANN EL-NEMR lives in Shrewsbury, Massachusetts with her three children. She started writing two years ago as a hobby, but within a time span of a year she has turned into an author. She has had two other books published, *Betrayed* (January) and *Forgiven* (June), by Jan-Carol Publishing, Inc. *The Pledge* is her third novel. She loves to delight her readers with her stories. You can contact her on Facebook, or at her website www.annelnemr.com.

LONESOME VAGABOND

COMING SOON FROM ANN EL-NEMR

Logan and Riker are twin brothers. They inherited an empire of wealth from their grandmother when she died. The brothers are complete opposites, Riker likes power, money, greed and he is head of their company. Logan is an easygoing simple man who doesn't want to be known for his money but wants to be loved for who he is. His only desire is to be left alone by his brother. He sails around the world from one place to another with his boat.

He unexpectedly meets Bailey in Barbados and immediately falls for her. Riker arrives to meet up with his brother unannounced in the Caribbean Islands. He immediately despises the woman his brother has fallen in love with because of her simplicity and her social status. He schemes to break them up by hiring Ruby, a ruthless woman who never fails to accomplish her clients wishes. Will Riker succeed? Will Logan be too late when he finds out about his brother's dubious plan? Will Logan be able to convince Bailey it wasn't his fault? Will Bailey ever forgive Logan for his actions?

CPSIA information can be obtained
at www.ICGtesting.com
Printed in the USA
FFOW05n0141150415

9 781939 289582